An Asylum of Sorts

Sorts

American Menagerie

John D. Lowe

This book is a work of fiction. Any resemblance, herein, to a real person whether living or dead or an event, other than historical, is entirely by coincidence. Some of the locales mentioned may exist but the characters within never inhabited them.

An Asylum of Sorts

ISBN: 978-0-9914818-2-8
Copyright © 2017 by John D. Lowe

Dedicated to:

Anne, Marc, Oliver, W.S. (USMC, 2nd Marine Division WWII) and John at the bar. It is also dedicated to Tommy Freeman, my childhood friend who was like a brother and who died too young; and to the state of New Jersey, the home of all of the aforementioned. Also to the Dugout on Comm. Ave. Boston.

I also have to thank Roger Morelli and Dr. Julia I. Mutzbauer, both of whom saved the book from my impatience and rush to finish.

Chapter 1

The House, Late Spring 1977

"Do you have a room for rent?" she blurted out almost before the big red front door was fully open to reveal Rodney Cornelius Luger the IV. Rodney, now 38-years-of-age, was still daydreaming of his glory days at Brown University, some 17 plus years earlier, when he heard the tail end of the question.

"For rent? No, the house is not for rent but I have rooms for rent," he stated, his mind still on the campus of almost two decades past.

"That's what I meant, a room," said Alice Prodnick, a rather short and chunky yet not unattractive woman in her mid-twenties.

"A room for rent,...... yes I have a room for rent," Rodney answered as though finally coming out from under anesthesia. "Who told you I had a room?"

"God did," said Alice.

"Well come on in," said Rodney without even so much as a blink of surprise. Rodney probably heard the word God as Bob; he wasn't always in the present as you may realize. Not that God is a bad sort but folks who happen to talk directly

with Him or, worse, those who hear Him talking to them regularly should make the average person a little nervous. But
then Rodney probably did hear the name Bob, which sounds a
little like God if you're Rodney.

***

Rodney's spacious Victorian home was nestled in between
several century plus old oaks with a waist high hedge, backed
by a wire fence from the same era, protecting it from the street
and the flagstone sidewalk out in front. The backyard was
graced with the oldest magnolia in the town, which had spread
out like a gracious fan instead of growing straight up. The front
hall was lit by a stained glass window in the front of the house
which rose two floors to the second of three floors. The wrap-
around porch, which ran two thirds the length of the front of
the house then around and down half the side nearest the
magnolia, finished the elegance of this old Englewood, New
Jersey estate. The fresh green of late spring set the house off just
enough to make any passerby smile with appreciation for the
Victorian period.

Rodney Cornelius Luger the IV. had grown up in Englewood as a youngster, went off to Brown and came back a man
to live as the third generation of Lugers in the town. The
Victorian he now lived in was not his first domain in the town
as a man even though it may have been his first choice. No,
Rodney and his wife Helen had first moved to the cheap
apartments on the main cross street across the main boule-
vard, entering town and going out of town from south to north.
It was just this side of the railroad tracks in the White section
of town and not far from the hospital, the Englewood Field
Club and the cemetery all in a neat little quadrangle. They
called it, very cleverly, 'Better Slums and Gardens' after the
magazine with a similar but yet different title. This made it
uniquely chic for the young generation of Englewoodians
trying to move up onto 'the hill' and into the wealthy section
of town. Rodney was married then but now at 38 he was di-
vorced for utterly stupid reasons as all three of his brothers,

including the youngest, Jake, would admit; simply because he was late as usual. Some years before he had had an affair at the Wall Street firm he worked at and when Helen gave him an ultimatum, and a second chance, with a specific deadline attached he delayed until 24 hours past the deadline. Helen rightfully told him that he was a day late and shut the door as she left. But we get ahead of ourselves.

The days of 'Better Slums and Gardens' were interesting. Everything was new and exciting after being out of college and truly on their own for the first time in their lives.

Rodney had been a big star on campus with his athletic prowess and he had taken full advantage of it, that's how he had met Helen who was going to Pembroke College at the time. Pembroke is now part of Brown or was incorporated into Brown in much the same way that Radcliff was incorporated into Harvard during the feminist movement, which later angered Helen as she was left without an Alma Mater. They met in their junior years and Helen soon became pregnant, much to the consternation of her father who had some international acclaim and wanted an abortion. Rodney's parents, especially his father, were a bit more pragmatic and Rodney the III looked at the premature entry into this world of, possibly, Rodney the V. much as he would a business problem and gave the couple his support. Both made it through there senior years, graduating to get to 'Better Slums and Gardens' with their first born in tow and more than a year old on move-in day. Helen was bright with a Pembroke sheepskin in her bureau draw but she was content to sit at home with little Rodney the V. and exercise with Jack LaLanne through the miracle of her black and white television during the day. It was late 1961 after all.

Rodney got a job in the elite client loan division of Manufacturers Hanover Trust Company, or 'Manny Hanny' as he called it, and started making his contacts. Brown had greased the skids right into the top division at the bank. His athletic prowess was again part of the matchmaking and the bank allowed him special time to wear the red winged foot and run with the N.Y.A.C. Rodney, after all, was not only an Olympic potential but he had been a shoe-in for the most recent Summer Games until he came down with mononucleosis; now his sights were on the next Games, almost three years off. He was expected to win a silver medal in that upcoming Olympics against one of the all time great distance runners but it was not to be in the end. Rodney partially ruptured his Achilles just days before the Olympic trials. His path to athletic stardom was washed away with this simple yet excruciating injury which occurred on a cool-down day. He felt and heard a pop as he experienced a slight tearing -- and went down like a sack of potatoes on the track. To end up like a helpless lump on the track after all of those years of training was difficult. Immediately after he fell on the track he was mad not fully realizing what had happened. Then as he tried to get up he started to understand the impact of this great injustice that just befell him and he screamed inside full of anger for his misfortune. He then pegged God for a mistake and, eventually, swore at the Almighty before dragging himself off of the track dripping in self-pity.

During those Olympics an American hero was born in the race Rodney was to have run. This runner ran against one of the greatest distance runners of all time and in a dramatic final kick he closed the gap, passed him on the straight and headed home across the finish line into immortality. He was an American runner Rodney had run against many times and vanquished with ease and now he was the greatest distance runner of the day standing on the podium where Rodney knew he should rightfully have been.

The spectacular black and white footage of this American, passing one of the greatest in the sport with such finality, became the backdrop for any show on great sporting events well into the future. And every time Rodney watched one of these shows he was forced to once again relive his missed glory in life. His name would not become a household name as did the name of the man he had always beaten. He would sit in his den in future years with the walls covered in frames filled with medals of his past triumphs. And he would not let it go even when thieves broke into his home and stole most of these medals thinking they were made of precious metals and not just of dreams. He would become stuck in the past and the past would take more and more of the present away from him as time progressed.

Rodney and Helen would have a second child soon after Rodney V. It would be another boy but this child would not have the weight of a roman numeral after his name to tote around, he would just be called Jack.

Rodney moved from the bank to Wall Street within ten years and joined the syndicate group in a brokerage firm which was made up strictly of Brown University graduates. They would sit on the top floor of their building on lower Broadway with their feet propped up smoking cigars. They would do this while reminiscing about the Providence, Rhode Island campus on the hill as they placed large blocks of newly offered stocks at other Wall Street firms with little effort. It was the good times and the bonuses were some of the largest seen on the Street up to that point. This is where Rodney gained his penchant for smoking cigars whenever presented the chance, even if they were of the quality of a cheroot or less.

Life became relaxed and routine and Rodney and Helen and the two boys were finally able to move to that big Victorian house on the hill after one intermediate stop on a street between "Better Slums and Gardens" and that wealthiest part of town. They had arrived at their destination in ten short years; what now?

Things would change as Rodney's greed and feeling of entitlement took hold one summer three years after they had moved to that big house with the red front door. The head of his group would be forced into rehab for alcoholism by the firm and just before he committed to rehab Rodney took the opportunity to make his move. He wasn't going to let this slip by like that Olympic medal. Not knowing that his boss had admitted his alcoholism to the firm whereby the firm decided to back him completely for a shot at rehab, Rodney proceeded to spread rumors about his drinking and debauchery. Then he made a play for the top position. Here, his world would start to come apart.

He was caught in this manipulating charade and condemned by the firm. He stayed on the floor with the boys from Brown but he was no longer quite one of them and sat at the bottom of the food chain. This is when he started the affair with Wendy Brinker a 25-year-old secretary who stood 5'10" with blond hair halfway down her slender back pointing to legs that just captured the eye of any man she passed. Her emerald green eyes were seductively mesmerizing and she had had them on Rodney from the beginning. She now knew that it was her time to enter his world, when he was weakest.

Not only was she attractive and intelligent, and young but Wendy was a Smith graduate and this clinched it for Rodney during one of her several passes while he was at his weakest. In reality, she probably could have enticed Rodney earlier as his passive narcissistic character was his major weakness.

His world went deeper into chaos when he failed to meet Helen's second chance ultimatum over Wendy. Helen had found out about the affair from Rodney himself. Rodney was turning into quite the drinker and alcohol was always getting the better of him, especially the night he drank himself into a state of self-sorrow and was washed over by an utter and absolute feeling of guilt about his affair. This was when Helen was enlightened as her drunken husband, the great Brown athlete, cried like a child and spilled the whole story. He had become the story he had spread about his boss.

He waited an extra day in the end to be with Wendy once more and then break the news of the end of the affair. That night when he returned to the grand old Victorian, Helen was gone. Just like the Achilles this could not be happening to him, then the reality and possible finality of it all started to sink in as he started to wrap himself, once more, in self-pity.

Now three years down the road Helen still hadn't returned and as the house was becoming a financial burden, due in part to his reduced status at work, Rodney decided to rent more rooms. Alice Prodnick would be his second tenant. Carter Mills was his first tenant and a long time tenant who had been rented a room as a request from one of Helen's friends several years before Helen's ultimatum. Helen eventually left and Carter stayed. Carter ran around in tennis whites most of the time even in winter, on occasion, as it had been summer the last time that he had truly been sober and he had been a fairly good tennis player at the time. Now he busied himself by throwing parties at the Englewood Field Club. Carter was from a wealthy family and he had little need or concern for toil. Rodney Junior, whom everyone called V, and his younger brother Jack were both in boarding schools during the year and on Cape Cod most of the summer so the house was wide open. V had taken the past year off from school to sail as part of the crew on a 12 meter sailboat so he would finally attend his last year in prep school after the summer.

***

Alice walked into the main receiving hall following Rodney on his course to show her the room that God, or Bob, had mentioned. She looked up and all around, with awe shining on her face. Then she saw the stained glass from the inside and she whispered to herself, "My church to me it will be…"

"What?" asked Rodney automatically, not really looking for an answer.

"This is my church."

"Oh, good," said Rodney still not listening, "and it's only a hundred twenty-five a month."

Alice just smiled to herself and followed behind Rodney up the stairs past the stained glass and to the left of the second floor landing. At the top of the landing, with Alice standing behind him, Rodney turned the knob to a door which opened up into a room facing the front of the house.

"This will be done," whispered Alice looking past him and into her new home.

"Oh yes, you're right," replied Rodney not listening to the inflection in her voice. The inflection was caught in the deep recesses of his mind but not readily acknowledged as familiar and similar to the intonation of the voice of Dr. McGee, the priest at St. Paul's Episcopal Church when he was a kid. He hadn't been back in many years so the subconscious warning did not register. Nothing registered except the thought of another one hundred and twenty-five dollars a month.

"Can I move in tomorrow, my doves need their sanctuary?"

"Doves?" questioned Rodney.

"They are God's doves, they exist in His sanctuary."

"Sort of like in the Bible; you mean Biblical not real...."

"They are Biblical in every sense."

"That's nice," said Rodney with a smile, envisioning a religious picture containing doves, "You can move in tomorrow but I'll need a check today."

"How is cash?" offered Alice.

"Cash is even better," said Rodney smiling again as he saw his electric bill and gas bill being paid off.

Alice Prodnick was not one for propriety as she turned slightly and reached down into the front of her tight red leather Capri style trousers. She smiled with slight delight on her face and her light hazel eyes closed briefly as she touched herself while retrieving a small cardboard tube. Rodney did not notice this and even if he had it would not have connected as he was visualizing one hundred and twenty-five dollars and some paid bills. He never would have recognized the slight joy which registered on her face as she touched herself with intent while retrieving the item, as he was never in tune with a woman's needs and joys.

Rodney focused on the tube as she twisted the head of a small bearded figure that looked strangely like Jesus and then pulled the little figure, no larger than a large paper clip, from the tube with bills attached. Rodney could only think how clever to have a small item attached to the bills in order to twist them smaller when extracting them from a tube. The fact that it looked amazingly like Jesus Christ in a white robe was not important.

Separating two one hundred dollar bills she said, while handing the bills to Rodney, "My first offering, but I only have hundreds."

"Not to worry, I'll have seventy-five back to you by the end of the month or deduct it from next month." Rodney knew that he would keep it deciding that he would apply it to next month even before he finished the statement. He could use the money but he didn't think to ask for a deposit. Nor did the fact that Alice called it an offering make him think beyond his immediate needs.

As Rodney pocketed the money, Alice shoved the little Jesus back into the tube and the tube back into the front of her trousers with a slight sigh of eyes closed joy as she lingered for just a second. Rodney smiled at her as if she had just made a friendly remark with regard to her happiness about moving in. Alice was happy alright but it was a bit more involved than Rodney could ever perceive. She was in what she called 'exquisite joy'. The little Jesus was back in her pants where he belonged and made her happy all day long. And now she had a home for everything 'exquisite' including two live white doves.

***

Rodney would, initially, think that the 'birds' lived outside of her window and think nothing of it. Then he thought that he was imagining the doves as he saw them at night through her bedroom window when he arrived home from his demoted position on Wall Street. He would think this for days, not connecting what he had seen on different occasions, until one morning when one flew past him while he was on the way down the upstairs hall to the spare bathroom. He was headed to the spare bathroom because the pull chain to the tank, five feet above his Victorian toilet, had separated from the lever and the height of the lever was too daunting, in his condition, to try to reach up and hand manipulate. The bird had flapped its wings against Rodney's left ear but it had not phased him as he was feeling ill from a severe hangover as he headed to the porcelain bowl of the spare toilet. And he would from then on think the birds' presence in the house as normal. He had had a rough night and had taken a cab back from the city. He had the cabby drop him off at another address and then he had fled while the cabby screamed after him waking two people in the neighboring homes. They were awoken for a brief moment before they turned and went back to sleep while Rodney slinked through the adjoining streets until he found himself once again in front of his white stucco Victorian in the dark of night. The stucco, which had been added in the 1920's, helped the house to stand out at night with the slightest moonlight.

***

As Alice left the house Rodney told her he would have a key to the front door for her the next day, in time for her to move in. It would be a Saturday after all and he could have a key made at Demarest Hardware in nearby Tenafly.

Alice left with a smile knowing that she now had a home for her Jesus, her princely white cat and her two Heavenly white doves and it was a glorious summer to come. On top of this she was only a couple of blocks from the big stone church called St Paul's. She had walked right into the nave of the church the previous day and into the vestry where she had found a robe in the priest's closet. It was a robe that she had then carried to the back of the church, covering herself with it, while she took delight in herself and her surroundings. The secretary across the hall, in the converted gymnasium, had thought she had heard the organist doing something strange with the instrument. She thought this for one brief second before she went back to work on her paperwork in follow-up to the leasing of sections of the large structure as the number of parishioners had fallen off dramatically over the past several years. But then it had been good old Alice Prodnick. When she left that day she knew that she would come back for the robe once she found it a new home. Well, she now had that new home and once again returned to the vestry, put on the robe, and walked out; as simple as that.

Carter Mills was walking along the upstairs hallway late that Saturday after Alice had retrieved her key and come back in a Babe's Taxi from Fort Lee, near the George Washington Bridge, where she had been living with an aunt. He was walking along the hall in an energetic alcohol induced high when Alice topped the stairs with her two white doves on her right shoulder and her white short haired cat cradled by her left arm. In Carter's alcoholic world this was not abnormal, nor was it real. He found it somewhat strange, nonetheless, that she was wearing a robe with a cross on the back, but 'what the hell', although there was something unsettling about this unreal figure.

The rest of Alice Prodnick's belongings, which did not amount to much, were out on the driveway but Carter did not offer to help nor did he introduce himself because Alice was not truly real to him in his state. She was more like a moving part of the scenery. Carter was a gentleman but this could only be noticed with people he knew or those he was forced to interact with purely by accident or due to no fault of his own. These people became real and his instincts kicked in, the instincts ingrained in him as a result of his good upbringing, the instincts that came out of his youth. They were automatic and it made him happy to practice them on a level not altogether conscious but someplace else deep inside his being where he was taken back to happier times, innocent times. But as stated, they were not conscious thoughts but yet relationships to a better time; he didn't know why he felt better, he just did.

Carter was aging, he had seen combat in WWII in the Pacific as a Marine. He had left The Choate School for Boys in Connecticut in early 1943 and lied about his age in order to get into the fight. Carter was smart and knew how to talk his way into anything in those days. He had talked himself into a hell that he could not have dreamed of and that hell had first found him in a shallow, sandy hole with his buddy on an

atoll called Tarawa. Historians would later call it Terrible Tarawa. His buddy had been hit in the head by a random Type
92 heavy machinegun round from harassing fire during the
first night. The 7.7mm bullet struck in such a way that it had
covered Carter with his buddy's brain matter. Carter had the
rest of the night to think about this and those brains on his
striped sage green cotton herringbone twill Marine utilities,
brains which had carried the memory of him and everything
that they had experienced together as friends. The next morning nothing would quite be real again. The Marines took Tarawa in three days and Tarawa took Nevin Harper's life and
Carter Mills' dreams.

Alice felt Carter's presence and glanced over her shoulder,
between the two doves, to give him a knowing smile that was
somewhat demonic and which had a startling effect on Carter.
This 'what the hell' became chilling. It reminded him of a
similarly chilling experience he had in the Pacific when a
Japanese soldier came at his location with a knowing demonic
smile on his face and a grenade in his hand. He had been cut
down by six or seven Marine M1 Garands whose 30'06 rounds
all hit within two second of each other as he kept coming. The
smile was still on his face as the grenade went off held close to
his chest as he went down. Carter was chilled once again with
sudden fear and this time by a rather short and chunky yet not
unattractive woman in her mid-twenties with two white doves
on her shoulder, a white short haired cat under her other arm
and a knowing smile which stopped him cold. It stopped him
cold like she knew about that chilling smile he had seen back
in 1943 on that remote Pacific atoll. She had, all-of-a-sudden,
became somewhat real for one brief moment and then again
slipped back into the unreal.

Carter nodded out of fear and dismissal and continued on
down the hall and downstairs. He knew that he needed a drink.
A glass of Johnny Walker Red would help. He did not need the
demons to come back, not now. He was starting a new
relationship with a younger woman who loved him as he was
and the demons were not welcome.

Alice's room faced the front of the house. She had a large window directly across from her door. It gave her a pleasant view of the hedges out front and the large oak tree at the corner of the driveway. Something was missing and as that same knowing smile, that she had given Carter, flashed across her face Alice Prodnick knew just what it was and that she had seen it in the nave at St. Paul's.

Just as she set the doves on the empty curtain rod across the window, after having put the cat on the bare white mattress, Rodney appeared at her door.

"I see the key works okay," he said, not noticing the cat and thinking the doves were actually on the outside of the window. "We have nice trees here," he continued pointing to the window, "and a great many birds that go with them," he added trying to make an excuse for the two white birds that he thought he saw right outside of her window.

Alice just smiled. "It works fine and I love the trees, they are God's artwork."

Rodney received the same demonic smile that Carter had been given but he was not chilled, he was not moved and barely noticed it. He had not seen the smile on that Japanese soldier's face when he had blown his chest and face apart with that grenade many years before. Rodney just turned on his heel, without offering to help her with her things, and walked away adding, over his shoulder, "You have one of the nicest rooms in the house," forgetting to add that it was as well the smallest.

Alice walked up to the window, looked at her meager belongings still on the driveway and then thrust her head between the two white doves and moved it from side to side until the doves spread their wings into her face to hop further out to make room for her. As they did this Alice just giggled like a child might who had their face tickled by soap bubbles for the first time.

That evening Alice walked into the smaller chapel attached to St. Paul's and when she had left there were several objects missing, to add to the robe which she had come back for earlier, and one was the smaller altar cross. It did not have Jesus on it but it would do and would have to be in the room that night. She could get her Jesus cross at another time.

That night Carter stumbled in a controlled manner past Alice's room and noticed, through the crack in the door, a large gold cross, maybe sixteen inches high, gleaming dully in the light of the full moon now at its highest point of the evening. Carter stumbled subtly in his gait at the sight and continued on as though he did not notice, but something registered which told Carter that he would probably exit the house from the back staircase, instead of the front, from now on.

Fortunately Carter did not really see Alice dancing in the light of the moon later that night by the big old magnolia tree in the backyard. She was naked under a semi-sheer white cotton dressing gown. She had her arms wrapped around her ample breasts and she turned slowly on her bare feet with her head tilted upwards smiling in the soft light of the full moon as though it were fresh rain falling on her face. She could feel her feet on the cool grass tickled by the residue of the fallen and dried magnolia pedals which Rodney had failed to rake up. If Rodney had looked out the window into the moonlit backyard he would have thought that everything was normal, such was the state of his existence.

"Moon and sky and earth beneath my feet frame me for God's rapture and angels above come down and turn with me," Alice muttered as she slowly turned while cautiously moving her left arm and hand down from her breast towards the dark triangle just below her waist.

"Jesus is man, Jesus is King on the cross he is prostrate for me," she muttered with growing intensity as she reached that triangle with the stubby fingers of her left hand.

"Oh, stars in heaven and earth below these leaves tickle at my thoughts and caress the bareness of my feet." She now spoke in a clear voice growing with more intensity as she manipulated the soft crevice of the dark triangle with her fingers.

"Moon to caress, God to delight, oh come Jesus, come to my pleasure and feel my rapture," she now spoke out in a high voice growing in volume with the last word. "Make me the Mary, make me the vessel and take delight because I am yours," she intoned loudly with her head facing the moon and her legs spread apart as she stood in one spot with her short, thick fingers working quickly up and around and over the triangle now clearly visible through her now dampened semi-sheer cotton dressing gown.

"OH MY GOD rapture me, rapture me OH MY GOD," heard Carter coming from the backyard through his late evening stupor.

"Oh HEAVEN move earth, move earth Move, Move, MOVE, MOVE, Moooove......................," and it was gone punctuated with a shriek.

Carter thought for a moment or two and then lifted his head up above the window sill from the sun bed he was laying on. He looked into the backyard in time to see the flowing tail end of a semi-sheer cotton dressing gown as it disappeared towards the house. Briefly thinking it must be a ghost he fell back to the bed.

Alice sat up against the house cross-legged and all done in. She had shrieked her last words to the heavens and a light went on momentarily from the house next door. She sat holding her breasts and swayed back and forth with a smile of contentment on her face both for her physical joy and for satisfying the heavens.

Rodney just turned in bed when he heard something minor make its way briefly through his wax earplugs: something like a cat, he thought, as he fell back to sleep.

***

Carter woke before dawn not really having slept but having tossed in a semi-drunken stupor most of the night. His lips were stuck together and his tongue was dry and sandpapery; time for a 'bit-of-the-dog' that bit him. He grabbed the damp washcloth that he kept close to the bed. It was sage green and never failed to startle him every time he brought it to his lips in order to unglue them. It startled him and for less than a nanosecond he was a Marine in the Pacific on god for-saken Tarawa where everything was green, brown, white or red. It was so fast that he never realized why he was startled. He never connected the dots and would never get rid of that 'Marine Corps utility sage green' terry cloth washcloth as the woman he loved had given it to him. She was both young and attractive and she took care of him, outside of the carnal, in a way that he could not take care of himself. Margaret was sent, if not by heaven, by whatever power it was that kept Carter moving unknowingly in search of the young man that he had once been.

The damp cloth succeeded in parting his lips and the sub-conscious shock sent him for a drink of scotch to not only rid his mouth of the sandpaper tongue but quell his, once again, rattled nerves. And the cycle started again. He was always in a sweat whenever he woke whatever time of year it was; mid-winter or mid-summer it did not matter. He could not re-member his dreams but his dream world and his daily world had become one in a cycle of 24-hour pieces. There was such great similarity between the two worlds that he could not separate them from each other even if he had thought to try to do so.

Alice was now quite still in her bed at the front of the house. She was still like a corpse but with a wisp of a smile, or a smirk, as the only evidence of life. Alice always smiled in her sleep but when she was overly excited her eyes would remain open as well. Looking dead, except for that smile, could be disconcerting to some and in particular the occasional boyfriend in the past. It would be downright frightening if her eyes were open as well. But men, except for Jesus, were crude and simple and she now preferred the company of her cat when she was without her Christ.

***

Alice was in this deathlike sleep, with a smile, late one Sunday afternoon a week later when she was awoken by voices at the front door of the Luger house. They were talking with Luger and the other male voice sounded like Luger. As Alice came out of the depths of her sleep world she started to tune in to the voices which talked and laughed with familiarity. She could not make out the conversation, thanks to the thickly built Victorian walls and doors, but she could detect the fact that they knew each other. This unsettled Alice as she knew that she had a certain power over individuals but not several people at once who shared any type of bond. She listened intently in fear that her new world was being invaded even though she had invaded the world of the Luger house just recently herself. Getting up off of her bed and throwing her semi-sheer white dressing gown over her leotards and tank top, to give her some protection against the strangers, she headed for her door to take a look, grabbing her cat on the way.

As Alice came out of her room she could hear that they had gone to the back of the house so she walked in that direction. She came to the backstairs to the kitchen just as Luger was coming up with a very attractive woman in her early twenties followed by a man in his early twenties looking a lot like Luger himself.

Looking up at Alice and stopping on the steps with the young woman Rodney Luger hesitated looked down in brief thought, then looked up at Alice again and said, "Alice is it? Right, it's Alice. Alice this is Kate, my little brother's girl-friend," and turning and pointing to the man behind him he added, "and that is my little brother Jake." Then looking back up at Alice he finished, "This is Alice", and seeing that she was also carrying her white cat, "Alice and her cat."

"Nice to meet you Alice," said Kate as they continued up the steps past Alice headed for the third floor.

"Nice meeting you," said Jake as he passed her. And as his head turned back in the direction that Kate and his brother were headed Alice whispered so that only he could hear, "You are in my church and you are not welcome."

She then turned leaving Jake standing there stunned as she headed down the hall to her bedroom with the unbuttoned ends of the semi-sheer dressing gown following in her wake.

Rodney and Kate were already up the short flight of steps to the third floor while Jake was still standing there mouth all but agape.

"Jake, are you coming?" Kate's appealing voice softly queried. Her voice matched the soft beauty of her blue almond shaped eyes and she was told, on too many occasions, that she looked very similar to that Bond girl Jane Seymour. Although the color of her eyes were not different to offset each other by tone one eye, on occasion, would look slightly smaller offsetting the other in a way which Jake found quite sexy. Kate was also 5'8" to Jake's 6'2" but her long brown hair gave her even greater stature as it fell a third of the way down her back. Their eyes were both the same shade of blue which helped to make them look as though they were related and belonged together.

"Yeah, yeah I'll be right there," he said as he started to head up the stairs then halting to look back down towards the kitchen. "Oliver, come here boy, where are you?" With this, heavy paws and thick dog toe nails hit the lower stair case and headed for Jake's voice.

"Come on boy, that's it," and Jake headed up the short flight of stairs to the third floor with a large black Newfoundland now trying to edge by him as he heard Kate's voice as she talked to Rodney.

"Jesus Oliver," gasped Jake while catching himself from going over the side of the narrow stairs as Oliver rushed by in a squeeze.

By the time Jake got to the third floor Rodney was already showing Kate the bedroom to the left of the stairs across from the small bathroom and at the other end of the third floor hall from another room.

As Jake entered the room Kate's voice became clear and was alive with interest. "Can we easily fit a queen bed in here?"

"No problem," said Rodney smiling, just before Jake's

voice, sounding similar, pointed out, "Only if you can make it up those narrow stairs."

"As I said, no problem," came Rodney's voice all too quickly in response.

***

One week later found Kate, Jake and Oliver ensconced in the third floor bedroom to the left of the steps coming up. It was one bedroom of two on that floor, with one of the two chimneys of the house coming up through the middle of the room. The queen did not make it so they had trouble shot the situation and pushed two doubles together. This made their young energetic love making a bit tricky as things had to be negotiated so that neither one nor both fell through the crack between the beds to the floor. Locking the wheel on the frames only allowed them advance warning before a true breach occurred.

It was night and Oliver slept to the side of the beds which were shoved against a wall and up under a gable. Now, after a week, this spot had become his.

Jake slept with a 12 inch KA-BAR knife under his pillow the previous night, along with this night, with memories of Alice's words still echoing between his ears. And it hadn't helped that the previous night, as he headed down to the kitchen, Jake almost ran head long into Alice as she walked past him at the bottom of the third floor stairs wearing nothing but her flowing semi-sheer dressing gown. It flowed back away from her caused by the slight breeze coming down the hallway from one of the front windows and most likely hers. This sight made the small hairs on the back of Jake's neck stand up and it wasn't her nakedness that caused this but the cross that she was clutching between her breasts with her left hand and her trance like appearance. She just went right on by without so much as a slight flinch in her step with Jake just short of running into her and clearly within her vision.

Jake, wide-eyed, had backed halfway up the stairs, turned and went back to the bedroom to pull the KA-BAR from his pack to put under his pillow. Making some noise as he opened several zippers in his hiking gear trying to find where he had last put it he had woken Kate.

Groggily, "Wha, …..what are you doing…….?." queried Kate.

"I, ah…, ah looking for knife."

"Oh, ok……what?"

"Knife, I'm looking for my KA-BAR, that woman is nuts."

"What woman, what are you talking about?" asked Kate as she came more awake.

"Dracuqueen."

"Who?"

"Alice the nut who whispered that we weren't welcome in her church."

"That was days ago, forget it."

"You didn't see what I just saw."

"Go to sleep……..I'm tired."

"She was basically naked in a trance with a cross stuck between her breasts"

"What, stuck where?"

"A cross between her breasts………..Did I tell you she was in a naked trance? Jesus."

"Go to sleep," said Kate as she turned to face away from Jake.

Jake just whispered, "Yeah, that's easy for you to say, you didn't see it."

Just then Oliver, stretched out and asleep next to the bed, started whimpering and running in his sleep.

"Oh no, now Oliver's dreaming of her. Dogs are intuitive, you know."

"Go to sleep."

"Love you, see you in the morning," Jake had said as he walked towards the bed with knife in hand and then knelt next to Oliver shaking him, "It's alright boy, it's only a dream, come on." As he shook him Oliver let out one more big whimper and then settled down, and Jake went to bed with his knife for the first time.

Jake's dreams were not good that night as Oliver started to once again run in his sleep and Jake joined him as they ran across vast lawns at night with a full moon and Alice following slowly behind in a trance. As fast as he ran he could make no headway with Alice close behind him steady in her pace. Kate finally shook him awake as the sun was starting to come up. This would not be the last time that he would have his Alice the living dead dream.

The character of the house was establishing itself with Jake, who was working as a freelance reporter; Kate, who was working on her masters in psychology and Oliver who was working on anyone he could for a snack, along with the assortment of eccentric individuals. It was an asylum of sorts.

It was Victorian and it held a guy still in a gun pit on a far flung pacific atoll in the Gilberts by the name of Tarawa, a woman who was having an affair with Christ and someone living in his own world 17 years in the past. All three were living in the past, in one form or another, while the house moved on and Jake and Kate worked to deal with the present with an eye towards the future.

Carter, although somewhat insane by appearances, was the sanest of the lot, outside of Jake and Kate. He was intuitive like a barometer and Jake felt safe as long as Carter did not seem to be too disturbed about something, anything.

Rodney on the other hand had a few screws loose and Jake was fully aware of it experiencing its many manifestations as he was growing up.

Jake remembered the time that Rodney had slapped him across the nose and bloodied him once when he was eight-years-old. He was spending the day at his older brother's house while his Father was on a day long business trip. Their Father had picked Jake up shortly after he was bloodied and upon inquiry Jake had just told him, "Ah..., slipped while climbing a tree." He knew that if he had told him the truth his Father would have torn his older brother, by eighteen years, apart. He hadn't wanted his father to get upset.

Rodney was jealous of Jake and his relationship with their

parents. As a younger son to older parents their relationship was more than a good one. Jake loved his parents and his Father had once turned to him and shook his head with a warm smile and said, "I don't know what it is about you but you are special." He just did not want to upset this man he loved by telling him that his older son beat on him emotionally or physically whenever he had the chance. Jake learned to deal with it, or live with it, and accept it as one of the several weaknesses of his older brother.

In the early years Jake had gone to his older brother with ideas and dreams only to have them shot down. The last time Jake asked his older brother for advice had been seven years earlier when he was in high school. He had been accepted into an honors program in film making. It was a class that only took students who consistently hit the honor roll in other subjects. Jake's imagination had finally been released and he knew that he wanted to be the next John Ford but Rodney stepped in and for the last and most devastating time.

Jake had made a film that his professor loved, a parody on McDonalds. The professor said it was so good that he should try to get it to McDonald's. Rodney had worked on the initial public offering of the stock so Jake thought he'd show him the film, which was a mistake never to be repeated again.

After setting up the commercial and showing his older brother, Rodney had just laughed and called Jake naive, "How can you be so simple as to think that they may want this as an ad. They sell to kids anyway and besides the movie is not too good."

Jake had the beginning of tears in his eyes that night and it was long before he rationalized everything that his older brother did to him. Over the years Jake would see his brother as both weak and envious in a very destructive manner. He would also see 'his film' come onto television as an ad for McDonalds but it was someone else's idea, apparently someone with an older brother who was not quite as vindictive. Rodney always seemed to have a couple of drinks in him as well and this would add more acid to this vicious brotherly bath.

By the time that Kate and Jake had entered the house both were aware of Rodney, the true Rodney and they just walked around it as best they could. The fact that one of Jake's other two older brothers was also jealous and vindictive allayed a little of the fear of Rodney as they both realized that it was viral in the family. That is, with the exception of the second oldest brother Tom who was Jake's protector. The other troublesome brother, Brian, as a last parting blow, before moving west, had done his best to talk Jake out of attending law school. Jake had been accepted to three but with concern about more college debt he had over researched the situation to the point of setting up appointments with law firms to get an idea of the business side the profession. Firms that he had visited were impressed that someone would do this so they entertained his interview requests. Brian had told Jake to stay away from the law as 'there are too many lawyers out there.' He did this as he did not want his 'baby brother' sharing in any of the pride that he felt he had instilled in his father not understanding that their father had pride in all of them. But Jake would always be special just because he was last and late. Years later a high powered corporate attorney would ask Jake, after a long discussion on economics and history, why he had not become a lawyer. Jake told him what his brother had said. The attorney smiled and replied, "But he failed to tell you that there are very few good ones out there." Jake would always rely on his own heart after that conversation but that was yet to come.

Two weeks after first entering the house Jake walked past Carter struggling to hang a picture and he heard, "I'd buy one of their damned hamburgers after seeing that movie."

Jake stopped dead in his tracks, back stepped to Carter's door and looked at Carter smiling broadly. It was the first time that he had seen Carter smile a real smile, it was rare.

"I'd buy one of those damned hamburgers," he repeated while holding the framed picture of a young woman up against the wall with one hand with a hammer in the other while a nail stuck at a crooked angle out of the old plaster wall. "That was a good movie!"

"What movie Carter?"

"The one you made, I was sitting outside and could see it, I could only hear your brother, don't worry about him, he's a drunk." And Carter smiled a broad smile again and then turned his attention once again to the hanging of the photo.

"That was seven years ago," Jake said with amazement, for the first time fully realizing that there was someone intelligently lurking behind those eyes, someone who had just come out, if briefly, from seven years earlier as though it happened the same day. Changing the subject while he took this revelation in Jake added, "It's plaster you know."

"What?" asked Carter still trying to bang the nail into the wall and having a large chip of plaster jump off and hit him in the chest.

"The wall, it's plaster. You need to drill a whole or use the ceiling molding which has a ridge in it to hold hangers."

Carter stepped down from the chair he was on which was at the wall across from his bed and he walked over to Jake.

"Maybe you could do it for me," said Carter who grew up in subdued wealth and wasn't used to doing things such as drilling into plaster in order to hang a picture. Things like that had always been taken care of and in many ways he hadn't progressed past those years, especially since 1945 when the war finally ended.

"No problem, I'll get a drill from the basement and do it later for you if that's okay?"

Instead of answering Carter held the picture out towards Jake and just said, "That's Margaret."

"She's very pretty Carter."

"She's more than that."

Jake noticed that Carter was sober when by this time in the day, or any time in the day for that matter, he was usually in one degree or another of intoxication. At least this was the impression that he had for the two weeks that he and Kate had been there and every time he had seen Carter at his brother's house over the previous seven years. Carter was changing.

"I've seen her before."

"At The Club, she just joined this year, she plays tennis. She's from North Carolina, my home."

"I didn't know you were from North Carolina, Carter."

"Not originally but I was planning on going to Chapel Hill in '43 the year Guadalcanal ended. I never made it. It was my last year of prep school and I wasn't old enough for the service but my roommate was. We were talking about the Marines on Guadalcanal that February and the next thing I remember, the next day, was my buddy and me in front of a Marine recruiter after leaving school. He told the truth and got 4F...........I lied and got Tarawa..........but I did get Chapel Hill later," said Carter with sadness in his voice talking about something in one complete thought that he never talked about. But it came out in relationship to Margaret.

Jake could hear Carter's voice change as he uttered the name Tarawa and he could see his eyes change at the same instant. His soft brown eyes seemed to sink back into themselves leaving behind in their wake, fear, sadness and anger as they moved away from the present. His tall slim frame seemed to have less strength to it as it sagged under the weight of the name.

"Tarawa? I've heard the name but, but I can't place it," Jake said with hesitation as he realized how disturbing this place was to Carter.

"Harpie," Carter whispered in a barely audible voice. "Harpie died there and I didn't," said Carter in a stronger voice but still a whisper as he looked off in the unfocused distance with a stare that scared Jake.

Nervously but knowing he had to Jake asked, "Who is Harpie Carter?"

Carter snapped his head. "What, what did you say?"

"Harpie, Carter,................... who is Harpie?"

The light had gone from Carter's eyes even more as he looked like he was looking for an escape, a place to go but there was none. He looked at Jake with no choice in the matter, "Nevin Harper, he was a friend of mine."

"What happened Carter?" Jake asked feeling that no one had ever asked him this question before.

Carter's eyes started to tear up as he tried to hold a memory back. "I let him down," mumbled Carter remembering the sick smell of blood and brains and vomit the next morning when he saw Harpie's eye looking at him. One eye was closed and distorted by the bullet that had hit dead center through the back of his helmet going through the back of his head and exiting to the side of the now disfigured eye, throwing out brain matter with vaporized blood and disfiguring the eye. The helmet had barely slowed the 7.7mm bullet hitting dead on. It had happened while they were hunkered down with Harpie resting with just a small piece of his helmet sticking above their two man hole. Carter was on guard and he had let it happen even though it was random harassing fire. He had told Harpie not to worry, to get some sleep. Carter had started to see things move in front of him that were not there in the fading light of that first day and then he heard the slow methodic woodpecker like stutter of the gun come out of the dark. He heard the whomping of rounds, in rapid progression, into sand and palm logs that were scattered about. Then he heard the unmistakable whack against Harpie's helmet that had thrown the helmet spinning off splattering Carter with blood and gray matter as it threw Harpie's head against the back of the hole in the direction he was facing to rest. Carter hadn't moved that night. Before the light completely faded he could see the blood and brains on his Marine dungaree trousers and jacket and he added to this mess by reflexively throwing up on himself. He now remembered the smell of it all and the first sight of Harpie the next morning. He froze facing forward shaking that entire night. Tarawa was his first experience with the horrors of WWII in the Pacific.

But there was something else even darker than this event that Carter was hiding from. It crossed his   subconscious quickly but just slowly enough to cause a great wave of emotional pain. It clouded all rationale and took Carter to the edge of utter despair and the bottle which was part of who he now was.

"I killed him and I'll kill her," Carter muttered then left the room handing Jake the picture of Margaret on the way out.

He had changed that quickly and Jake realized that he had made a mistake. He had gone too far both because he wanted to know and because he thought that he would be kind and help Carter in return for his random kindness to him, which was great in its uncommon character.

Jake stared at the picture then went to the basement for the drill. By the time Carter returned to the room that night, after sitting at the bar in The Club all day, Margaret's picture was on the wall. It then dawned on Carter that he had not killed her; things were where they should be. He had sat at the bar in The Club mumbling to himself that day with occasional outbursts. He was known by everyone and was liked enough just to be considered to be eccentric and his parties were always open to everyone. Sam behind the bar knew better. Sam had been one of the first Blacks in the Marine Corps during the war in the Pacific and saw active combat with a Marine Corps combat support unit on Saipan, even though they were supposed to be just support as the 3rd Ammunition Company. They brought ammunition forward into combat. He and Carter had both been with the 2nd Marines on Saipan. He just smiled to himself when Carter mumbled and he controlled his drinks but did not stop them. Sam knew how to answer his outbursts and because Carter knew he understood he would say more in front of Sam than anyone else.

"I killed him, I screwed up."

"The Japs killed him Cart and there was nothing that you or I could do about that, it was going to happen. It's just in the cards man," put in Sam with a tone of camaraderie.

Sam did not have to be curious, unfortunately he knew too well, on a personal level, what Carter felt but he had just figured out how to deal with it inside himself. He had also figured out how to get completely rid of that feeling of 'everything is useless' that many feel after experiencing the brutality of war. Sam got to know everyone. He became one of those exceptional individuals who one feels lucky to meet once in life. He was that person who would make you feel as though you were special and that he knew you as a good friend. He had a way of making everyone feel this way and in doing so he moved forward leaving his ghosts behind too involved with the living to be held back by the dead. But he did not have that burden that Carter had that went beyond Harper and something that no one knew, not even the few who knew about Harper and they numbered less than the fingers on one hand.

Carter smiled at the picture now on his wall looking back at him saying to himself, 'it's not a dream, it's okay, I'm here and I understand'.

Margaret understood without having to understand. She did not ask about Harper and on the rare occasion with her when the name did come up she would just touch his arm smile and pull him gently into her arms almost like a child and that would end it. Margaret knew that Carter had been on Tarawa as well as Saipan but it was Tarawa that was trying to take over his life not only in dreams but in full daylight. She read about Tarawa without letting Carter know. She read about it and cried but never let Carter see her tears. She read about the Marines wading ashore and not stopping even while they were getting raked by machinegun fire. 'Such a small place for hell to exist' was all she could think.

Carter's ghosts fit right in with the Luger house, they were at home there and less intrusive than if he were living in a normal house.

As he was looking at the picture of Margaret he heard music forcing its way up the front staircase, from the den, and down the hall into his room. The music sounded somewhat martial and was accompanied by an audible grunt floating up with it. It made Carter sweat a little as he was magnetically pulled down the hall towards the sound. He heard more grunting in quick succession and started to sweat more with worry as he now hesitated but yet moved down the hall pulled by forces beyond his control. The grunt dragged him back to the war again but it was something he needed to face; his help was needed. This was the driving force that walked him down the hall although he did not consciously think that someone needed his help, it was automatic and driven by a deeper feeling of guilt. It was a feeling of guilt that he had over friends who had died while he lived to see the end of the war and go home.

He came to the stairway leading down to the front hall lit by the large stained glass window which graced the front of the house. The window which reminded Alice of a church and brought her to the front door that day that God had told her that there was a room for rent.

Carter stopped and through the throbbing martial music he heard a rush of grunts which had him take two steps at a time as he headed down the stairs to the den. As he touched the ground floor he heard one loud final death grunt. Just as he realized that he was too late he heard the flutter of wings as two white doves flew across the opening to the den and landed on Henry's antlers. Henry was the Lugers' stuffed deer head hanging over the den's fireplace. No one seemed to know where or how he got that name, he was just Henry to most.

Carter's nerves were frayed as the sight of doves in flight confused him while he stood briefly at the entrance to the den in his tennis whites. He turned the corner to the den and stopped in fear of what he might see. But, there sprawled back in the den's overstuffed brown leather chair backed up against the built in Victorian book cases was Alice Prodnick. She had her hands resting between her legs and as Carter's eyes fell on her Alice's eyes came up looking directly at Carter as a demonic grin came across her face. Then she laughed at Carter's frozen and frightened figure.

Carter did not see an unreal Alice anymore, he saw a

skinny, sweaty, little man in a Japanese army uniform laying back in the overstuffed chair clutching a grenade in his groin and now laughing with that still demonic grin. He just froze and mentally vanished as though he were not there at all but someplace else. Alice had become that fanatic Japanese soldier from long ago.

Carter was still frozen in place as Alice got up and passed him with her long robe flowing behind, a robe with a cross on it and a small tag inside saying: PROPERTY OF ST. PAUL'S CHURCH. As she cleared the doorway she laughed, not even looking at Carter as she passed him. A moment or two later, still frozen in place, the doves flew past the side of his face. They alighted on Alice's right shoulder side-by-side as she reached the first landing four steps up on the main stairway before turning right to the large flight up to the top landing.

Carter came back to where he was as though he had snapped awake. He truly did not know why there was martial music on. He headed to the stereo receiver located in the bookshelf behind the overstuffed chair and turned it off, letting the record on the turntable next to it continue to turn.

Just as Carter looked up, Rodney turned the corner from the living room. He was dressed in a frayed and torn pink Oxford button down shirt, which came from Brooks Brothers many years ago now, and a strange patchwork pair of Brooks Brothers trousers made up of yellow, red, blue and green squares of identical size. It was still late spring on the calendar but summer days were already starting and Rodney had just come back from The Club which was becoming more active as some kids had finished school for the year. The pants made Carter smile and brought him back to Margaret in his mind as he remembered her once saying, "Who dresses Rodney, Helen Keller?" She had said it to get Carter's attention when he had gone into one of his trances at The Club and Rodney had just walked away from them after talking to Carter and not realizing that the conversation was all one sided. The comment was ridiculous enough to get Carter's attention; Margaret had learned this. A childlike comment   would always connect when he was lost inside of himself.

"What were you listening to Cart? It sounded rather snap-py."

Then Carter noticed. Rodney was having his dinner. It was ravioli out of a can. The man bought cans of ravioli, the Chef Boyardee brand and ate directly out of the can, sometimes with a spoon and sometimes with a fork. Carter found this odd and then again it took him back in time to eating 'Meat & Spaghetti in Tomato Sauce' C-Rations while sitting in Saipan in 1944 and he would gag involuntarily.

"I don't know, it was on when I came in," Carter snapped as his eyes refocused on Rodney's ravioli can as Rodney brought it up to his mouth and shoveled more of the red covered grayish white ravioli into his mouth. As in the past Carter could taste the C-Rations and started to gag once again.

"Something caught in your throat Carter?," Rodney queried, not remembering that this happened every time he ate ravioli out of a can in front of the man. It just did not connect. As Carter was trying to escape the world he had lived in from 1943-1945 Rodney was running deeper and deeper into the world that he had lived in from 1958-1961 while trying to re-write 1964 and the Olympics. This running to the past created a disconnect for Rodney in the present.

"No, no, I'll be alright," he said as he looked down and away after starting to move his hand up, in an aborted attempt to block out the sight of the can going up towards Rodney's gapping mouth, as though he were going to try to block out the sun.

"Hey Cart," Rodney blurted out with a mouth over full of ravioli, so much so that he had to tilt his head back to keep it from spilling out, " if I go to your shop can I get a discount? I need a new shirt or two."

"Yeah, yeah, no problem, maybe some new trousers as well, I'll call Bea and let her know," said Carter with quick authority ending the question in order to get Rodney to move on with his can while still looking down to avoid seeing it.

Carter was fully back in the moment and thinking about his small specialty 'preppy clothing' store in the next town over. Carter's family had owned a company that manufactured hinges for doors that were used throughout the country. It was a 100-year-old company and Carter had no worry for money; the shop was somewhat of a life preserver for him. It sold items for or of attire from topsiders to Lily dresses and items not found at Brooks Brothers to people who, for the most part, worked on Wall Street and summered on Cape Cod when not at The Club. During any holiday sale from Christmas to Easter Carter could be found, on occasion, passed out between the aisles in the old revolutionary home converted to a store with its narrow halls. Everyone who shopped there knew Carter so they just stepped over him on the way to the item they were interested in as though he were just a bump in the floor. He was actually asleep more than he was passed out on these occasions. Having so many people come up to him over a short period of time during these sales, as well as the celebratory atmosphere of the holiday, just had its inevitable end result on Carter. These were usually the only times, along with part of some of the winter months themselves, that Carter would be found not wearing tennis whites. During Christmas he would dress up as Santa and borrow any large dog that he could and dress the dog up as an elf. It seemed the dogs in the area all knew Carter as well. The elf dog, whichever dog it was, would inevitably stand guard over Carter when he passed out forcing the shopper to get past both Carter and his elf. Easter was different. He'd wear worn out kaki slacks and a nondescript button down shirt, the same one every year, along with these big hairy, grey and white, rabbit feet. Now, seeing Carter passed out with those big rabbit feet helping to block the aisles was a funny sight. If you were in the store during Easter and you heard a surprised, 'Haooha', followed by a chuckle then you knew someone had found Carter on the floor with those feet.

Carter spent most of his waking hours in his own inebriated world but he had the respect of those around him as though he were a good spirit who was there but wasn't. People could feel the man's good heart even when he was in a slight rant fueled by alcohol and even though his voice was mostly gruff in nature.

Rodney took his last bite and dropped the spoon into the can with a hollow metallic sound, and Carter's stomach jumped. "I'll head to the Owl tomorrow. Thanks," he said to Carter indicating that he would take advantage of the shirt discount at Carter's store 'The Wise Owl' the next day.

"Hey Cart, you want any raviolis, help yourself," said Rodney in a falsely benevolent voice to equalize Carter's promised discount as though he were offering something of value in return. Magnanimous was not in Rodney's vocabulary. Not being able to simply accept this offer was one way he showed his lack of knowledge of the word. The other was taking too many things personally and not forgetting them even though they became greater in importance only in his mind.

Carter just gagged again as Rodney turned around to the direction from which he had come and, not recognizing the gagging, left. Carter gagged a full ten seconds after he left which left him covered in sweat and wondering what the hell had just happened. He saw that Jap from hell with the grenade again, he now remembered, and Rodney eating C-rats, the ones he hated in particular. It was time to head to the room and get a drink.

While Carter was headed toward the back stairway Alice came back down the front stairs minus her doves and robe. She had dressed to go out among people and was headed for the church once more, for candles this time. Although it was night she knew that the church would be open as it always was.

***

"I think I pressed Carter too hard," admitted Jake to Kate as he sat on the bed reaching down and combing Oliver's thick three layered black coat, typical of a Newfoundland.

Without putting her book down, "I'm sure you didn't," replied Kate automatically.

"No, I really did; I thought that I was helping but...but... he said, 'I killed him and I'll kill her.'"

Kate lowered her book into her lap and looked at Jake. "What do you mean he'll kill her?"

"I don't know. I do know who 'him' is, I think. It's someone by the name of Harper, he calls him Harpie, in a place called Tarawa."

"No, what do you mean 'he'll kill her?'"

"Oh, I don't know, didn't make sense," Jake said half paying attention while trying to think about everything. Turning to Kate with Oliver's brush in hand as Oliver looked up waiting for the next brush stroke Jake added, "Tarawa, I think it has to do with the war."

"WWII if you have to pick a war," put in Kate with a changed voice. "I remember my Father mentioning a place called Tarawa........."

"Your Father?"

"Before he went to medical school he had been in the Navy as a Corpsman, the word Corpsman just stuck with me as a child. He was only eighteen at the end of the war and never left the U.S. But he had heard stories which made him thank God that he never went to the Pacific and many of the stories had to do with a place he called 'bloody Tarawa'."

"I never heard him mention that."

"He only mentioned it to Mother when we had problems as a family. But it was enough that we would hear it, and it stuck out especially with the word bloody before it."

"I didn't even know that he was in the Navy."

"He didn't really talk about it. I asked mother about it. But then he did not leave the States so it was a minor blip in his life. But thinking back, the stories that he heard about that place had had an impact."

"Tarawa?"

"Yes."

"So it was bad. I'll have to go to the library and check it

out."

"What do you think he meant by saying he would kill her?" queried Kate with more concern in her voice.

"I don't know but it was more fear of doing so than stating fact. But it was also enough to be more than just a passing response."

Chapter 2

The Church

Alice turned the large medieval style knob to the small iron bound oak wood door on the side of the main church of St. Paul's, which would allow entry directly into the nave. She pushed and the door gave but barely a fraction of an inch before stopping fast against its dead bolt.

"Bastards, how dare you," she mumbled to no one in particular.

She tried again and then smiled and giggled, her demeanor moving from anger to gaiety in a matter of seconds as she turned and headed to the back of the church. There between the main building and the small attached chapel was a wooden grate which stood three feet off the ground set into the stone of the church and maybe five feet in height and two feet wide. The grate was in the shape of the stained glass windows on the sides of the main church building, or long and narrow with the apex forming a wide point. The wooden slates to the grate ran horizontal, canted down to keep rain out, and they were bisected by a thinner piece of wood running down the middle and all was painted a dark gray- brown. It looked like a vent but for the most part it was ornamental, unless one looked much deeper.

Alice giggled again as she put her strong stubby fingers up against the grate. She then moved forward and up with her entire body weight moving the grate up just enough for the bottom to come free of its stone base for removal. Alice had figured this out one recent frustrated night when again the doors to the church had been locked. In anger she had simply pushed up against the grate trying to break it when it had moved. The church itself, unknown to her, was, for the first time in its history, keeping its doors locked due to the recent theft of items such as an altar cross and priest's robe.

The grate had been designed this way when the structure had been put up in 1856. It was designed this way not only to facilitate easier replacement of the grate, if too worn by weather, but as well to allow the 'knowing' access to a secret passageway in order to be able to move in and out of the church, and the nave, without being seen. No one knew about the passageway except the current priest and one of the church's oldest parishioners who knew the history of the building as his family had been members since the early 19th century, before the current church had been built. They both felt that it had to do with the effect of the Underground Railroad which passed through these towns with a secret hideout below a barn and one behind the wall of a Revolutionary home. As these were small places to hide it was felt that the clergy in the 1850's decided to quietly add to the "Underground" space available in the area. There had been no record of this made and it did not show in the architectural drawings of the structure still held in the church's vault. Only the priest and the parishioner knew and now Alice knew. After all of these years the grate had never been replaced but diligently scraped and painted and the passageway was never discovered by accident until now.

Alice lifted the grate leaning it part way across the opening and then squeezed in. After getting in there was plenty of room to turn around on a stone floor covered by years of bird feathers and other remnants from nests abandoned or discovered and removed from the grates. She turned and grabbed the two wooden handles running laterally down the back of the grate and placed to give the average person enough leverage to lift and pull the grate in and slide it back down in place. The handles were amazingly strong after all of these years. Once she replaced the grate, Alice smiled a sinister smile as she pulled her shoulders close together and hugged herself. After her first visit she realized that she could not see anything inside and had returned with a flashlight which she left just inside the removable grate. That first discovery was just that, a need for light as she could not travel through the darkness without a torch or now a flashlight. The church and all of its mysteries and treasures were now hers for as long as she chose, or at least for the night. Alice felt that she knew everything that there was to know about the church but there was another mystery to the passageway that Alice did not yet know. It was one that would be surprising in ways Alice could never have imagined in her most sinister of moments.

Alice walked along the narrow corridor partially stooped, even for as short as she was. She walked maybe 20 feet until the corridor turned left, opening into a room with old straw on the stone floor where maybe ten people could sit comfortably. She bypassed this going to the left-hand corner of the small room where there was an obvious gap where the two opposing walls met. She pushed the right wall of stone with her shoulder and a section of wall balanced on a short and narrow pedestal easily gave way pushing a line of stone, which had been part of the wall, out into the room. This newly revealed stone would allow a person to close the hidden gap upon exiting simply by pushing against it. Once again Alice squeezed through and found herself in a small stone box behind an old wooden panel whose middle section sat between wooden rails only visible from the inside of the box. She pushed the tight fitting panel aside and found herself in a small closet, containing the priest's vestments, after which she slid the panel back into position. She smiled with glee once again knowing that her Jesus had shown her the way in a way that no one else knew about, so she thought.

She would not take anything from this little closet as she wanted to protect the secret of the passageway.

Her task to devotion, as she saw it, was to find appropriate candles for 'her church' in the Lugers' house.

She left the small vestments closet and entered the priest's chambers. She looked around briefly then giggled once more as she headed out and to the back of the pulpit. Bypassing the pulpit she ran with a flow to the center aisle ending in front of the pulpit. She stopped here looking at the darkened Tiffany stained glass windows of different biblical scenes with Jesus. As she glanced around she started to turn with outstretched arms accompanied by a demonic laugh. "Mine, it is mine and I am here to be seen as glory," she spoke in more than a whisper ending in another full turn and an extended giggle as though she had lost control of it.

She stopped, facing the pulpit, and eyed the gold capped candles to either side as well as those back further on the altar. The larger candles further back on the altar would serve her purpose. She would take them and possibly come back for the candle holders which were just too large to handle altogether.

She stepped up onto the platform leading to the altar, stopped, looked up at the domed white vault above her head and smiled. She then proceeded forward and removed each two foot tall three inch in diameter candle from its holder with a little giggle of conspiracy. Then she stepped back from the altar and looked up at the stained glass behind it while pulling the candles to her bosom, hugging them tight to herself exhibiting complete glee. She was not done yet. She had discovered the ladder off to the side of the main door of the church which was topped by a trap door. She knew that this was the bell tower and now was her chance to reach the highest point in the church.

Placing the candles at the base of the wooden ladder, built into the wainscot board ceiling, she started to climb, pushing the trap door open at the ceiling using her back. The trap door easily pushed up and fell back against the opposing wall just above it. The long ladder climbing to the tower was just to her left next to the trap door so she simple moved her short, thick, strong fingers over and continued climbing and then transferring her feet to the long ladder all the way up. She could see the actual color of the bell rope traveling up through the ceiling now below her. It was a richer brown than the blackened end that ended five feet above the floor off to the left of the main entrance. Rodney Luger, as an altar boy, had pulled that rope many times on Sunday morning as had many from generations before him. Now Alice Prodnick was in the bell tower where few of these young boys had been, except for the most daring among them. Of these boys she would notice two sets of initials and dates in caulk. One was R.L. 4/8/51, just off to the left of the ladder one third of the way up, the other was T.W. Dec. 24, 1872 although covered by soot. Alice had discovered these initials near the top of the ladder just under the belfry's platform. She climbed up through the floor of the platform and stepped off the ladder and among the three bells of the belfry, and smiled to herself.

Alice could not see through the slats of the belfry's elongated vents for any distance but she could look down through them and see the street below. She could also see the stone owl attached to the wall of the tower just below her and meant to chase birds away from any instincts of nesting. Alice decided that she wanted that owl then turned and forgetting about it walked to the largest bell and ducked under and into it's inner dome standing next to the clapper. She wrapped her arms around the clapper and started to recite slowly so she could hear the enclosed echo speaking back to her: "My domain is within", she then giggled, "I control all with reverence for woman." She then screeched excited by what she had said. She stood there silently for a moment then let out a primal screech again followed by, "I-I-I-I umph" followed by a full throated scream and then a pause, then, "I-I-I-I umph" and another scream.

While she was doing this an old couple was taking their

nightly stroll past St. Paul's. The old woman stopped first as the old man's hearing was not quite what it used to be.

"George dear, listen."

"What Gladys?" he said as he stopped, saying it as though he had said it a million times in the past.

"Did you hear that?"

"Hear what my love," he said with condescending love in his voice.

"That!" directed Gladys.

"I-I-I-I umph," was heard followed by a muffled scream coming from above the church.

George heard it that time and his face became serious as he barely heard, "I-I-I-I umph, the Devil will not have me, I am the Devil." This was followed by a blood curdling scream, which he heard clearly, accented by the muffled deep tone of the bell Alice was still under, creating an acoustic mirage as though the sound was coming from the heavens well above the church.

George, being partly deaf, grabbed Gladys by the hand. Hearing this female yet masculine voice coming from the heavens beyond the church steeple and invoking the Devil was enough. Legs that had been unsteady for some years came quickly back to life as he almost tugged Gladys off her feet yelling, "Come on girl that damned ghost is real."

George thought he was sprinting as Gladys trailed behind barely keeping up when a car, obeying the 15MPH speed limit in front of the church, slowly started to pass them and one of its passengers remarked to the other, "Look, that poor senile bastard looks like he's wading through a tide while dragging that poor old lady." And the car was past.

As George and Gladys started to pass the funeral home, located in the old Victorian next door to the church, George got the shivers up the back of his neck and tried to throw it into third gear. But he just kept dragging along at the same speed until they were both well past the funeral home.

As Gladys and George disappeared into the night, with a new and frightening story, Alice came out from under the bell giggling. She tilted her head back and stepped around in a controlled twirl with her hands uplifted as her giggle turned into a full throated demonic laugh.

Descending the ladder Alice stopped two thirds of the way down at the initials R.L.4/8/51 and giggled again.

"I know who you are and I am the devil," she uttered, and then laughed again as she pulled a red colored piece of chalk from the left hand pocket of her slacks and while holding on with her right hand drew a crude Heptagram over the initials and date.

She giggled the entire time that she was drawing and as she finished she whispered, "I fear no trap." She then leaned over and touched her tongue to the 'Devil's Trap' and giggled again as she straightened up, returned the chalk to her left pocket and started down once more.

Descending the final ladder she lowered the trap door behind her as she went. Coming back to the floor she smiled a self-satisfying smile and retrieved her prize candles from the floor.

She had more to do, as she had purposely brought along the short fat piece of red chalk.

Alice did not put 666 or any demonic sign on anything but she did have her own sign and it was simply a red circle the size of a thumbprint. To her the circle represented fertility and woman and the red meant power that could not be intimidated and only she knew what it all meant. She would put these little red circles out of sight so only she would know they were there and no one would remove them as they would never see them to remove them. They would be there for all time and so would she. She laughed with satisfaction as she drew her last circle under the eagle lectern whose wing's held the large bible on the pulpit platform. It would never be seen here, hidden in the dark but present for every sermon. She delighted in the thought.

She allowed herself one last twirl in the aisle, just in front of the altar, giggling once more to herself. She then collected her candles from the side of the altar where she had left them before putting her chalk to work. She tucked them under her right arm secure by her right hand as she headed for the priest's chambers, the vestments closet and her secret passage.

She would not leave a trace behind other than the missing candles, a small red Heptagram in the bell tower, which would not be noticed for many years to come, and little red circles that would never all be discovered outright but would all disappear in the same year that she had put them there.

She entered the closet and slid the panel back with her left hand to reveal the small entry box behind it. Once again she slide the panel back in place behind her after stepping in and making sure that the clothing on the hangers were spaced the way she had found them to prevent any attention to the panel.

Once again she entered the Underground waiting room and closed the stone corner behind her so that the room once again looked as though it only had one entrance and exit at the far side. As she crossed the room to head for the narrow passageway, and the removable grate, she thought she was in control of this secret room and passageway and that she knew all its secrets but she did not. Not yet at least.

After replacing the outside entrance grate she picked the candles up from alongside the wall of the church where she had laid them and stepped back to view her handy-work. She was satisfied that the grate looked perfect and that no one would notice anything and that no one would ever know that she was there. She looked around in the dark moonlit night and saw no one who would see her and smiled as she headed off the property towards the street and back up the hill to the Luger house.

Chapter 3

The Club

The next day Carter shuffled through the front door of The Club and across the 100-year-old oak floor which was always kept at a shine. He passed George and Gladys Johnson sitting in overstuffed chairs and speaking with the Coopers on the sofa across from them. Carter was headed for the bar dressed in tennis whites and George Johnson was animated in his speech as he passed.

"I tell you Whit that damned ghost is in that tower!"

"Now come on George," said Whitaker Cooper in a calming voice.

"I heard it too," put in Gladys.

"It was a declaration and a scream part man and part something else, I have never heard anything like it."

"Whaddaya mean declaration George? Like, 'I have arrived'"

"Very funny Whitaker," said George using his full name as he did when he was not happy with his friend.

"It was something like the guards chant in the Wizard of Oz, couldn't quite make it out."

"And it ended with 'I am the devil'," put in Gladys who

was not prone to exaggerate.

"You mean to say George that you found the Wicked Witch?"

"Yeah, and she's alive and well, I tell you", finished George with a smirk.

"Maybe we aught to talk with Reverend McGee; maybe he needs to do a dance or something around the church."

"Very funny Whit."

Carter knew the Johnsons and the Coopers and could hear their voices from the bar where he now sat but he could not make out what they were talking about even if he were trying to listen. And if he did listen and did hear what they were saying he would have thought that it was all normal. As it was he was seeing that demonic Jap with the grenade from his past and that was real. He was also seeing birds flying around the Lugers' house for some reason and this seemed normal and fit in with all the other chaos that was going on in his head.

Carter hadn't sat for more than a few seconds when Sam came over and threw a coaster down on the bar followed by a rock glass with just a couple of small cubes. He followed this with a good two shots of Johnny Walker Red. No need to ask. Sam knew by Carter's haggard look that this was a rock glass day. Sometimes it wasn't.

"How are things Cart, you look tired?" put in Sam. But he knew.

"Saw that damned Jap again last night. He laughed at me and had birds flying around him and then Rodney shows up eating C-rats, Jesus Christ Sam," declared Carter as he started to sweat all over again thinking of the grenade clutching Japanese soldier. He also started to feel a gag coming on at the thought of flat monotonous C-Rations. He reached for the drink and put half of it down with one swallow leaving one of the cubes in his mouth to help cool himself. Before he even put the glass down he had the other cube in his left hand and put it up to his forehead.

"The Jap's dead Cart, he can't hurt you unless you let him.

The bastard 'll try and try but he can't do anything, you guys killed him. You told me."

"The son-of-a-bitch just wouldn't go down Sam, he wouldn't go down. Everyone shot at the same time that morning and I heard two enblocs ping out of their M1's they fired so much and the son-of-a-bitch still came forward until that damned grenade went off."

"He's dead Cart and they probably hit him a few times, a couple of those guys probably didn't have all eight rounds in their rifles so you'd have to hear a couple of enblocs pop out."

"Jesus Sam." Carter said just before he lifted the rock glass and drained it putting it back down again with his hand around it indicating that he wanted Sam to fill it again so he could take another sip immediately.

Sam knew this and looked at Carter with bottle in hand ready to pour but he wasn't pouring. Sam added a smile that lifted his salt and pepper mustache in a way that always made Carter smile, no matter what state he was in. This meant, 'take your hand off the glass, slow down and do not take another drink as soon as I pour it or I won't pour it.'

As soon as Carter smiled Sam knew he was back and poured the drink. Sam noticed that Carter was getting more of the crazy periods lately. When he had met Margaret he settled down to a degree and was happier most days but recently he was seeing that Jap with the grenade, a story that Sam had only heard once before this recent period. It was a story that did not come easy from Carter and only came because he had to get it out for some reason that day and he knew Sam was the only one who would understand, he was the only one he could tell. After the War Carter kept everything in, along with his nightmares. He even denied his nightmares. They did not happen he would tell his wife or he would tell her that he didn't know what they were about when she became so worried that she tried to force him to talk about it. He was angry a lot and she knew that this was the war. She knew Carter well as she had known him as a young girl. Their families would summer together on Cape Cod in the years before the war. Carter had married Jean after the war because she knew him enough to understand him and he knew that at some level she had always loved him and he needed that. But Carter was a bad husband, no fault of his own. It was partly the fault of the war and the lost love of a woman he knew that he would never see again, and that was his fault.

Carter and Jean had two beautiful daughters late in their marriage and Carter had a soft spot for his daughters, their presence kept the monster inside him at bay most of the time. He knew that if he had a son he would make impossible demands on him knowing that he could never stand up to the men he had known and fought with and now loved more than brothers. He knew that he was blessed by having his two daughters.

Jean lived many years with Carter's night sweats, fitful sleep and escalating nightmares. She tried to get him to talk with someone and this only angered him more. Who the hell could he talk to except his buddies and most of them were dead. Once, the fear was addressed when he went to a reunion and met some old buddies. The Jap and the grenade came up, there was something about that lone Japanese soldier first thing that morning, and how '...the bastard wouldn't go down', and they all laughed, even the ones who did not see him as they had seen their own. They laughed but it was not a comfortable laugh and Carter never went back to a reunion. He just started drinking more and talking in drunken stupors to his closest buddies who were all dead.

Jean finally left Carter when the girls went away to boarding school. She had tried. Carter only blamed her for not leaving sooner because he did not consider himself a good cause.

Over time he became almost numb to the nightmares. And his guilt of surviving became manageable and acceptable as he had no choice but it remained lurking in the corners like a big black dog ready to come out of the dark and put its shadow over him. This thought gave him a small flash of fear at least once a day although usually brief as he subconsciously kept the dog at bay. It was manageable and he found a fine balance with drinking. Drinking became an escape but he usually did not allow it to go far enough where it only brought everything back and amplified it.

Now sitting with Sam he was starting to walk with the black dog again and Sam knew it. The Club knew it. Most people in The Club had known Carter for years and they knew the bad times. They were glad to see them go for Carter's sake but they could see them returning even after a period of unbridled happiness after meeting Margaret.

"I'm tired Sam but I'm edgy, I can't get away from it.'

"I know buddy, I see 'em too and I'm here to tell you that the bad guys are dead and gone and our pals will keep 'em that way."

"Whaddaya mean?'

"When you get angry about losing a friend and all the shit that happened do you for one moment ever feel that someone is looking after you and the only thing you do is feel even more guilty because you know it is a buddy looking after you who didn't make it and you did?"

With a slight slur, "It's not that easy Sam."

"It can be if you can find a way to understand it."

"What the hell is there to understand when you see what happens to a guy when he gets hit hard?"

"Ya gotta find something there Cart, don't look too hard. Feel any good you can and let it wash over you. There's gotta be a reason why you and I are here and they are not or you'll truly let them down," finished Sam.

"Christ, that's too much to deal with," mumbled Carter looking down at his drink as a cherry plunked into his scotch.

"What the hell, said Carter now fully alert and looking up to see Sam's big smile, "Why'd you do that?"

"'Cause you're a cherry asshole," said Sam and then he smiled again.

There was one brief moment of silence then both Sam and Carter broke out in laughter enough to turn the heads of the Johnson's and the Coopers.

"Carter's back," said George Johnson with a smile.

Looking up towards the door Sam said, without changing his direction of sight, "Don't look now Cart but here comes Margaret."

Without looking, because he did not need to, Carter pushed his drink forward to Sam, "Sam take this. Give me a ginger ale will you."

Sam filled a rock glass half full of ginger ale and swapped out the two before Margaret's line of sight would have seen the exchange. Margaret would not ride Carter on his drinking or for that matter bother him about it. She would subtly try to help him manage it when she was present and when she was present he did not need it as much and he would feel like he let her down if he drank too much.

As she approached, Sam found himself appreciating the easy beauty of this woman just past her thirtieth year but years ahead of most 50-year-olds in her understanding. She complimented his friend well as her 5'7" frame and warm smile moved towards Carter. Like most women at The Club, she was slim and fit and could be found most weekends either swimming laps in the pool or on the squash court. She kept her brown hair short in a pixie, which framed her light blue eyes and radiantly attractive face. She was also a trust child who had no need for money but she did need Carter to fill that place in her soul that nothing else could touch.

"Hi Sam, how's my favorite man doing? He's not telling you stories about me is he?" said Margaret as she reached Carter and kissed him on the cheek as he turned his head towards here voice. She knew that Sam was the only person who he could really talk to about his ghosts and she thought that's probably what they had been talking about so she changed the subject to herself to make it easy for them to change there conversation.

"He hasn't caused any trouble yet but I have my eye on him, he can be shifty," said Sam as he smiled his mustache smile with both hands leaning on the bar.

As Margaret sat she reached for one of Sam's hands and squeezed it warmly, "Only to be a fly on the wall when you two boys get together," she said with a warmth that softened the content of their previous conversation and helped to relax Carter.

"What can I get you Margaret?" offered Sam.

"Can I get one of those fresh squeezed orange juices?"

"I always save the best oranges for you Margaret, will my boy be okay while I step away?" asked Sam with a knowing smile.

While Carter still looked at his glass listening to the two of them Margaret smiled at Sam, "I'll make sure that he is." And Margaret and Sam gave each other a conspiratorial smile with a mutual glint in the eyes.

As Sam walked off to the end of the bar and to the hand levered juicer, which had been at The Club as far back as anyone could remember, Margaret rested her hand on Carter's left arm as both of his arms rested, stretched over the bar in support of his torso. She squeezed his forearm lightly and Carter smiled as he turned his head in her direction.

"I think I love you Margaret," said Carter softly followed by another smile.

She could tell that he had been feeling pain before she sat down. She squeezed his arm even more and she could feel her eyes start to tear as she thought how dear this man was and not only to her. He was a good soul. 'Cart' was all that she said as she smiled at him with moist eyes.

She then stood up from her tall bar chair and stood next to Carter wrapping her arms fully around him kissing him on the side of his head and then holding him tighter as he leaned his head into her cheek.

Sam, looking down from the end of the bar as he pulled the lever down on the last orange half, just smiled at the two of them. 'There is good in this world' was all that he thought in that brief moment that he pulled the handle down completing the filling of the glass.

As he tossed the last orange half in the garbage, and picked up the glass of orange juice and headed back towards Carter and Margaret he had a smile on his face.

Putting a napkin on the bar as a coaster, he placed the glass of orange juice in front of Margaret, who was still standing. "My best for you Margaret, you'll need the fortitude to deal with this guy," said Sam nodding his head in Carter's direction.

"Sam, you can put it under my number," said Carter looking down at his rock glass again briefly.

"It's on me Cart."

"Are you boys fighting over me? A girl like me needs to come here more often when you two are together."

Sam and Carter just smiled at each other.

Margaret looking out at the red brick and white painted concrete patio said, "Isn't that Rodney out there on the concrete end of the patio?"

"Yeah," said Sam, "he's with some English friend from Bermuda".

Just as Sam said this Rodney noticed Margaret at the bar standing next to Carter and raised his hand in a wave as he pushed back his chair and said something to the man at his table. As the man at the table turned to look Rodney came around his table and started into the bar and towards Margaret and Carter.

Sam seeing Rodney come moved away to the other side of the short bar and started to dry some glasses with a small bar towel. This was more to give them all privacy, now that it was becoming a group, than the need to dry glasses. As Rodney arrived at the bar and looked towards Sam, Sam threw his head up with a smile and said, "Hi Rod."

"Hey Sam," said Rodney before looking at Carter and Margaret as he leaned against the bar in his tennis whites covered in red clay. Rodney always dove for the ball on the clay courts. He was competitive that way. He would dive for anything even if it was physically impossible to get it. After midday tennis on weekends, people could always see Rodney coming from a distance like a neon sign of red clay.

"Hi Margaret," he said looking at Margaret then looking down at Carter, "Carter, you wanna meet Clive Hawthorne? I

know him from Bermuda and you mentioned that you wanted to rent a house down there for a season."

"Sure, why not," said Carter after a second or two as he
turned and smiled at Margaret and started to get up.

Grabbing Margaret's right hand in his left and his ginger
ale with the right he started to follow Rodney and then stopped
and turned, "Thanks Sam."

"For what? Talking with a pal?" and he threw Carter that
mustache smile.

Carter just smiled in return and so did Margaret looking at
Sam. Then they both turned and headed for Rodney's table at
the closest part of the brick and concrete patio to the great lawn
in front of the tennis courts. The portion of the patio that they
were headed for was past the red bricks and was simply
concrete painted white. The patio was bordered by long
trough-like concrete planters which were knee high and
planted with red geraniums.

As they neared the table Clive Hawthorne turned in his
chair, not getting up even with Margaret present.

"Clive, this is Carter and Margaret, Carter lives in my
house; he's interested in a seasonal in Bermuda," said Rodney, not bothering to introduce Clive to Carter and Margaret.

Clive appearing fairly drunk extended his hand in Carter's
direction and blurted, "I say ol' boy, you look familiar." As he
shook Carter's hand he nodded at Margaret.

Clive was just a little younger than Carter but not by much
and he looked as though he had been at sea a long time with
leathery sun browned skin accompanied by the telltale broken
capillaries, under the skin, of an alcoholic more so than Carter.
Carter could clearly see this even through the tan, which was
not a good sign for Clive if he cared to know.

"I shouldn't, I've never been to Bermuda," responded
Carter a little aggressively detecting Clive's arrogance, which
was always something that Carter could not handle well.

"Could be it was the Army. I was in the British Army just
before that Korea folderol, would have gone too if not for my
appendix, had it burst you see, bad show, peritonitis and all

that you know."

"No, I don't know, I still have mine and I was in the Marine Corps and never met a Brit in my wonderings," replied Carter matter-of-factly.

"Surely you met Brits in Korea if you were there and of course not me," Clive pointed out with a laugh.

"I was in the Pacific during the war and there were no Brits, there were only Japs."

Margaret's hair went up on the back of her neck, 'uh-oh' she thought but it was too late.

"Surely you experienced the great forces of His Majesty," shot Clive with defensive arrogance.

"They were nowhere to be found. As I say, the only foreigners I met, outside of a few Australians, were Japs and never made it to Australia unfortunately as the few Australians that I did meet were great people, no doubt from a great nation," Carter stated knowing that Clive would not like the high exult that many Americans have for Australians.

Clive started to steam. "Well, I guess Monty, being the great man that he was, stole the British thunder from the Pacific. Europe was the heart of the whole party and once again you Yanks came late to the show," he said finishing with his nose actually up in the air to try to get his head higher than it was.

"Europe wasn't our war you horse's ass," Carter intoned as Margaret bent her head and Rodney shot back in his seat, "but yet that bastard FDR sent you limey bastards all our resources while our guys died on Bataan and Corregidor and the death camps that followed. You tell the thousand guys that died around me over three days on Tarawa that Europe was the heart of the war," finished Carter with more clarity than he'd shown in weeks.

"Settle down ol' boy, it's just that the Nazis were the big enemy and thank God for Monty as he made the show work. You Yanks did help with your great resources I must admit, but the real genius was Monty not Eisenhower or that charlatan Patton."

"Why you little shit," loudly returned Carter.

By this time Rodney had his hands up thinking what to say other than the extended flat palm for stop. And Margaret? Well Margaret just held Carter's hand.

"Where was Monty when our guys were pushing through Omaha Beach?" Carter continued, "Where was that little weasel when we broke out of the hedgerows and started charging forward? He was still stuck outside of Caen even after having it bombed into oblivion. We had to slow our breakout, turn left and relieve his right flank to pull his bacon out of the fire."

"That was all in Monty's plan ol' boy, to keep Jerry in check so you Yanks could attack. He set them up for you," Clive stated with increasing arrogance.

"Monty had no plan. He was getting his ass handed to him as he would again in Holland after letting an entire German army escape twice."

The Johnsons and the Coopers were now watching through the open window as Sam watched from the corner of the bar. The only thing they could all hear was Carter at first and only certain words and phrases where he raised his voice such as '...YOU HORSE'S ASS' and 'WHY YOU LITTLE SHIT.'

"Holland was a bit of genius that was partly unsuccessful."

"That's like a WHORE saying she's partly pregnant," shot Carter using whore with emphasis and starting to get angrier.

They all heard 'whore' too.

"You don't know your history," Clive intoned in a louder firmer voice but yet noticeably drunken.

"I lived my history and I had a buddy in the 101st Airborne in Normandy and Holland and then the Bulge where Monty fucked them over again with his ignorance and misuse of airborne," Carter stated in raised voice to compete with Clive.

"You Yanks are all alike, you show up late with all your toys and we do all the fighting," Clive stated even louder so that now everyone could get most of the conversation even the hard of hearing George.

"Why you pompous little shit," blurted Carter as he moved closer to the table ready to reach out and grab Clive.

All eyes, including two more sets from a young couple on the other side of the patio, were on them as all onlookers, except Sam, reared back in protection from the final blow which would come any second.

Clive in response reared back in his chair in fear and fell over backwards.

"Appendicitis! You aren't worth the time. Forget Bermuda if it's full of self-important little shits like you. Let's go Margaret," he said as he reached for her hand whose grip he had broken when he had moved closer to the table in anger.

"Sorry Rodney," whispered Margaret to Rodney so Clive would not hear as she was not sorry for him.

"Well, well, I don't know what to say," said Rodney to no one in particular as he turned to look at his Bermuda society connection, Clive, on the ground.

As Margaret and Carter walked back to the bar Sam had a big smile on his face as he could clearly hear everything after the voices fully elevated but mostly he heard Carter as he was the loudest.

"What are you smiling at?" said Carter as they entered the bar and he saw Sam still smiling.

"Semper Fi," was all that Sam said, shaking his head sideways with an, "Umph," as he closed his mouth in satisfaction.

"It looks as though we tried to sit at the wrong table," put in Margaret as they sat at the bar again.

Sam just laughed again. "The guy deserved it. He's been serving up that English garbage for a couple of days now. I'm surprised you hadn't run into him before this Cart."

"He's not at the house, I would have noticed."

"Jesus, that's all you'd need," said Sam, and then looking at Margaret with deference, "Can I get you a fresh orange juice Miss Margaret?"

"Now you are having a good time Sam," said Margaret with a smile, as he would address her this way when things around Carter and she got to be a little crazy.

"Carter said it all for me, the man has made me a happy man today," responded Sam.

"How about a 'real' ginger ale Sam?" put in Carter.

Sam looked briefly at Margaret for an 'OK' and she just smiled.

"Coming up and this one is on me too, you can pay for Miss Margaret's orange juice though," Sam said as he smiled again.

"Now you're just trying to confuse me."

Just as Carter said this a deep bark came from the entrance to The Club and before Jake and Kate could stop him Oliver bounded across the room towards Carter. All 150 pounds of Newfoundland came barreling across the floor at full speed slipping and scratching at first on the polished oak before his paws took hold.

Even coming from full speed Oliver was able to stop, without slipping or bumping, right at Carter's seat. This joyful charge by Oliver always made Jake nervous until Oliver was at a full stop. He once saw Oliver take off like this towards a group of kids no more than seven or eight years-of-age and he almost closed his eyes as he screamed at Oliver. But Oliver stopped perfectly among them as they proceeded to laugh and giggle and pull at his ears as he just sat there, panting from his short run, taking it all in. He loved kids and Carter, and he loved Jake and Kate but he would not come to a stop when he ran at Jake, he would bowl him over as his playmate and they'd wrestle.

Carter turned to see Oliver looking up at him and just smiled down at that big Newfoundland, "Hey boy, how'd you get here?"

Oliver barked again and looked up waiting for Carter to rub the top of his head and his ears, which is what he started doing.

"Hey Sam, you have any of those stick pretzels?" asked

Carter looking down at Oliver

Before he could finish his words Sam had one in hand and was tapping the top of the bar with it like a drumstick.

Carter looked over at the pretzel said, "Oh good," and grabbed it.

Just as Jake and Kate reached the bar he was feeding the pretzel to Oliver.

"Oh, not again. You're going to spoil that dog if he doesn't choke on the pieces. He inhales you know, he doesn't chew," said Jake as he came up and rubbed the back of Oliver's head and looked up at Sam.

"What'll it be Jake?" inquired Sam while Kate gave Margaret a hug and talked briefly with her.

"A Heineken Sam, and put it on 224."

With Kate now looking up, "Kate, can I get you one of my special orange juices? I only make the special ones for you and Margaret and I have some that I just made."

"They are especially good today," Margaret put in with a smile.

"Sounds just right Sam," answered Kate.

Looking out to the patio as he now rubbed Oliver's ears, and Carter went back to his scotch, Jake noticed his older brother and Clive.

Flipping his head in the direction of the patio and his brother as he rubbed Oliver's head with both hands Jake said, "You meet Clive yet, Carter?"

"Oh did he," said Margaret while Sam just laughed in agreement as he put the open Heineken on the bar top and headed to the orange juicer and a small pitcher of fresh juice. "It was something," continued Margaret.

"You didn't miss anything," added Carter bringing his scotch up to his mouth as he looked straight ahead.

"I think it shook up the Johnson's and the Cooper's," returned Margaret.

"The guy is a blowhard, I met him yesterday," said Jake grabbing the Heineken and using the cold bottle to cool his forehead as he waited for Kate to get her drink before he took a sip.

"You can go ahead," said Kate, knowing what Jake was doing.

"No, I'll wait until you have yours. I can't help it, I'm just built that way," he said as Kate leaned over and kissed him on the cheek.

"Oh, God," said Carter now looking at the two of them.

"Ah, young people," commented Margaret with a smile as Sam came back with the orange juice handing it over the bar to Kate with a napkin under it.

"Try it first then I'll put some grenadine in it for you," Sam said knowing that Kate liked orange juice and grenadine.

Taking a sip while Sam waited, she took the glass from her lips and said, "It's too magical Sam, I don't want to ruin it."

Sam smiled and as he started to walk to the other end of the bar Carter, with a delayed reaction said, "The Johnson's and the Cooper's, I thought I heard their voices."

Sam without stopping or turning laughed and said, "And they sure heard you Cart" as he continued to the end of the bar.

"They had a history discussion," said Margaret to Kate and Jake in answer to their now, questioning expressions.

"His history, not mine," put in Carter as he lifted the rock glass to his lips.

"I can imagine and I bet it had to do with how the Brits won the war in spite of the late Yanks," guessed Jake, knowing.

"Jesus, you got that too?" said Carter now looking at Jake with his rock glass hand supported by his elbow on the bar and holding the rock glass at face level.

"That appears to be his mantra."

"His what?" questioned Carter, his face screwing up.

"He says it a lot dear," said Margaret interpreting for Carter "Oh."

"Sort of if he says it enough by magic it will become true," added Jake.

"Well, like I said I never saw a goddamned Brit in that hellhole," said Carter before draining his rock glass.

"The war in the Pacific," Margaret interpreted for Jake and Kate.

"Rodney's bending over backwards to this guy's BS and you know he's trying to get something," said Jake.

"I would guess a cut rate on a house in Bermuda later this year," noted Kate.

Margaret laughed. "He does try to cut corners."

"He's cheap," confirmed Jake. "Never go anyplace with the guy if they only take cash because he never has any with him and he knows where all the bars are in New York that only take cash."

"We've already had the experience," Margaret said as she laughed again.

"The best was trying to make my, at the time, 16-year-old 6 foot tall nephew pass for an under 12 when they showed up at the airport to go to Bermuda and the kid knew nothing about it. When Rodney got caught he blamed it on his secretary, who made the reservations."

"And he eats C-rats," noted Carter as he held up his glass and pointed to it while looking down the bar and getting Sam's attention.

"He eats what?" asked Kate horrified.

"Horrible canned military food, dear," explained Margaret.

"I know, he eats ravioli out of a can," said Jake.

"That's it," said Carter now turned to look at everyone with his empty glass down on the bar.

Carter then turning back said, "Just half," as he held up the rock glass when Sam stopped in front of him.

Glancing sideways at Margaret Sam could see her smile. She knew Carter was reducing his drink and momentum now that the turmoil with Clive had passed and was all but forgotten by Carter.

"Rodney's going to have a party next Saturday," said Jake.

"I heard. Is that English fellow going to be there?" queried Carter taking a first sip of the new drink.

"Yup, I think that's what it's about."

"Wonderful," commented Margaret.

At that moment Oliver, not having gotten any attention, stood up from his lying position, announced by a shuffle of nails on the oak floor and barked.

"Good comment Oliver," noted Margaret.

"The dog is smart," added Carter.

Kate just glanced over at Margaret and raised her eyebrows and Margaret nodded in agreement that this party could be interesting, keeping everything in mind that was just said.

Sam just standing there and putting it all together said, "Oh boy!," and then pushed off the portion of bar that he was leaning on and headed back down to the other end.

"The guy controls a lot of the liquor down there," said Jake.

Hearing 'controls a lot of liquor' got Carter's attention as he turned his head and asked, "Who?"

"Clive, he apparently derives most of his income from liquor imports into Bermuda besides the two seasonal homes he rents out."

"No wonder he's a drunk," noted Carter just before he took a sip of his scotch.

Margaret just smiled, adding, "And that's nothing we'd know about."

"Not like that," grunted Carter.

"And you are right. You would not have fallen back over your chair."

"You got that damned right and that's not the only thing bassackwards about the guy."

"He does have a challenge when it comes to history but that's not all," hinted Jake.

"And what else should we know before this party?" queried Margaret.

"Women!"

"What?" asked Carter.

"You missed him at the house when he stopped by Carter

but he didn't miss Alice."

"Who?"

"The woman with the birds and the crosses."

Carter did not answer,as he was still trying to put the pieces of the puzzle together in his head. He still confused the girl with the crosses with a Jap with a grenade.

"That'll be interesting......, if she's there," said Margaret.

"Oh, she'll be there," said Kate, "She passed me in the kitchen and giggled and said something about 'the rapture of the upcoming festivities..........' At least I took that to mean the upcoming party."

"I guess it will be interesting," said Jake as Oliver lay down on the cool floor again accompanied by the sound of his nails giving way across the hard wood allowing his bulk to ease to the floor.

Chapter 4

The Party

Saturday, the day of the party, Jake's older nephew Rodney V, or V for short, showed up. Even though he had finished school early for the year and was on the Cape for the summer he came back to bartender the party with a neighbor friend. It was still June.

Jake realized that V was home right after a speeding white cat turned the corner from the wet bar/pass-through from the large living room to the kitchen. As he jumped out of the way of the little white maelstrom flying for all it was worth he looked up to see his six foot tall, and still tow-headed, nephew in pursuit. V was at full tilt with a BB gun in hand loosely held against his right shoulder and pointing down. As he saw Jake he came to a stop out of breath.

"That damned cat……….., it crapped right in the middle of the den……….., Jeeesus," he said in all seriousness, then looked at Jake eyes wide and they both started to laugh.

"Did you get him?"

"Naah, just trying to scare the crap out of it," said V, and they laughed again.

"So, you're home. What's up?"

"I've got the bartending job tonight along with Sally Nichols."

"Ah, sweet Sally Nichols. The party oughta be interesting."

"Especially if I control the drinks," said V followed by a big exaggerated grin."Yeah, Sally is something else," he added as an after- thought.

"Ah no, that's trouble," said Jake smiling conspiratorially.

"Sally or the controlled drinks?"

"Both!" And they both laughed again.

"Are you and Kate going to the party?" queried V.

"I don't think we'd miss it, at least to the point where you start manipulating the actors."

"Yeah, I like that. Sorta like marionettes."

"Jeez," commented Jake shaking his head subtly with a short smile.

"Bring Oliver too will you. I don't get to see him much."

"Will do,.. now I'd better run to pick Kate up at the bus stop. Your grandmother has Oliver by-the-way and it's tough to get him away from her. They really bond, those two. I'll bring him along though."

"Good, see you tonight," and with another thought as Jake started to head for the door, "Hey, did you meet Clive?"

Stopping and turning Jake questioned, "Yeah, why?"

"What an asshole."

"I guess that puts it where it belongs," followed Jake.

"I'll fix him tonight, but he'll be his own undoing."

"Ah Jeez, I don't wanna know anymore. See you later," Jake said as he went through the mud room to the side of the kitchen heading for the driveway.

V just exited the kitchen, with BB gun in hand, in the direction the cat had headed.

***

Early that evening Jake was back with Oliver in tow. While Kate stayed on the third floor to do some work on her papers Jake and Oliver went in search of V and they found both he and Sally setting the bar up in the small pass-through between the living room and the kitchen. It had a sink and had been a wet bar, Jake guessed, since the 1930's. Oliver actually arrived first. Hearing V's voice, he took off when he and Jake were just at the foot of the stairs leading down from the second floor to the entrance to the kitchen.

"OLIVER!" Jake heard from the bar area more expecting the sound of a crash than anything else.

By the time he caught up Oliver was on his hind legs with his front legs resting on V's shoulders as V scratched his back and talked to him like an old buddy who he hadn't seen in years. Sally was there and she just stood and smiled looking as intelligently beautiful as ever.

Oliver was a big dog, as V stood six feet tall. Sally was also tall at 5'9" and she was athletically thin and in great shape as a state ranked middle distance runner on her school's new girl's track team. She had one of those faces that drew you in. If it were not such an intelligent face it would have been angelic. Her hair was light brown and fell behind her in a single French braided pony tail that helped to frame a face filled with charm, character and self-assurance. This face was offset by the most stunning blue eyes that Jake could recall ever having seen.

"I see he found you," Jake said seeing V and Oliver first, as he entered the bar area, and then seeing Sally, "Hi Sally."

"Hi Mr. Luger," said Sally as V still talked with Oliver.

"Oh, God Sally, don't call me that. Jake or JL is fine," he said joking a bit.

She smiled. "Ok then."

"What's wrong," said V still scratching Oliver and looking at Jake from the side of Oliver's head which was resting up against his, "don't you like the Luger name?" and he laughed.

"I'm barely five years older than you. I don't want to get old too fast."

"Sorry Mr. Luger, I won't do it again," said Sally with a laugh.

"Oh smart," said Jake smiling as Sally had known him for years as Jake and was simply having fun.

"So, do you know what your partner plans tonight?" Jake asked Sally.

"Mischief no doubt," replied Sally.

"I think they call it madness with this crowd."

"Ah, harmless really," said V as he lowered Oliver and reached for a Ritz cracker box near the sink.

"Oh no you're not going to feed him that stuff….. Between you and Carter."

"It's good for him, it cleans him out."

"It gives him gas and believe me when you are sleeping in a tight third floor room with little ventilation and a 150 pound dog, with gas, laying on the floor next to you, it gets noticed," said Jake.

V just laughed and fed him the Ritz.

"It's going to be hell tonight," finished Jake just shaking his head.

An hour later Rodney senior showed up at the bar, in the pass-through, with Clive while Jake was on the third floor with Kate. V and Sally were just finishing the set-up, which should have been done a half hour earlier if Sally and V hadn't been fooling around with each other.

"I say ol' boy you are the image of your father," stated Clive gratuitously to V as he ogled Sally.

"Oh, God," whispered V to Sally.

"He's not staring at you," said Sally under her breath so only V could hear.

"Thanks Mr. Hawthorne," returned V.

"Right-oh, now what's your name my sweet young lady?" asked Clive as the doorbell in the front hall went off and Rodney headed in its direction.

"Sally."

"I once knew a Sally during my time in hospital in Kenya."

"Oh, God," whispered Sally to V.

"Clive, Clive come and meet Dick Baxter," said Rodney

appearing at the entrance between the den and the living
room with a tall thin man next to his side.

Clive just nodded his head at Sally and headed for Rodney
and his friend.

"Saved by the bell, hey Sal," said V laughing. "Ah, we'll fix
him good tonight."

An hour later Carter came in the front door just as Alice was
halfway up the front stairs headed to her room. At that same
moment her two white doves flew across the main hall from
their perch on the top of Henry's antlers above the fireplace in
the den. Their destination was Alice's shoulder. Carter did not
see Alice but he saw and heard the flutter of the white motion
going up to his right which only made him move faster across
the hall towards the backstairs. He thought again that he was
seeing things. He would come down later once Margaret
arrived but right now he headed to his room for a Johnny
Walker Red.

By 9 o'clock that night the party was underway with maybe a hundred people, more or less. Carter and Clive had man-
aged to avoid each other as Margaret would deftly steer Carter
in the other direction when she saw Clive. Kate and Jake, along
with Oliver, were on the veranda taking in the cool evening
and waiting for the voices to start rising to that unmistakable
pitch when people start getting stupid in funny ways. They
could see and hear Clive through the wide open French doors
bragging to someone about something when something else
caught his eye and a hush came over him as his head fully
turned towards the staircase in the front hall. There descending
the stairs, between the two landings, was Alice with a semi-
sheer, white, ankle length dressing gown flowing behind her.
It was a semi-sheer dressing gown from the 40's with white fur
trim that had a slight yellow tinge to it. It looked like it
probably came from the second hand shop downtown.
Underneath this she wore red leather slacks with a matching
red leather button-down shirt that accented her cleavage. Her
smile was almost from ear to ear accompanied by a strange
twinkle in the eye that gave Jake the chills.

Clive liked the twinkle in the eye as he headed straight for Alice, after most everyone had turned individually to see who was coming down the stairs before turning back to their conversations.

"May I introduce myself, I'm Clive Hawthorne from Bermuda," Clive said with a short bow as Alice giggled with a bit of the devil in it.

"Bermuda, where's that? Do you know the King of Kings?" questioned Alice making it more a statement than a question.

"A bit of an odd thing, I say," said Clive with a smile realizing that the question did not require an answer.

"What do you 'say'?"

"It's just a figure of speech my dear."

"I like your accent and I like older men," she chirped with a smile.

"Jolly good," said Clive hamming it up. He then took a gulp of his scotch as he fixated on Alice's cleavage.

Alice watching him stare at her chest giggled. "My breasts are very nice," she said as she ran her index fingers around the circumference of her nipples starting from inside and moving her fingers in unison out and around.

"I should say," said Clive as he continued his stare for another moment before grabbing hold of her arm.

With Alice in tow Carter headed to the bar. He had grabbed her around the wrist and headed off in the lead but to anyone looking on Alice was the one in complete control. She was the one manipulating Clive for her own entertainment, or fascination.

Arriving at the bar in an excited state, Clive held up his glass and then put it on the bar saying, "Another one if you will young Rodney, but a short one."

As Clive turned to look at Alice V smiled at Sally and filled the glass three quarters of the way full knowing that Clive would bring about his own downfall with a little help.

To Alice Clive queried, "What would you like my little wood nymph?" He was already three sheets to the wind.

"A Shirley Temple."

"A what, my dear?"

It was quiet enough around the bar and V could hear her and said, "I got it."

V did not add anything alcoholic to Alice's Shirley Temple, she didn't need anything. She was in her own world and in control of that little world in its own twisted up way. It was the real world to her and V had a good idea about it even though he had only been home one day and had run into Alice only once. After picking up the chase of the cat he had run into Alice in the hall instead. She had no idea what he was up to but smiled that wide frightening smile that sent chills up the back of V's neck. He had come to a halt and introduced himself and moved on quickly. V was perceptive and this brief encounter, along with Jake's description, was enough for
V. She did not need any alcohol and Clive was in for a surprise, however that came to fruition.

Clive handed Alice her Shirley Temple holding it up close to his eyes to try to figure out what it was before he did so. He handed it to her without even making eye contact but turning quickly to get his little brownish yellow Scotch bomb into his hands.

"I say ol' boy, that is a whiskey," said Clive, holding the drink up and viewing it as one might a precious gem in the light, and seeing that the glass was anything but a short one.

"No, it's scotch," said V with a smile.

"Ah, off to see the stars my dear," said Clive to Alice as he grabbed her once more to head off to the French doors.

Before trailing off behind Clive, Alice turned and looked at V and gave him that same frightening smile. It reminded V of a nightmare that he once had about being chased by bad guys. Every time that the bad guys caught up with him the Cheshire Cat would appear sitting high up on a limb in a large tree and giving him that same frightening smile Alice had. It was a smile which stated that she had complete control over the recipient of the smile.

"God, she gives me the creeps," said V to Sally after Alice turned her head away again and followed Clive to the French doors.

"I think she likes you," said Sally with romantic exaggeration in her voice.

"Funny."

"Hey V, can you load 'er up!?" said Dick Baxter coming up to the bar as Alice and Clive disappeared out the French doors.

Behind Dick was his wife. She was holding up her hand with her thumb and index finger indicating 'just a little'.

V recognized her sign to make it a small drink and nodded to her. Then he poured Dick an extra fat scotch. She didn't see it and V knew that Dick would enjoy it. V liked the Baxters. Dick was probably the most intelligently funny individual that he had ever met and probably ever would meet. He was a Park Avenue advertising executive and an imaginative one.

V liked his television ads and he did not like ads as a rule, like everyone else. He knew Dick would handle his booze okay but get even funnier which his wife Kathy wanted to keep down. V wanted to release the complete package because he knew that eventually Dick would have a large group around him listening to his stories, which would elevate everyone's energy level. He knew that if he started loading drinks, in that type of evolving atmosphere, that he and Sally would have one hell of a memory to laugh about for years to come.

Jake came to the bar next. He and Kate were still situated out on the veranda and had been talking with Carter and Margaret who had just come out, missing Clive by seconds. And neither Jake nor Kate had noticed Clive and Alice either, as they passed to their left and into the blackness of the deep backyard.

"So, the volume is increasing V. Voices are sure getting louder, I doubt that you had anything to do with that," said Jake with a smile.

V just smiled back. "What can I get you uncle?"

"Two Heinekens so you can't mess around with the   alcohol."

"Ah, you never know," said V with a laugh.

"He's getting out of control Mr. Luger," joked Sally.

Jake just shook his head and smiled as he picked up the two Heinekens and cocktail napkins. "Have you seen Clive?" Jake asked thinking of Carter.

"He headed out to see the stars with the bird lady."

"Oh Christ," Jake thought out loud about Clive's future while looking at the two of them. Then he said, "Oh well," and they all laughed. V had filled Sally in on Alice.

As Jake turned and headed back to the French doors he said over his shoulder, loud enough for them to hear, " The bar is open with complete discretion." Everyone else was oblivious.

V just smiled behind him.

Stepping out on the veranda Jake looked at Margaret sitting in a wicker chair and said, "Fee-fi-fo-fum there is an Englishman lurking about the yard," while Carter talked to Kate from the matching wicker chair across from the matching love seat where both he and Kate were sitting.

"Thanks for the warning," responded Margaret, "I saw him heading off into the back with that young lady,... what's her name? Alice is it?"

"That's it among a host of other names I assume," responded Jake.

"Then they may find each other interesting," commented Margaret as she smiled and reached over and touched Carter's leg affectionately more to let him know that she was there as he continued his conversation with Kate. Jake handed Kate one of the Heinekens as he took his spot next to her on the love seat.

Not even recognizing that Jake had sat back down, Carter continued on his conversation with Kate whose younger brother had just moved to Tucson.

"I remember traveling to Tucson with my family before the war when I was a kid, but I never went back later. I don't know why. I remember that I was intrigued by the desert but later things changed. I'm sure your brother will like it there." Carter took another sip of his scotch and continued, "I remember these falls, I think it was called Bear Canyon, I'm not quite sure but we rode horses there from a spot just outside of town. Wait, it was called Sabino Canyon, I remember now. They had just finished building these four foot bridges and we were told we had to see the canyon now that access was easier. I guess it was 1935 or sometime around there." Carter went on as Kate smiled.

Carter liked Kate as though she were one of his daughters and she strongly reminded him of one. The two women had actually gone to the same preparatory school but never met or never really got to know each other so that Kate would remember. Kate's presence would stimulate Carter to talk and reveal feelings that he kept from his daughters. With Kate it was all in one package: he had another daughter and one he could talk to about things like "before the war" or even touch on the war itself. Carter's daughters would never hear him go that close to the subject as he protected them from it, nor would he take them back to his years before the war. They actually did not fully appreciate that he had been right in the middle of it. His nightmares and personality problems, as they saw it, were due to the fact that they had a very bright and very eccentric father. He worked hard to keep the war from them. Kate missed the closeness of a father, as hers had been painfully distant from her. As a result they both helped each other and Jake and Margaret were always glad when they engaged in conversation no matter how mundane the topic.

"I visited that canyon and I know the bridges that you're talking about," Kate said with a sparkle of recognition in her voice and in her eyes. "The falls seem to step down from the top of the mountain. We actually swam, or really waded, in one of the pools after sliding down a chute between two pools."

Seeing Kate's joy Carter said, "I'll have to go back there then."

Feeling Margaret's hand on his leg Carter turned to her and said, "We'll have to go to Tucson sometime soon."

Margaret knew that as something attached to a memory before the war it was unlikely that they would go although Kate was helping him to open up and see some good memories for the first time since 1943.

"I've always wanted to go and the falls sound wonderful," agreed Margaret not pushing the topic but hoping that it would stick enough for Carter to act on it.

"Jake, you're lucky to have Kate," said Carter now acknowledging Jake's presence.

"I know," said Jake unembarrassed as Kate became a little flush.

This was punctuated by a big roar of laughter from a small group around Dick Baxter, just past the French doors in the middle of the den, followed by Dick declaring, "Did a bird just fly by and crap in my drink? This scotch is a hammer. V knows how to make a drink. Are those two white doves on the deer antlers or V's drink? I better lay off this stuff. Hey V," screamed Dick back in the direction of the bar by turning his head part way over his shoulder, "whad you put in this drink?"

There was a roar as Dick then made a gesture to the birds that everyone had seen, or Alice's doves.

Followed by this roar of laughter came a screech from the deep recesses of the backyard and it was a man's screech. It was loud enough and ominous enough to turn the heads of all on the veranda, including Oliver who had been asleep next to the wicker love seat to the right of Kate and who now brought his head up to look.

The screech was followed by an emerging Clive. Coming out of the dark and into the light, given off from the inside of the house, Clive looked to Carter as though he'd seen a Jap with a grenade. And for some reason Carter just laughed and then yelled, "Say ol' boy seen a live ghost?" and laughed again.

Everyone else watched with flat expressions as Clive came

up the first of the three steps to the back veranda, leaned against the wall, seeming out of breath, and said, "She's a bloody demon. Good God, she has a figurine where one should not have a figurine…and what she said…."

"And what was that Clive?" queried Jake now very curious.

"We're in mixed company. She is a demon I tell you." And with this Clive pushed off the wall with his right hand and headed back inside towards the bar.

Margaret could see Alice coming up the driveway in the back by the garage to enter the back stairway and everyone on the veranda could hear that demented giggle as she neared the house.

"What a horse's ass," was the only comment that Carter made as Clive left the veranda, cutting to the right in the direction of the living room and the bar.

"What figurine and where I wonder," said Jake to everyone but to no one in particular.

"I think we're better off not knowing," said Margaret.

"The man had fear written across his face," added Kate.

"Ha," was all that Carter added, then, "Where the hell's Rodney?"

"I haven't seen him in the past hour," noted Jake and then as on queue Rodney entered the den mumbling to himself and dressed in running shoes, shorts and a running top.

"Woooha," and a laugh came from Rodney as he walked around in circles dazed. "Woooha," again and it wasn't V's doing. Jake knew immediately what was going on and most people at the party knew as well.

"Oh Christ, another insulin reaction. I'll get the glucose tube,.. be right back," said Jake as he headed into the den and past Rodney on his way to the kitchen. As he passed Rodney he got a personalized, 'Woooha' in the ear. At least it was a friendly insulin reaction, they were easier to deal with. Also, for some reason, Rodney would only listen to Jake when he was in insulin shock. One night the EMT's were called when Rodney was at The Club and their Mother had called Jake from Sam's phone when the EMT's could not even get close to him. Once Jake showed-up Rodney calmed down and let him get sugar down his throat. Jake always thought it strange how his old-enough-to-be-his–father brother would torment him constantly but when he needed advice he would come to Jake and Jake was the only one he would let near him when he was in insulin shock.

Jake was back in a flash with a tube of glucose as Rodney just stood there in a daze with his hands held up bent at the wrist and limp like a marionette. And now there were shorter periods between his 'Woooha's'. He'd say 'Woooha' like it was an uncontrollable rush of adrenaline. He was a bad diabetic when it came to balance. He was slim and athletic and that was part of his problem. He'd take insulin then exercise and leave the insulin nothing to deal with in the form of sugar so it would turn Rodney into something else and not someone else. Jake remembered the time he let Rodney continue to progress into an insulin shock when they were dealing with someone who had always been a jerk. Rodney started to get confrontational as the insulin started to overtake him, and the guy got defensive not knowing what was going on. It was actually pretty funny and once Jake got him out of the guy's office and to the elevator in the Manhattan office building that they were in, he gave him a candy. As Rodney started to come out of it he just asked, 'What happened?' 'Oh, nothing really,' Jake had said and smiled.

Now he just went up to Rodney, who held still seeing it was Jake. He automatically opened his mouth, as Jake brought the tube up to his face, so Jake could squeeze some of the liquid glucose into the side of his mouth where it would force him to swallow it. A couple of shots of this then Rodney opened his mouth for more like a baby wanting more, and not being prompted to do so. Jake gave him more, then stood with him as he started to come around. 'He'd have one helluva headache from this one,' was the only thought Jake had.

His face still looking dull, like he was stupefied, Rodney uttered, "Ah hell, where am I?"

"You're getting ready for the Marathon, we better get to the start," said Dick Baxter, and those who knew them both laughed.

Rodney looked down at the way he was dressed, "Shit, I forgot to eat. What the hell am I dressed like this for?"

"Beats the hell oughta us," said Dick with a smile like it really doesn't matter.

"You probably started going into insulin shock, went into automatic and put your track stuff on," was all that Jake could offer. "You okay now?"

"Yeah, yeah, thanks," said Rodney as he was still collecting himself and Jake headed to the kitchen to put the glucose tube back where everyone knew it was located. Rodney came out of this one fast.

When Jake came back through the room Rodney, not bothering to change, had a drink in his hand and was laughing with Dick.

"The bastard's going to kill himself one day," Jake muttered to himself as he walked by headed back to the veranda.

"To the rescue again, how many does that make this month so far?" asked Carter.

"Too many, he's gotta learn to eat."

"And not C-rats," put in Carter punctuated by a slight involuntary gag at the thought.

As Jake sat down he heard that familiar escape of gas and knew what was next, "Ah, Christ Oliver!" And Oliver came part way up to look at Jake with questioning in his eyes as the smell hit.

"Oh, God," said Kate with a deep intelligent laugh as she got up quickly and moved past Jake.

"Jesus Oliver, you been eating those C-rats too?" put in Carter with another involuntary gag.

"Ugh," said Jake getting up and moving back as Margaret and Carter did the same. "V fed him Ritz."

"What?" asked Carter.

"V fed Oliver Ritz crackers and this is what happens, every time."

As Kate, Margaret and Carter moved up against the large Victorian window, to the side of the veranda, Jake, with exaggerated importance and fury, grabbed up one of the cushions from the wicker love seat and started violently fanning the air above Oliver. Oliver just lifted his head again and closed his eyes to take in the breeze being made.

They all laughed.

"Totally oblivious. Jeez Oliver," said Jake.

"Poor guy," offered Margaret.

"Who, me or him?" said Jake turning his head back to look at Margaret and avoid the smell at the same time, as he continued to fan.

"Well, that's a good question but I think the trophy goes to the big black one on the floor who feels that everyone ran away from him for no reason."

"Yeah, but he finally got our complete attention," said Kate laughing in a manner that got them all to laugh as Rodney came out on the veranda.

"Gawd, what is that fowl odor? I thought we had a sewer system here," stated Rodney standing on the veranda in his track shorts sniffing the air and screwing up his face at the same time, while teetering a little in his wobbly stance.

"If it's so bad stop sniffing it," commented Jake.

"V fed Oliver Ritz crackers," added Kate.

"Whad?" asked Rodney.

"Your son fed the dog Ritz crackers and it makes him fart," injected Carter.

"Who Fard?"

"The dog Rodney," said Margaret ,"and you will not get me to say that word."

"Whad word?" asked Rodney somewhat out of it from a combination of the insulin shock and V's drinks that had hit him fast.

"FART for chrissakes," said Carter.

"Oh....., I see," said Rodney. "Have you ah...., have you seen Clive?"

"Heading for the bar...., awhile ago," said Jake as he stopped fanning.

"We're gong ah.. swim…ming," said Rodney.

"What?" asked Jake.

"Yeah, everyone's dah..cided to go to the ah……….. Major's so we can…,ah, swim in their pooool."

"Count me out," said Carter, and by their silence everyone else on the veranda was in agreement.

"Suit yurrrselves,… I'm off."

"Hope you're not driving," said Jake.

"Na, we're all wa…..king, ahh," said Rodney as he barely negotiated the left side French door before going back in with a little wobble to his walk. One large drink on top of the shock had taken its toll.

The air was clearing as Jake threw the cushion back on the love seat and they all returned to their seats.

"They're really all leaving," noted Margaret who faced the den.

Jake turning and looking thought for a moment and then said, "Well, waddya suppose is up with that? I wouldn't think they'd all really go."

They hadn't been sitting on the veranda all that long but it was long enough for V to work his magic and set everyone on a course.

"Maybe it was Oliver," remarked Carter with a smile. And Kate emitted that flat intelligent laugh of hers again.

"Poor Boy," said Margaret.

As Jake turned around to face Carter and Margaret, V appeared at the French doors. He leaned out to the veranda and, supporting himself in the door frame using both arms like he was crucified, just laughed. "Well, those people are blitzed," he said with a smile on his face and then he laughed again as Jake turned to look at him.

"How many were you feeding extra heavy drinks to?"

"All takers," V said as he laughed.

"Christ, that's going to be hell to pay," Jake continued as Sally appeared at the door to V's right. "What are they up to besides swimming, do you know?"

"I think I do. I know Mr. Flynn has eyes for Mrs. Dockray and vice versa. I heard them whispering by the side of the bar about skinny dipping. At least they thought they were whispering but they were loud. V really fed them as they kept getting larger drinks for each other and getting louder as they went," said Sally finishing with a humorous grin.

"Well, there it is," said V.

"But they all left," observed Margaret.

"Well that may be a problem," followed Jake.

"Well, there are a couple of people in that group who are hot on someone else's spouse. I see them together in the store sometimes when my eyes are focused," added Carter.

"How big is that pool I wonder?" commented Kate with a laugh.

"Jeesus V, you might've set some dynamite off."

"Hell, I'm just the bartender," said V with a devilish smile. Then, turning his head toward Sally while still leaning into the veranda supported by his arms on either side of the opening he said, "Hay Sal, wanna follow them and see what they're up to in that pool, oughta be funny, and it might be better than driving the Aston Martin."

"Jeez V," responded Jake not only to the fact that they found humor in all of this but also realizing that they had intended to take Sally's father's Aston Martin, and pride and joy, out of the garage for a spin.

"Yeah, why not," replied Sally looking at V with a smile.

"See you all later," said V looking back at everyone on the veranda as he pushed with his arms, straightening his lean and turning to Sally before they both headed for the front door.

Margaret turning to Carter said loud enough to be heard by everyone, "Hey big boy, wanna come over to my place?"

"Why not," said Carter.

"Just why not," returned Margaret, and Carter just smiled.

"Maybe we'll see you two at The Club tomorrow," said Margaret as she rose to get ready to leave.

"And make sure the big boy there gets something to fix his stomach," said Carter nodding towards Oliver now raising his head again as Carter stood.

"His stomach is almost a done deal for the next few hours. V gave us a gassy 150 pound dog for the night and a lot of others a helluva headache for tomorrow. By-the-way, I never saw Clive again nor did I see Alice," said Jake as he and Kate stood.

"I don't want to know," said Margaret as she collected her cloth bag from the side of the chair.

"Nor I," added Jake with a laugh.

Margaret and Carter left for Margaret's shortly after. And Kate and Jake took Oliver for a late night walk in an attempt to defuse a potentially gassy night. Exercising Oliver always helped and, besides, it was a beautiful starry night.

V and Sally followed the drunken group to the pool, but not all went. There must have been fifty of them that went to the pool. The others filtered off to their homes, most of which were within walking distance while some drove.

V and Sally were able to sit in the woods, no more than fifty yards from the edge of the pool. This was well within hearing range considering that everyone was talking at exceedingly high decibels due to V's influence.

What they saw was something out of the history of Caligula, which V had just studied. Even though V knew that the sexual stories of Caligula may not have been true what he and Sally were seeing was.

They just remained quiet until, "Oh God Sal, I wonder what's going to come of this? Do you see what I see now, I thought it was someone else?" whispered V to Sally, although everyone was so loud they would not have heard them talking at a normal volume.

Sally's eye brows just went up as they watched. "Yeah, she gives me the creeps," said Sally, "They'll forget about all of this like everything else." And then she just chuckled shaking and lowering her head to look at the ground and think for a brief moment.

"If nothing else, this stuff will lie under the surface, it'll be interesting to watch them at The Club over the next couple of days. Too bad I have to go to the Cape this week."

"I would rather be on the Cape," said Sally now looking at the pool scene as they both watched what was happening for a few moments before speaking again.

"Did you see that?," said V in disbelief followed by a splashing sound, "Jeez, now she's gone and done it," added V. "Jeez, she just kicked him in the nuts," added V again as swearing could be heard coming from the pool area.

"We better sneak oughta here and besides, she gave me the shivers before I saw this," said V a few seconds later as he got up from his squatting position, turned and moved off at a low stoop with Sally following in the same manner. They left to the sounds of all sorts of invectiveness coming from the pool area now behind them. It had been an interesting night.

Chapter 5

The Event

It was the next morning, Sunday; and Kate, Jake, Oliver and V were headed to The Club for brunch with a little trepidation, both Kate and Jake having been given an overview of the pool episode by V. At least Jake and Kate had trepidation. V was filled with curiosity and Oliver was filled with a bowl of bland but safe food.

Sam ran the brunch, having some of the members' high school age children work for him. V had been one of Sam's best workers the previous summer and when they went up to Sam's table, across the ballroom now set for brunch with round tables, Sam's eyes brightened even more.

"V, why are you home?" Sam declared as they came close.

Laughing, V said, "I thought you'd be happy to see me. I came all this way to see you. Hell, I'll just turn around," he finished as he started to turn.

Sam laughed and warmly said, "I thought you'd be on the Cape, you're a sight for these old eyes."

V turned, laughed and walked over to Sam who gave him a big back slapping hug. "He was my best worker," said Sam looking at Jake and Kate while still hugging V.

"Hell, I thought I was your best Sam," stated Jake laughing.

"You were until V." Then Sam laughed winking at Jake and then releasing V.

"How long are you down for young man?"

"Now I get 'young man'."

"I think you earned it."

"Just for another day then I'm back to the Cape. I bartended last night at my Dad's"

"I heard," said Sam with his eyes smiling and a closed mouth grin.

"It was an experience," added V.

"I've heard some rumbling, something went on," commented Sam.

"You don't want to know," said Jake.

"Hey ol' boy," said Sam as his attention changed to Oliver who had sauntered slowly across the room to joint the group. "I've got something for you," added Sam as he went behind the temporary counter.

"Just so it's not a Ritz," said Jake looking at V who just smiled.

"Naw, a nice Milk Bone biscuit," said Sam as he came out from behind the counter.

Oliver's tail started to wag so hard he almost came off of his front paws. He was a chow hound.

Feeding Oliver the biscuit and looking up in Kate's direction Sam asked, "Kate, fresh orange juice and Eggs Benedict?"

"That sounds perfect Sam."

"And the two of you?" Sam queried looking at Jake and then V with his voice dropping for effect as though it was a chore to have to ask them. "The same sound good?"

"That'll do me," returned V as Jake nodded in agreement.

"I'll have it sent over when it's ready."

"Thanks Sam," said Jake as they turned and headed back to the table as Oliver stayed behind to clean the floor of any crumb that still existed.

The main dining room was actually a ballroom built in the

late 1800's with a large window seat and shallow oriel bay window at the far end and back of the room. The window seat was 26 feet from end to end and could seat 15 people comfortably on its window box seats. To the far side, away from the front of the clubhouse, was a large fireplace, six feet from the base to the bottom of the mantle. It was large enough to heat the entire room in the 1800's. From the mantle to the ceiling the wall was covered by a large piece of oak contoured to match the mantle and the surrounding molding with the crest of The Club at its center. Along the walls of the room where old framed pine boards with the names of Club champions painted on them and the year that they were either tennis or squash champions. The Club had one of the oldest squash courts in the country.

During the 1919 flu epidemic the ballroom had been converted into an infirmary accommodating mostly returning soldiers from Europe. This was the same room where both Jake and V took dance lessons as small children. In later years Jake and V had found a 'secret passage', kept secret by the older kids, that would allow you to get to a small catwalk above the ceiling of the ballroom so you could kneel down and look through a small hole in the ceiling at the goings-on below. As teenagers they found it quite funny to watch the little kids from above going through the same process that they had as little kids. The Club, besides having its large spring fed pool, hockey rink, paddle tennis, squash and tennis courts, had its special places to those who had grown up in the place.

Now it was the scene of Sunday brunch and all was relatively calm until Rodney walked in followed by Clive with Alice in tow.

"Oh Christ," said Jake looking up in the direction of the front door after looking down, for one second, at Oliver who just returned to his side.

"What," said V turning to look in the direction of Jake's stare. Kate had already turned sideways and did not say a word.

"Well, we know where Clive is," commented Jake.

"Yeah, with Beelzebub," snickered V.

With this Kate laughed a hearty laugh. "Oh come on, she can't be that bad, you and Jake are too much. Did you know Jake sleeps with a knife under his pillow because of her?"

"Jeesus, unck," said V turning to look at Jake.

"Well hell, I have to sleep in the same house and she gives me the creeps. I think she even gives ol' Oliver the creeps and that says something."

Looking back at them as they passed a couple of tables out towards the fireplace to get away from everyone V commented, after a moment, "I say, I have to agreed with you," he shivered, "ah, she does give me the shivers."

"The two of you," said Kate. "She can't be that bad, strange but not that bad."

"Time will tell kiddo but I don't think we want to be around when the tale is finally told," said Jake with V nodding with a smile in agreement.

"You two are too dramatic."

Rodney, taking a seat, saw Jake, Kate and V and waved briefly as he sat. He then turned his attention to something Clive was pontificating about as he was using great hand gestures.

"That damned woman!" came a familiar female voice. It came from the table behind and to the side of Jake, closer to The Club's brick patio, and only three tables away, so it was loud. Someone else had noticed Alice's entry with a similar lack of empathy.

It was Charlotte Campbell. She was with her husband Charlie but as Jake took a sideways glance he noticed that the atmosphere at their table was frigid. The Campbells had been at the party and had left along with everyone else.

V, hearing and seeing Charlotte Campbell, all of a sudden looked like he had just remembered something important that he had forgotten to do. "Oh," said V in a lowered voice that would not carry past their table, "forgot to tell you, Clive and Beelzebub made it to the pool last night."

"Oh, that must have been interesting," commented Jake in the same hushed tones realizing that the Campbells were probably involved in some way.

"I would say it was a bit more than interesting, it was interactive."

"Who was interactive with whom?" queried Jake.

"A few people with a few people from, sorta different couples."

"I'm not two years old you know," noted Kate in a normal voice alienated from the conversation.

"Yeah, but your Kate, I don't want to say this stuff in front of you," said V taking the flat of his hand and moving it in a down motion trying to tell Kate to keep it down.

Kate just gave him a stupid grin.

"Okay, Okay," said V in hushed tones.

"Well, what happened?" continued Jake.

"By the time we got there things were already progressing a little as they all had a jump start at the party, if you know what I mean. Then Clive and Miss nymphet from hell come across the great lawn to the pool area. I could see them coming sixty yards away in the night because she was wearing this familiar great robe which was too big for her as she held it closed with her arms wrapped across her chest. I thought it was Reverend McGee for one brief second then I realized who it was. It had the cross on it and everything, Jeez. They came up to the pool and ol' Beelzebub went right up to old Charlie Campbell back there and opened one side of that damned robe and she had nothing on. And................."

"Well what?" asked Jake.

"You're both not going to believe me."

"I will and she probably won't because she doesn't believe me," said Jake nodding in Kate's direction.

"Oh, shut up the two of you. Just say what you're going to say V," commanded Kate.

"Well, she brought out this big long candle with a gold cap on the top like the kind you see in church and she handed it to Mr. Campbell as a big smile came across his face, as if his wife wasn't standing there."

"Why would she have a church candle?" put in Kate.

"Well that wasn't all. She gave Mr. Campbell the candle and pulled a large cross out of a pocket someplace. I didn't know those things had pockets. Anyway, she pulls this out, like the one on the altar in the small chapel, and holds it between her breasts with her legs now spread and says something to Mr. Campbell."

"Oh, this is not good," said Jake in a voice even more hushed than it had been while taking a sideways glance at the Campbells as the tension at their table grew.

"Well, then he takes the candle with one hand and wraps his other hand around the princess of darkness, inside that damned robe ."

"I don't know if I want to hear anymore," Kate said in a hushed voice.

"Oh, no, now it gets good. Ol' Mrs. Campbell comes up, grabs the candle away from Mr. Campbell with both hands, chucks it in the pool, says something to Beelzebub that gets her hair in a tizzy and then turns and kicks Mr. Campbell right in the jewels. Man did he go over. When we left the hell queen was trying to get her candle out of the pool, it sure changed the tone of things and we don't know what happened from there but we could hear some nasty words coming out of Beelzebub as she tried to get her candle. I was afraid her head might start to spin around throwing out projectile pea soup or something."

"You and your uncle, both the same."

V just smiled.

Then Mrs. Campbell let loose, "You WHORE!" She could not hold it back any longer as she had to stare at Alice from where she was sitting. And the more Mr. Campbell tried the calm her, the angrier she got until it came out in an explosion with Mrs. Campbell standing and staring directly at the Rodney, Clive, Alice table.

As though it were not loud enough the first time, "You WHORE, you walking piece of BLASPHEMY," Mrs. Campbell screeched with vigor.

Now even Oliver was worried because Charlotte Campbell was one of Oliver's food benefactors so her voice in despair or stress was like Pavlov hitting the bell with a sledge
hammer. Something seemed to be wrong in Oliver's world and
it certainly was in the real one. Such words were never, in
recent memory, heard at such a volume with such directed
focus in The Club.

Now, along with everyone else in the ballroom, Rodney's
table was looking at Charlotte Campbell as it hadn't all yet
connected, while Charlotte continued to head to a melt down.

"Yes, you. You little frumpette from Hell," she continued.

V smiled and looked at Kate because even Charlotte
Campbell got the Hell connection.

If by now Alice did not realize it was she that was being
singled out she soon would as Charlotte Campbell started to
head for her table with Charlie Campbell's hands just missing
the grab of her arm as she escaped his reach. She then flew past
Jake's table with Oliver now sitting up, his eyes alert.

She made it to Rodney's table and looked down at Alice,
"You sick little twisted WHORE, how dare you come here."

By this time, with her voice at its highest, Oliver was up and
gone, and at her side in case she was in trouble.

Alice turned sideways in her chair and looking up at
Charlotte just giggled that demonic giggle of hers as though
she had been waiting for this to happen.

As Alice reached her hand down into her crotch and continued to giggle an over shadowing noise erupted from the
field in front of The Club's patio. The noise was so great and
further amplified by the funneling effect of the low striped
awning over The Club's patio and wide opening into the ballroom that it was almost painful. Along with the noise came a
rising of dirt and grass off of the recently cut lawn which rose
in a cloud as a medevac helicopter dropped into the center of
it. Everyone's attention turned to the sound except for that of
Alice and Charlotte Campbell, and Oliver. Even Clive and
Rodney were held by the helicopter's appearance even

though they were in the eye of their own storm. Once everyone realized it was that rare entry of the emergency helicopter
for the hospital across the street the attention went back to
Charlotte and Alice, and Oliver just in time to see Alice show
Charlotte a little figure and laugh.

There was a five second gap in the event so no one other
than Charlotte and Oliver saw what Alice had done with that
figure or where it came from and Oliver would never talk. So
only Charlotte, among the talking, saw it and one could only
guess as Charlotte froze for one brief moment with her eyes
wide open. Then she screamed as Oliver started barking at
Alice. She screamed again and then ran out to the patio on the
way to the helicopter as Alice laughed. Oliver was in close
pursuit of one of his benefactors.

Oliver was a protector of the vulnerable as well as those
who provided him with food. While on the Cape with Oliver
the previous summer, on Sunken Ship Beach directly across
from the well-known 'target ship', Oliver had left Jake and
Kate's side only to be seen 100 yards down the empty beach
barking his head off at the water's edge. When Jake ran to see
what was wrong he found a little girl, maybe three-years-old,
wading into the water and giggling with glee. Jake grabbed her
out just as the parents realized that she had gotten away, heard
Oliver and then saw Jake grabbing her out of the water. Oliver
saved the day and the mother hugged Oliver so tightly he
almost choked. Well, Charlotte now fit into that category and
Oliver was her guardian.

She ran down the aisle between the tables, right past Charlie Campbell oblivious to his existence as he reached his arms
out for her. She flew first across the red bricks then the white
painted concrete of The Club patio. She barely touched a brick
and little of the concrete surface on the way, and as the patient
was pulled out of the helicopter on the flight gurney Charlotte
leaped in taking its place followed by Oliver. The rotors were
still winding down as the two of them made it aboard. Oliver
just sat there in front of Charlotte looking out the open door of
the helicopter.

"Oh crap, I'll never get him out of that thing," said Jake just staring at the end result of the dash: a big black dog sitting in the helicopter's doorway with his tongue out catching his breath.

"That was cool," said V.

"My God, this is awful," said Kate.

Clive was just staring over in the direction of the helicopter in shock while Alice looked at him and giggled. Rodney taking the first intelligent action he had taken in days got both Clive and Alice up and out the door. This happened while most everyone else was once again staring at the helicopter which was now carrying Mrs. Charlotte Campbell and a 150 pound black Newfoundland with his tongue out, panting from his rush to follow her onboard.

By the time the first person turned back to Rodney's table to see what was now happening there, it was empty. Sam was left just standing behind his makeshift counter with his hands on his hips shaking his head thinking that it was lucky that his friend and fellow Marine Carter had not seen this. Who knows how he would have seen the madness. It may have seemed normal to him or he might have had a flashback, although they did not have helicopters until the end of the war and he and Carter had never seen one during their time. You would never know with Carter. Sam thought it interesting how his first thought was of Carter. There was something uniquely special about that man that seemed to touch everyone. He couldn't put his finger on it. As he thought about it he just chuckled, smiled and took it for what it was. He then headed back into the kitchen as the helicopter went completely silent, except for the consoling words of the crew trying to get Charlotte and Oliver off the helicopter.

"He's your dog," said Kate laughing.

As Jake got up V said, "Offer him a Ritz."

"Very funny," said Jake as he came to his feet and headed past a stunned Charlie Campbell. He walked across the patio to the now quiet helicopter and its crew talking to a big black dog in an overly friendly tone like they knew Oliver or something. They didn't get it. Oliver knew Charlotte as the provider of food and these people in uniform were unknown to him.

"Here boy, come boy, that's a good boy, come on........." they were saying in chorus when Jake broke through their semicircle at the helicopter's loading door.

"Oliver damn it," said Jake, "what the hell are you doing?"

Oliver just sat there and panted.

Looking at the crew Jake said, "It's really difficult to get him out of anything that he ran into out of fear, his fear or someone else's"

Jake remembered the time that he and Kate and Oliver had driven down to Puerto Penasco, Mexico two summers previous to this one. They had bought prawn shrimp and red snapper for a dollar a pound along with five sky rockets for a dollar a piece. As the shrimp and red snapper was baking in a sand pot Jake made of hot coals, stones and seaweed, for added flavor, the sun started to go down and the time was perfect. Jake had reached behind his back and pulled out a rocket, set it in the sand and lit the fuse. Within three seconds the fuse ignited the propellant and it took off in an arc towards the sea with a mighty SWISH then out over the water it blew up with a concussive BANG and with this Oliver was gone. Jake and Kate watched as Oliver, back lit by the flash of other rockets, hugged the top of the dunes as he ran low and fast to the parking lot. By the time Kate and Jake got there Oliver was taking up most of the interior of an English Mini. 'Is he yours?' asked one of the previous occupants. 'Yes, are you all ok?,' responded Jake. 'Yeah, he just blew in as we were getting out, he looks like he's shaking,' said the other previous occupant. It was the SWISH-BANGS that got him. "Jesus, come on Oliver it's okay, come out," Jake had coaxed to no avail. After a half hour they gave up and started to walk away with purpose. Oliver had a greater fear of being left behind after the SWISH-BANGS had stopped and hopped out to follow them. This was Jake's first experience with Oliver taking refuge and not budging.

"What?" said the older of the three people at the   helicopter's door.

"He's neurotic, what can I say, he grew up only knowing French," said Jake with a smile.

"What, the dog speaks French?" one of them harped in.

"No, forget it," Jake wasn't going to explain how Kate on-ly spoke to Oliver in French during his first year while Jake was away at school as a joke for his homecoming. She had a subtle sense of humor.

"Oliver come on, get out here."

He wouldn't budge just sitting there in front of Charlotte panting.

Another tack. "Mrs. Campbell, are you okay?"

"She's a demon!"

"I can't agree with you more," confirmed Jake.

"Do you know what........., what that creature just did, my God.........my God?"

"I really don't want to know but I have an idea that it wasn't cute."

"My God!"

"An understatement I know, are you okay?"

"Is that thing still there in the ballroom?"

"No, they left and will never be back again."

"That was scary. I don't know what happened to me. I don't want to face those people," stated Mrs. Campbell.

"It's okay trust me," said Jake and he looked down and thought for a moment, then looked up again, "I have an idea."

Once he explained this to Mrs. Campbell she hugged Oli-ver ,who was sitting, and she got up. Then Oliver got up wagging his tail, excited that his benefactor seemed to be okay.

As she came to the door of the helicopter Oliver moved to let her pass. She stepped down with Jake's help, although she got in with no problem, and Oliver just stood taking up most of the cargo bay wagging his tail and not moving.

"You too Oliver, now!" But Oliver wouldn't move.

Jake started to move away from the helicopter with Mrs. Campbell, and with purpose, leaving Oliver. Then he added by yelling back, 'WANNA RITZ/BISCUIT!' Oliver took a leap like he was diving off a rock ledge into water. He landed in a run, which braced him against his weight when he hit the ground, and he took off out in front of Jake and Charlotte. V had him trained well. V's subtle sense of humor was making the word Ritz a word of reaction for the big dog.

Jake, muttered to himself, 'that was easier than I thought', then he yelled back towards the helicopter over his right shoulder, "Sorry fellas, take it easy."

He heard them muttering to each other and laughing as he headed back to The Club with Charlotte in tow and Oliver now in the lead.

"Now smile and try to laugh a little," whispered Jake to Charlotte before they walked back onto The Club's patio.

Oliver led the way to the interior of the ballroom and by the time Jake and Charlotte entered, with Jake's arm around her shoulder, Charlotte was a beam and smiling.

With everyone watching, and before a word could be said, Jake shouted out, "Now did that catch you or what?" And then he laughed, after which the staring faces seemed to question his statement and the laugh that followed. It wasn't working.

"Charlotte and I had a bet, with my brother's guests' collusion of course, that she would not do what you just saw her do. It was brilliant and I can't believe it but she did it and to top it all off we had the added benefit of an emergency helicopter for her to run to which was a complete adlib on her part by-the-way. And Oliver here would follow Charlotte anywhere once she mentioned BISCUIT." And with this Oliver had prefect timing looking up at Mrs. Campbell and offering his paw. Initiated by Oliver everyone laughed with relief and one or two even applauded, now fully appreciating the story, as Jake returned to his seat.

"How did you come up with that one?" muttered Kate as Jake sat down.

"Out of pure desperation or Oliver would still be on that damned helicopter," muttered Jake back.

"Alright unck, that was beautiful," said V as he started rubbing Oliver's ears and head after Oliver took up a seat next to the Ritz man.

Having everything out of her system Charlotte allowed Charlie to reach over and kiss her on the temple and then hug her briefly while she sat in her chair with a warm glow about her face.

Charlie looked over at Kate, as Jake's back was to him, and smiled realizing and appreciating what he had done.

Kate smiled back then facing Jake she quietly said, "I think you have two lifelong friends and it would appear that the Campbells are okay." She smiled again, this time at Jake, and squeezed his left hand with her right hand.

"You aren't going to get sentimental in front of me," commented V reacting to Jake's warm smile towards Kate when she squeezed his hand.

"Oh hell V, there's never any down time around your world to let anyone get sentiment," noted Jake. And they all laughed thinking of the whirlwind that had taken place since V got home.

"Maybe I'm not so crazy sleeping with my knife under my pillow," added Jake as an after thought.

"I agree with you there," added V.

"You are both too much, you're like little kids."

"Ah, and that's why you love us," said Jake with a smile as Kate laughed and V added his smile.

"On a serious note…," said V leaning forward with his face scrunched up in exaggerated concern.

"Oh, no, what?" said Jake leaning back and smiling as he knew something was coming.

"I forgot to tell you and Dad never says anything."

"Uh-oh," groaned Jake.

"Well, he has a commercial scheduled to be shot in the house this week."

"Are you kidding?" said Jake.

"Well, this is nice to know," added Kate.

"Yeah, well Beelzebub and her birds and cat live there

now."

"Christ, it's her 'Church'," said Jake more thinking out loud than responding to V.

"Oh, no, not with that again," stated Kate.

French turned to look at Russell and started singing louder to drown him out. Zach and Jake looked at each other, smiled and then stood in unison and started singing Rule Britannia along with Russell, who was now trying to stand with great effort.

Within a matter of fifteen minutes of back and forth the French had Russell by all fours carrying him up and down the staircase, by this point passed out, with his head bumping on the steps while they sang the Marseillaise. The two girls were getting surrounded and Zach and Jake automatically started to size up the situation in order to determine who was the biggest French guy and what to hit him with. They thought the same. The only way to deal with a situation like this was to strike first and hard when the time came.

It happened, however, that they were able to extricate themselves from the restaurant after retrieving Russell.

Out in the street Zach and Jake looked at each other and laughed. "Which one did you pick?" asked Jake a little out of breath.

"The big ugly one with the mustache, I already tested the weight of the bench," said Zach, and they both laughed some more.

They could not leave Russell in the street with a pocket full of currency so eventually they found his room, which was a minor miracle with his state and all the one way streets in that section of Paris. Russell was awake and alert enough to get it right. After getting out of the car he lost his dinner but still had eyes for Sandy. Pressing his face up to the car's windshield with vomit still on his lips he pulled out his passport and told Sandy that he was giving her his passport and the only way to get it back to him was to meet him the next day. She was nice enough to say yes, just to calm him. He was a mess. Zach and Jake got him up to his room and dropped him on his bed but he bounced off onto the floor and passed out again. At least he had his passport and his cash. They never saw him again.

They got the girls home to their hotel room that night and

linebacker with curly black hair, a matching beard and wild eyes. They had a friendship that was tighter than brothers. Jake knew that he would get in the middle of hell for Zach and he also knew that Zach would do the same for him. They had already been in a couple of close shaves together from a potential brawl in Paris to being surrounded by Basque anarchists in Spain.

In Paris they were in sync with each other when they wound up at a restaurant called Le Sergent Recruteur. It was near St. Michel, and as Jake would remember, from a semi-inebriated haze, off of Rue de Henri IV; or so he thought. Earlier they had been drinking Scotch at a café along the Seine, not too far from the Louvre, when a Scotsman came up to them and inquired if they were 'Yanks'. Once he confirmed that they were American he asked if he could join them. His name was Russell.

So, the three of them sat talking about Paris and Parisian women among other things while Zach and Russell toasted anything that came to mind. Zach was smiling with every drink as Russell tried to keep up. Zach had a constitution like no other. Jake just took it for granted but the man could drink a half bottle of scotch in an hour and not show it; the only telltale sign was that his face would get a little red. He had a 'hollow leg' as Jake's Father would have said. Russell was a miner from Scotland on 'holiday' with a wad of cash, in three different currencies, to spend and it was all in one pocket. He worked an entire year just to come to the Continent and blow his earnings. He was a likable guy and Zach and Jake had taken to him.

Two tables down from where they were sitting Russell noticed two young women and commented on how he would like to meet them. Jake just smiled and said, "Hold on a minute Russell," as he got up and then headed to the table with the women. It turned out that they were both American from California and within a matter of minutes Jake had them joining his table while Russell sat speechless and smiled. With Kate the only woman on his mind, he took special effort to introduce the two young women, Barbara and Sandy, to Russell. They loved his Scottish accent so all was good until they got into the rental car that Zach and Jake had taken down to Pamplona, Spain. The driver side door had a dent in it and a jimmied lock where the Guardia Civil had broken into the car, which they had stupidly parked in front of the police station. The cash and passports had been left behind with the only missing items being their airline tickets, and there was no problem there other than a nuisance.

As Jake drove, with Sandy in the passenger seat next to him, Zach and Russell continued to make toasts in the back seat from a bottle of Dewar's that Zach had in his bag. With Barbara crammed into the back seat, in the middle of the two, they proceeded to drink without restraint. Zach would take a guzzle and Russell would reach for the bottle and try to compete. Jake had caught Zach's eyes in the rearview mirror and shook his head 'No' and Zach just smiled back.

By the time they had parked the car and arrived at the restaurant Russell was already three sheets to the wind. They headed for the basement dining room which was a large stone room at the bottom of a wooden switchback staircase. There were no windows and it was more like a medieval dungeon, but pleasant. The dinner started with raw vegetables, then pâte and so on through several courses all for 24 Francs. This came with all the wine that you desired, which was not a benefit to this group. Russell ordered a bottle for himself and sat it to the right of his plate. He was interested in the younger woman Sandy but Sandy was just being kind to him with eyes for Jake.

As they sat they hadn't noticed the twenty or thirty, or so young Frenchmen sitting at a long table across from them. They were all wearing stripped jerseys with the colors of sky blue and white. It would turn out that this was the French national soccer team. As they drank more, and Russell drank more, two ships were being set up for a collision.

When the French started singing the Marseillaise Russell's eyes lit up and he started singing Rule Britannia. With this the

Chapter 6

The Confrontation

The next evening found Kate, Jake, Oliver and Jake's college buddy Zach Epstein barbecuing chicken on the side lawn at the Lugers', just off the veranda in front of the French doors. Jake tended the chicken with Oliver looking on, closely, as Kate and Zach talked. Jake could overhear Zach talking about his part time job working in his uncle's shoe store and all the crazy people whose feet he got to see. He laughed as he told Kate that you could tell a lot by a person's feet. It was only part-time until he found what he really wanted and he had no idea what that was at this point. The three of them wrote their own schedules and would have the next couple of days with each other.

***

Zach and Jake had bummed around Europe together at the end of their junior year at Boston University. Jake had talked Zach into it and they did everything from run with the bulls to running off of a moving train or, that is, Zach running off of a moving train. That can be pretty funny when the person coming off the departing train, like a bullet, is built like   a now."

"Christ, it's her 'Church'," said Jake more thinking out loud than responding to V.

"Oh, no, not with that again," stated Kate.

"Alright unck, that was beautiful," said V as he started rubbing Oliver's ears and head after Oliver took up a seat next to the Ritz man.

Having everything out of her system Charlotte allowed Charlie to reach over and kiss her on the temple and then hug her briefly while she sat in her chair with a warm glow about her face.

Charlie looked over at Kate, as Jake's back was to him, and smiled realizing and appreciating what he had done.

Kate smiled back then facing Jake she quietly said, "I think you have two lifelong friends and it would appear that the Campbells are okay." She smiled again, this time at Jake, and squeezed his left hand with her right hand.

"You aren't going to get sentimental in front of me," commented V reacting to Jake's warm smile towards Kate when she squeezed his hand.

"Oh hell V, there's never any down time around your world to let anyone get sentiment," noted Jake. And they all laughed thinking of the whirlwind that had taken place since V got home.

"Maybe I'm not so crazy sleeping with my knife under my pillow," added Jake as an after thought.

"I agree with you there," added V.

"You are both too much, you're like little kids."

"Ah, and that's why you love us," said Jake with a smile as Kate laughed and V added his smile.

"On a serious note...," said V leaning forward with his face scrunched up in exaggerated concern.

"Oh, no, what?" said Jake leaning back and smiling as he knew something was coming.

"I forgot to tell you and Dad never says anything."

"Uh-oh," groaned Jake.

"Well, he has a commercial scheduled to be shot in the house this week."

"Are you kidding?" said Jake.

"Well, this is nice to know," added Kate.

"Yeah, well Beelzebub and her birds and cat live there

the next day headed for the airport.

They had had a trip together, everything from being shot at by the Guardia Civil with rubber bullets as they were in the wrong place at the wrong time in Pamplona to Zach forgetting his pack on a train in Germany. Zach had gone back to get the pack and by the time he came back to the door to get off, the train was picking up speed as it left the station. Jake had watched in amazement as Zach flung open the door and came flying out pack in hand and legs churning for all he was worth as though he were running in mid-air. He predictably hit the pavement with a thump and as Jake came up he said, "What the hell was that? Were you running?"

"Yeah, I saw it in a Clint Eastwood movie once and it worked," said Zach looking up and smiling with a drop of blood coming off of his nose where he had scraped it as he came to a stop.

"You're oughta your mind, but you'd probably be dead if you weren't drunk," Jake had noted.

They had been at the Munich beer hall earlier that day and had bet two German patrons their age that they could out drink them when the Germans had said that Americans couldn't drink. A stupid thing to do but, 'what the hell' as Zach would say. The Germans were done at four liters each and Zach and Jake just kept on going that day. The Germans just shook their heads and anteed up.

They had been through many things together in the three short years that they had known each other and they clicked.

***

Coming up the steps with the chicken now on a platter Jake said, with feigned concern, "You're not telling stories about me I hope."

Zach turning just grinned and said, "Who you? You're boring."

Kate just laughed. "I know better, especially when you two are together."

"Look at Ollie, he's looking up to you," noted Zach looking at Oliver and gesturing in Oliver's direction with his hand holding his rock glass of scotch.

Jake looked down at Oliver doing a little dance and looking up at him. "Yeah, he wants the chicken. Here you go grab what you want and salad is on the table."

"Is Jake always this domestic?" questioned Zach with the scotch still in his hand.

"Usually when he wants something," said Kate laughing.

"Ah, you know your boy. I thought so," said Zach with a smile.

Jake just shaking his head as he put chicken on a plate for Kate said, "You two are bad together, that's the problem, not me."

"So, what's this that I'm hearing about a commercial?" queried Zach punctuated by his satirical smile.

"I couldn't fill him in on the details," followed Kate.

"Is this Rodney revenue?" asked Zach followed by an even bigger smile.

"I'd say so, they want to shoot in the front hall with the backdrop of the stained glass window, so no free renovation work," commented Jake while handing Zach his plate and turning back around to fork a piece of chicken onto his own plate.

"He'd go for the hard cash anyway," said Zach now getting up to head to the salad.

Standing in place with his plate until Zach took his salad Jake replied, "You got that right, they shoot for a day or two and he has a year's worth of rent."

"How did he get this?" asked Zach now settled and forking some salad.

"It seems to be a cottage industry here," said Kate sitting with her plate on a side table while she calmed Oliver down and made him sit on the far side of her chair away from her food.

"That probably puts it plainly. Many a new kitchen in Englewood has been bartered for a soap commercial or whatever they want to peddle for kitchens. You can see at least two a week around Englewood this time of year."

"How'd that start?" queried Zach showing actual curiosity.

"You know Dick Baxter?"

"The guy who can make you cry with his stories?"

"That's him, the Park Avenue guy. He brings them out here."

"Well, not bad," Zach concluded.

Just as Zach finished speaking Rodney came in the front door with Clive and both had been drinking heavily.

"Where is that mad wench?" harped Clive as he fumbled through the front door behind Rodney, looking up the stairway towards Alice's door as he did so.

"Oh Christ," said Jake moving towards the French doors, with plate in hand, to close them.

"Is that, that English idiot you were telling me about?"

"The one and only," said Jake.

"He's a drunk," put in Kate.

"So am I, but I'm not a pompous Englishman," confirmed Zach.

"That's obvious," said Kate as she smiled.

Zach just smiled back with a little glaze in his eyes from the scotch.

Jake looking through the glass of the French doors could see that they headed for the dining room and most likely the liquor cabinet in that room. He knew this would be trouble. Whenever his brother came in this early with 'a load on' and searching for more it was better to leave the house even though it hadn't occurred since Jake and Kate had moved in. The man, when drunk and alone, had a mean streak when it came to his 'baby brother'. Jake could not pin down the reason other than the fact that Rodney was jealous of his little brother. As a small child he was frightened of his older brother and could not understand his meanness but now as a young man Jake understood it as a bazaar form of jealousy. His older brother grew up during the war with all of the household concerns that the times brought and he was also the first son of a man who was a builder, a man who got things done and was busy doing so. There may have been pressure on his older brother in those early years but Jake would be the first to say that he is not a shrink. As a young man in high school, his older brother started to take the world on. He had it by the horns as he evolved into one of the best distance runners that had been seen at the high school level in years.

He became the best in the state and was sought after by every college that had a serious track program. One coach, from Bates in Maine, had actually followed him into the shower trying to convince him to come to Bates as he got soaked in the process, totally oblivious to the water. The coach wanted this guy but he didn't get him. The Ivys got him and he excelled. He became the big deal on campus and there was nothing he could not have nor do. This followed him for a period after graduation even after his first setback before graduation and just before the Olympic trials when mononucleosis hit. He was out of the Olympics and after coming back would be out again four years later with a torn Achilles.

Now his older brother, living in the past, would get ridiculous and funny to his friends when drunk. But he would get down right mean to Jake at the same time, if he was not surrounded by a large group. Jake remembered his older brother drinking with his best friend one night and his friend Steve was laughing wildly as Rodney spun around on top of the kitchen table. Rodney with his arms out was spitting water out of his mouth, as he spun around, representing his take on the new fountain in downtown Englewood. It was a year earlier and Jake had stopped by to drop some information off for V. Rodney saw him in the middle of his fountain interpretation and stopped. He approached Jake and turned angry with some statement along the lines that Jake was just like 'his' father. Jake took it as a compliment and finally understood that there was a degree of jealousy which had affected his relationship with his older brother through the years. It all started to make sense as Rodney started to go after Jake. His friend

Steve had stepped in and stopped him asking him what he was doing, with critical concern in his voice.

Jake had left the house as soon as he could that night and it had been forgotten but not completely. Rodney had forgotten but not Jake and it had become part of the thought process before he and Kate had rented a room in the man's house.

Kate had calmed Jake's worries and convinced Jake that if he avoided Rodney, when he was drunk and not surrounded by others, he would be okay. The party had been fine as they were among many people and, besides, Rodney's state of mind was also affected by an insulin reaction.

Tonight Jake felt on edge. He knew that his older brother was in the perfect situation and state to blow up at him. Rodney was with one other person and he would be the focus of that other person's attention. But if he saw Jake that focus on him would get broken, in his mind, as Jake took away some of the spotlight and that would not be good.

They had their dinner in relative peace only broken now and again by booming drunken boisterousness coming through the French doors from the dining room. Even Oliver reacted to the loud drunks, occasionally lifting his head with ears perked in defense ready to run if necessary.

It was getting louder as Jake said, "I'd rather go. I don't feel good about this."

Although they hadn't quite finished, let alone sat back in relaxed conversation, it was time to go. Zach could see it on Jake's face and Kate just felt it intuitively.

They picked up their dishes and headed through the French doors, through the den and on to the kitchen through the living room and the wet bar/pass-through.

As they headed back towards the veranda to finish the clean-up, with Jake in the lead, they ran smack into Rodney and Clive in the den. They were trying, without much luck, to master the stereo system located in the book shelf.

Jake saw Rodney first and prepped himself. He knew something was coming.

Rodney, only focusing on Jake, stared and then said, with

everyone frozen in place, "What the hell....are you doing?"

"Having a barbeque big brother," Jake answered cordially.

"Trying,....... trying to be a smart ass?"

"No, we're having a barbeque," repeated Jake motioning Kate and Zach to head out to the veranda.

At this Rodney noticed the others, looked at them briefly as they headed out the French doors and then returned to Jake, "Who said you could have............a barbeque?! I didn't."

Jake's defensive fuse was now lit which would make him more direct.

Then Clive harped in, "Where's that....... Yank friend of yours?"

"I'm a Yank you asshole," retorted Jake and Clive shut-up.

"He's my guest."

"Then I advise you keep him under control."

"Listen here old man........," started Clive.

"Just shut up and listen," said Rodney overriding Clive as he moved towards Jake, who fell into the overstuffed leather chair in front of the book cabinet trying to avoid Rodney's advance.

Laying back in the chair where he fell, Jake looked up at his older brother and said, "The day that you finally listen to me is the day we will get along."

With this Rodney took a swing at Jake, bending down when he did so with his fist hitting the shade on the floor lamp long before it got near Jake.

Jake got up and moved to the main hall to try to avoid what was happening but Rodney tackled him right on top of the red Persian rug and they both went down.

As Jake maneuvered to get out from under his grip Rodney reached into Jake's pants and tried to yank off his testicles. Filled with disbelieving anger that someone would do such a thing, let alone a brother, Jake hit him with his fist, from a lying position, on the side of his temple. Rodney let go.

Jake scrambled out from under, and Rodney got up and lunged again slipping on the rug and going down.

Clive just stood in amazement backing into a corner.

With Rodney on the floor, trying to get up, Jake went out the French doors to Kate and Zach. "I think we'd better go," was all he said as they headed for the front of the house and Zach's Mustang fastback parked in the street.

Before they reached the end of the driveway and the street Rodney came storming out of the house, ran up to Jake, and acting as though he had been attacked, screamed, "I'm gonna call the police... and have you looocked... up."

With this, Jake blew. He turned and said, "Well then let me give you something to call them about." Jake gave him everything he had with a twisting fist right on the nose.

Rodney went down, flat on his back, and was only partly lucid as he told Clive, who was still in the house and could not hear him, to call the police.

Jake shook his hand out and all three walked out to the street, down to Zach's car and left until early the next morning.

The next morning found Jake and Kate and Oliver back on the third floor asleep. Zach slept on the couch in the second room on the floor located on the other side of the house. This room was separated from Jake and Kate's room by a bathroom in the middle. When they had returned at about 2:00 in the morning the house was quiet and they had crept up the back stairway not knowing where Rodney might be.

Now at 8AM they were rising, lead by Oliver. Oliver just decided that he wanted to be with Jake and Kate so he approached the bed from its foot and landed right between them, all 150 pounds, which quickly spread the two beds wheel locks and all. With panic on his face Oliver sank in the middle of the two of them descending slowly to the floor taking the blankets with him and effectively waking Jake and Kate. When they woke they saw Oliver sitting with his tongue out panting over his little experience with drama and patiently waiting to be helped out.

As Kate and Jake laughed Zach could be heard from the room at the end of the hall stretching and yawning loudly.

It was time to leave the house for the day in order to avoid any wreckage that would probably surface later that morning.

They left within the hour and, with all three of them having Monday free, went to Ed's Crossbow Tavern for breakfast. Zach loved the pancakes at Ed's so much so that he'd talk Ed's ear off about them. Ed was always happy to see them come through the door as a result. He ate up Zach's unusual appreciation for his pancakes as it was his mother's recipe and one of those that is handed down. Oliver was given special care and allowed under the table with his own plate of two hotcakes, to Kate's chagrin. Oliver could tell when they were headed to Ed's and in the back of that fastback with Kate he started bouncing around in anticipation as Kate tried to remind him of her authority by speaking French. Jake laughed to himself listening to Kate and then being reminded of the time when they had been driving their Opel station wagon, which Kate still drove, on a major highway with fast food in the front seat and Oliver in the back. As soon as Kate had pulled the little box of French fries out of a fast-food bag the view out of the front of the car went from day to night as Oliver joined them. 'Jesus Christ Oliver, I can't see, Kate get him to move, Christ,' Jake had yelled as Kate started yelling at Oliver in French while he stared at the fries not hearing a word. Then Kate got smart and threw the small box of fries into the back seat and as quickly as it had become night it was once again day. She was speaking French with him once again this morning but Oliver only had Ed's hotcakes on his mind even as she held him around the neck to keep him under control. As soon as Zach parked he got out quickly and pulled the seat forward to let Oliver out and the big dog shot like a black bullet towards Ed's front door.   .

That day offered a special summer competition held at a lake in western New Jersey and they had all planned to go, even before the 'confrontation', as it was a Newfoundland rescue and swimming competition.

Oliver had been dumfounded to see others who looked just like him and especially the puppies that he would go   up to, sniffing their fir to make sure that he wasn't seeing things. It was all humorous to watch until Oliver decided that he was going to take off and play with one of the competitors heading for the water with a life ring in his mouth. With this a whistle went off and the group was advised to control their Newfy or 'crate' him. Crate Oliver, that sounded interesting but they were able to get him to sit and watch as they spent most of the day in the company of black Newfoundlands. There was not one brown and white one in sight. It was late afternoon and it had been a good day before they headed back to Englewood and what might await them at the house.

Jake's hand was starting to hurt quite a bit by the time that they were back in Englewood. Late that day, almost into evening, he went to the local emergency room and had a half cast put on as he had flattened the socket to his right pinky. It cost him eighty-five dollars. Jake knew that sometime in the future such a procedure in an ER would probably be ten to twenty times the cost due to malpractice lawyers. As a young journalist he just shook his head at what was coming. He was already experiencing the early stages of it in some of his court coverage.

Later that evening after Zach dropped them off they saw Rodney sober with his nose taped up. Well here it was they thought. But as they approached the house, with Rodney on the side lawn lighting one of several kerosene torches, nothing was said.

Nothing was ever said of it even though Rodney's nose was broken along with the damage to Jake's hand. It may have been that Rodney did not remember what he did or that he did and did not want to go near that one especially with the attempted castration of his 'baby brother'. Whatever it was, that was okay. It was okay that it would go away by mutual agreement and maybe something was learned, thought Jake, until another drinking bout sometime in the distant future.

Others would find out about it by default, maybe not the specifics but they would know. You cannot hide a broken nose and a broken hand in the same room without immediate recognition and connection, especially when one knew the brothers.

Questions would be asked sometimes with a smile, as with V, or concern but the answers were vague and questionable and the whole affair would quickly blend into the background. The activity around the commercial helped to put the event in the background even with the ever present bandages that really stood out when both were in the same room.

Chapter 7

The Commercial

Wednesday, June 29th

It was early Wednesday morning when the commercial people arrived. Kate had already left with the sun just coming up in order to be able to audit an early morning class at Sarah Lawrence in Yonkers/Bronxville where she had obtained her Bachelor's degree.

Jake was getting prepared to write a human interest story about a man he had interviewed the previous day. He was finding that he had a talent to approach almost anyone and find a story inside, once he got them talking.

This particular story was from a diner in Greenburgh, New York, Westchester County. He and Kate had stopped into the diner while meandering around after her visit to Sarah Lawrence to make arrangements to audit the class the next day. Jake got to talking with the owner and before he knew it he had a story about Judy Garland. Jake knew enough about history, economics, politics, science, theatre, music and the arts in general that he could talk with anyone about their interests once he had a small piece to grab onto. Judy Garland would come into the diner, as she lived close by at the time, and sing. It became a place where everyone knew her, and she'd simply sing for them. It was a refuge for her when she was drinking and the stories were heartwarming although it was during a time of great pain for this woman.

He put the paper in the typewriter, pulling it up to the halfway point in order to start his story in the middle of the page. He had barely hit the first key when he heard an amplified voice saying, "Get that screen on the lawn in front of that stained glass window." It boomed and was followed by more words. Oliver's nails against the finished pine floor was the next sound that Jake heard as Oliver pushed his way up to a sitting position to hear better. Before Jake could get up to investigate Oliver was up and headed for the door and the backstairs down to the kitchen.

Jake could hear the muffled bullhorn as he headed down the backstairs behind Oliver. Oliver no doubt anticipated new people who might feed him. This was usually the case when people met Oliver for the first time, if they had food either in their hands or nearby.

Alice was at work waitressing someplace in Bergen County it was assumed but no one wanted to verify it either by query or by accident. And Rodney had taken a few days off using the commercial as a convenient excuse giving the black and blue time to go to yellow and then fade. Carter was at his store, or so Jake assumed, until he neared the kitchen and could hear Carter on the phone to Bea, his partner, "What do you mean you can't get that belt? For chrissakes Bea, they make the damned thing and you should be able to get it. And what the hell were you thinking by ordering two dozen of those damned bow ties that we'll never get rid of for Chrissakes!" There was a pause by the time Jake made it to the kitchen while Bea talked on the other end.

"I don't give a damn Bea, send the damned things back and get those damned belts," he continued.

Jake had heard a couple of these 'Bea conversations' over the weeks and Carter was always gruff but that was Carter and although it sounded gruff it was never taken as such. It was just Carter fueled by drink.

Jake peered into the kitchen more as a reflex to check for Oliver than anything else knowing where he would, in the end, be found. But he only found Carter on the wall phone dressed in his tennis whites giving his commands to Bea.

As Jake came out of the hallway from the kitchen and into the main receiving hall of the house he could see the front door wide open and the mud room entry way door wide open as well. The stained glass window rising two stories above the main hall and fronted by the stairway was lit in a bright garish light. And there was Oliver sitting with his tail wagging as two of the people handling lights were talking to him and feeding him potato chips.

Jake could see for a brief moment many more people milling about on the front lawn as he gazed out the front door before Rodney and another man came through the door. And it wasn't Clive. Clive it seems had gone to visit another 'Yank' friend.

"Oliver, come here boy," he said to get Oliver out of the way and out of sight to avoid any possible confrontation with his older brother.

As Oliver got up and turned in response the two people who had been talking with him and feeding him chips looked up and smiled. "Great dog, is he a Pyrenees?" asked the one who was holding the bag of chips that Oliver was staring up at.

"No, a Newfoundland, like the one Lewis and Clark had," answered Jake frustrated by the same question from others in the past and leaving the two confused with the 'Lewis and Clark' addition.

"Oh, great dog," said the one with the chips bag as he fed Oliver another one.

"Thanks."

They then turned back to the lights looking up at the stained glass window in response to the man with Rodney saying, "There is just too much glare, push the lights out and highlight the color in the stained glass."

Carter's voice now escalated from the kitchen enough for everyone to stop and look in that direction, "God damnit Bea, I said I didn't want any more of those things and for Chrissakes get rid of that goddamned Lily dress will you," and there was a pause while Bea spoke.

"Because I FUCKING KILLED HER and that dress reminds me..., get rid of it," and he slammed the phone down against the wall cradle.

It was stated with such conviction within ear shot of people who did not know Carter that a hush came over the room as Carter walked in wearing his whites and finally realizing that something was going on, but Jake had seen this once before. He was someplace else, and this time it seemed that it had to do with 'killing a woman' but it made no sense.

"Jesus Christ, kill that light, they'll see us. God we're fucked," commanded Carter and then he turned with fear written on his face and headed for the stairway between the kitchen and the main hall. Then up he went no doubt for more Johnny Walker.

It had left the small crew, that was in the house at this point, stunned.

All we need now is Alice thought Jake looking up and seeing her door closed to the right of the stairs. He knew that behind that door lurked a white cat below two perching doves and this brought a subtle smile of humor to his face.

The commercial was about a window cleaner on a stick designed to reach high places and Jake watched out of curiosity as they moved the cameras in place and set up two chairs for the 'actors'. They actually had two captain's chairs for the man and the woman in the commercial. They were supposed to be husband and wife with a plot centered around a discussion, initiated by the 'wife', on how revolutionary the cleaner, on an extension, was. 'Jeez', thought Jake, all this for that little revelation.

Rodney stood off to Jake's right as they took the first take, initiated by snapping a small gate down on top of a small attached chalkboard with the name of the product on it and a #1 underneath it.

The crew had been stunned by Carter and word had spread to the actors that there was a strange character in the house who was a 'killer'. Jake had heard one of these comments which was made with little attempt to keep it to a whisper.

As the man snapped the gate down on that little chalkboard and moved away the man who had been with Rodney said, "Andddd action." And with this the actress on the stairway started moving the cleaner on the extension up and down from the top to the bottom of the window. Then she collapsed the telescopic handle as her 'husband' came from the direction of the front door and said to her, "Hi honey, what are you up to?"

As the 'wife' turned she caught Jake's casted hand and Rodney's tapped broken nose together in her line of vision. This, fueled by the story of the crazy killer in tennis whites, stopped her in her action as she just froze and stared at the two of them. One could only imagine what was going through her head but the pause and direction of the stare was enough to get the man, who had said 'action', to say "cut." Then everyone turned in unison to see Jake and Rodney and what she had noticed. Mostly the two brothers were met with stares that targeted the bandaging with their focus followed by a polite smile from the particular owner of the stare. But in one case a young lady, who had seen the 'crazy killer', put two and two together in her head and the end result was horror on the verge of panic.

"Ok people, can we get back to this! Time is money!," yelled the man with a clap of his hands, the man that Jake now realized was the director.

"Claire, Claire, are you ok?" the director voiced directly at the young lady holding onto one of the lighting support poles. She had not taken her eyes off of the Luger brothers as she continued to stare, especially at the one with the face that now looked like a raccoon with a big piece of white running between his black and blue eyes .

Taking her eyes off of the Lugers she looked at the director with a blank stare, nodded her head and then returned her attention to the light that she was controlling.

Jake headed back upstairs, with Oliver in pursuit, to work on his piece right after Claire, the light girl, had turned her attention back to her lights. Oliver would be content with Jake until he smelled those sweet smells of lunchtime and then he would be back.

They seemed to have a lot of people, somewhere around twenty, for a little commercial with two people talking briefly about a cleaning item. Rodney had soon become bored and decided to have a late morning drink for himself. He would remember to give himself his shot of insulin, just before lunch. He wouldn't forget that even if he did have a couple of drinks in him.

Nothing out of the ordinary happened until lunch a couple of hours later when Oliver sat up abruptly and then followed his nose down stairs to the lunching crew to see what he could get. Jake was too immersed in his story to pay attention although he and Kate might pay for it late that night with a gassy Newfoundland.

Oliver made the rounds at lunch and got a lot of 'hey boy's' and 'atta boy's' and the one he understood, 'here you go boy'. He had a feast of bits and pieces before the crew went back to work.

Jake knew lunch was over when Oliver returned to the room. He was not paying attention while he just sat at the typewriter and looked out the window. Then looking over at Oliver, "Come here boy," he said and Oliver came over for his head and ear scratching which helped Jake think.

Nothing happened until a half hour after lunch when a buzz saw went off down the street. Jake smiled as he knew it was Billy Washburn who owned a tree service. Billy came from a well to do family of the same town and had decided to skip college and start a tree service. He was a couple of years older than Jake with a beautiful wife and the start of a nice family. His tree service was quite successful. Jake smiled even more as the noise of the buzz saw grew more persistent. V worked, briefly, for Billy at the end of the previous summer picking up after the guys trimming the trees as the Washburns were friends of the Lugers. V had told Jake to listen for the buzz saw at some point during the filming of the commercial. He said Billy would really crank it whenever he found a commercial in town until the director or other member of the crew came up to him and asked him to stop for the rest of the shooting. And of course they would cover his lost revenue for the day. Billy had a deal going with summer commercials.

After a while the buzz saw stopped and Jake went back to work.

Claire was staring at the actors and the effect of her light on both of them and the stained glass window when Carter, still in his tennis whites, all of a sudden appeared on the walkway way above the main hall and across from Alice's room. He paced out mumbling something then paced back again as the director yelled, "Cut........what the hell now?"

On queue Carter came back across the top of the main hall again with his eyes getting wider as he walked in great steps then he said to no one in particular, "Jesus Christ the Japs are all over the place. Christ............" and he turned and headed back down the walkway again and out of sight.

Poor Claire had now lost all concentration on her lighting and was just part of the scenery as Rodney stumbled out of the dining room talking to himself. He had a drink, or two or more, in him. And he had once again taken his insulin on time automatically but then forgot to eat and was having an insulin reaction on top of the alcohol. "What's this, haaaaaa, whooooo lights whoooo aahh," he blurted out as he looked up at the stained glass window all lit up.

The director was at a loss. "Are you ok Mr. Luger?" he said as though he were talking to a drunk while the crew once again stopped and stared. They had never had experiences like this although they had seen a strange thing or two   while shooting, but not this many in a row.

The director not being able to make any contact with Rodney remembering that his brother seemed sane and had headed up the stairway where he saw that big black dog heading after lunch.

Yelling up the stairway, "Hey, anyone up there, we need help down here with mister Luger, can anyone hear me?" He yelled again, now cupping his hands to his mouth and tempted to get the bull horn if this started to progress into a bad situation.

"You need help?" came a loud voice from the third floor as Jake had heard the cry as clear as a bell.

"Yes, yes, it's Mr. Luger, he appears to have had too much to drink," the director yelled back.

"Oh Christ," Jake said as he ran down the stairs from where he was standing to answer the cries of the director. Oliver pushed himself up and followed. He followed so quickly and so fast that the momentum was more than he could handle. As he made the turn to the last short flight of steps he plowed into Jake and both rolled out into the downstairs hallway in a crash to add to the confusion now taking place in the main hall.

"Insulin, not drunk, he's having an insulin reaction hold on," said Jake as he untangled himself from Oliver and headed to the refrigerator in the kitchen and the tube of glucose.

Grabbing the tube he then flew past Oliver who was now in the main hall barking at Rodney as he gyrated around with his arms out. Claire was now not the only one eyeing the exits. Jake ran in and got Rodney's attention. Rodney stopped and looked at Jake like a sick child would look at a parent waiting for a spoon of cough medicine. As Jake brought the tube up to his mouth the now calm Rodney opened up for that medicine in the form of a squeeze tube full of clear glucose. Jake squeezed some in and Rodney just stood there with his mouth open until Jake said, "Eat it Rodney, it's good for you." Rodney closed his mouth and processed the glucose and then opened for more like a child in a high chair.

Within a few minutes Rodney started to come around as Jake explained to the director loud enough for everyone to hear that Rodney was a diabetic and that this was an insulin reaction from not eating in a timely manner.

The director breathed a sigh of relief along with the crew but they were all now on edge, between Carter's wild declaration and Rodney's exaggerated childlike gyrations.

Jake decided to stay after getting Rodney to sit just in case something happened with his older brother.

Just before they started another take, just after setting up again, Alice appeared. Having gone up the back stairway unnoticed, she walked out of the hallway and across the elevated walkway to her room and entered closing the door behind her.

"Crap, who's that?" the director asked Jake after turning in his direction.

"A tenant, don't worry she'll probably stay there," said Jake.

And then they heard it, "The devil will not have me, I am the devil." It was muffled but one could make it out.

The director looked at Jake who said, "Oh, that's nothing. It's okay."

Then the same voice chanted, "I know the secret of the secret to the secret passageway," which was followed by a demonic laugh from behind the door. Just as she finished the door flew open and out came Alice in full robe, fully open, and naked underneath. She had a large cross held between her breasts with the two white doves on her right shoulder and the white cat in pursuit. She stopped in the middle of the walkway, above the main hall, and staring down at everyone decreed, "This is my church and you are not allowed here." This was punctuated by the doves taking off with a flapping effect heading for Henry in the den, flying right over Claire's head and that was it. Claire ran out the front door screaming followed by Alice's admonishment, "Leave you sin of incest." If Alice truly knew the other secret of the church's pre-Civil War passageway her invocation would have been a   different one.

Jesus, thought Jake, if only Kate could see this because she won't think it's such a big deal later. He smiled knowing V understood.

"Holy crap," said the director.

"What's going on?" asked Rodney holding his head and walking in from the dining room where Jake had made him take a seat.

Just as Rodney came out Carter came back down the walkway and passed Alice quickly with excited fear thinking she was that crazy Jap with the grenade. But he was fueled by Johnny Walker and the fear that other Japs were behind him so he had no choice and he flew down the stairway, past the actors still frozen on the stairs and now hugging the wall as he went by. He went out to the den, out the open French doors and to the back of the yard with the departing warning, "We're fucked!" and he was gone.

"Christ, what is this a joke?" said he director looking from where Carter was last seen back to where Rodney was standing in the threshold of the dining room holding his head with his nose bandaged.

"It's all yours brother," said Jake as he smiled and left leaving Rodney behind holding his aching bandaged head. Alice at the same time went back into her room closing the door quietly while leaving the doves on the antlers and the white cat to roam the walkway.

It was as though everything rose at once like a great storm and then the calm came like the passing of the eye.

The director fearful of what might happen next got the crew moving faster. "Ok people back to it. Get into positions please, we have a short window here," he announced and someone in the crew laughed. The director wasn't laughing. It became a mad dash to get it all done and get the hell out of the Lugers' house and in one day, not two as they had planned.

The director was never able to get that slight tone of fear, like an animal on the edge ready to jump for survival, out of the eyes of the 'wife' actress. The commercial would make it to TV quickly, near the end of the summer. And this was long after V had heard the full story from Jake which helped it to take on a life of its own with a small cult following. Also, soon after Carter first saw Alice as a Japanese soldier Jake had heard from Sam about him seeing the 'Jap with the grenade', especially when Alice was near. And soon after this they all knew about the 'Jap' in the house. They also knew about the 'Japs all over the place', as relayed to Jake by a member of the commercial crew. This had also added to the humor of the commercial although everyone who knew cared about Carter. Sam had only told Jake as he had known that Jake might be able to help at some point knowing that it would eventually get around.

For those who knew what had happened during the filming of the commercial, the fear in the eyes of the lead actor, like a lamb in a field with a prowling wolf, was irresistible to watch. Jake and V would actually run, with Oliver following, to watch the commercial for the first time when Kate, who was watching the evening news, let them know it was on. They just sat down halfway through the commercial laughing while Kate just shook her head with a smile commenting, "You are kids aren't you," while watching them watch the commercial. Then she smiled at them again and proceeded to scratch Oliver's head, who was sitting in between her and Jake on the couch facing the television in the small television room; the room that was located through a door to the side of the fireplace in the den and facing the front of the house.

As Jake watched the commercial the off camera words, 'I know the secret of the secret to the secret passageway' came across his thoughts as a tape through a recorder and for one brief moment he wondered what the hell it was that Alice had been talking about. This thought was followed by a slight chill up his spine. Then he was back to watching the commercial without a second thought about it.

Alice still did not know the true secrets held within the church. She knew the secret of the passageway and thought she knew all of its mysteries. She thought that she controlled them but the secret of what she thought she knew would change everything for her.

The member of the crew, Claire, running from the house had convinced Alice of her powers although she was oblivious to Carter's preparation of the scene and the effect that the bandaged Lugers had on the young girl. She had smiled with glee that day when she returned to her room. And she had giggled quietly as she listened to the rest of the goings-on until she fell asleep on her bed with her eyes open long before the end of the day and the completion of the commercial. Luckily, young Claire would not have to witness Alice as she slept with her eyes open nor would anyone else in the crew for that matter. Knowing that Alice was at the top of the stairs behind the closed door would make the commercial more suspenseful and humorous every time Jake or V watched it.

Carter was dealing with his own demons and unwittingly Alice was one of those demons, although in a different form to him with a grenade in her hand instead of a cross or a figurine. Carter had changed for the better when he had met Margaret but Alice was disturbing that serenity in ways that no one really recognized. How could they? They could not see what Carter saw and besides, he had his own secret which should have killed him outright during the war instead of killing him slowly over the intervening years.

The Luger house was its own human cocktail of wondering souls walking the fine line between heaven and hell, and sanity and insanity. Rodney was left in his own world. He would emerge to grab from the world around him then sink back into his world without the slightest understanding of others or the need to understand anyone else except himself. It wasn't selfishness as he believed every thought that he had to be right and to be magnanimous, in a way, even though those thoughts would twist everything his way. Some things were twisted so violently in his direction, without him seeing it, that others would just shake their heads and move away from him. It would have been easier for everyone, including

Rodney, if he were consciously self-centered and calculating in getting what he wanted knowing that he was wrong along the way but not caring. That type of person is easier to deal with.

All of this made Jake's head spin as he tried to sort it all out with a modicum of fear in the mix. Kate missed most of the drama and that which she witnessed she just shrugged off as human nature at different extremes. Like Jake she felt a particular fondness, but particular to her, for the gruff Carter who would drop his gruffness with her, not realizing it and treating her more like a daughter. There was something uniquely special about this man but it was buried deep inside. There was something special about him that everyone who met him felt, but only Margaret and Kate could bring about a change in his outward demeanor. Margaret knew who was inside and she would spend many a day trying to bring that Carter outside once again. She was trying to rid him of his demons and help him to find happiness and peace in every day that he lived for the rest of his life. This she would take before her own happiness even if her own happiness were not the reward for Carter finding peace and joy in his world. There was one demon lurking inside Carter that Margaret knew was there, the one that controlled everything going on inside his head but she could not find it nor could she scare it loose in order to try and defeat it. It remained a secret to her and maybe to Carter as well, as it seemed to be buried deep within him and protected like a splinter surrounded by a protective cyst unlike a grain of sand protected by a pearl inside an oyster.

The commercial would remain on television well into the Fall to continually provide entertainment to both Jake and V. Kate would just shake her head at their sense of humor, with regard to a commercial, and their nervousness over a young woman who was just, in her mind, 'a bit eccentric'.

Chapter 8

The Fourth of July

Saturday, July 2nd

July 4th was just two days away on Monday. It was nice for Kate and Jake to have a three day weekend even though neither was yet fully in the job force. The Club would have their yearly barbeque run by Sam followed by fireworks on the great lawn between the clubhouse and the tennis courts.

V was still on the Cape but Zach, taking a three day weekend from his uncle's shoe store, would be there for the barbeque. This barbeque would be a bit safer than the one just a week earlier when Zach saw Rodney get laid flat on his back by his best friend. He would not miss it as he had been to it for the first and last time two years earlier and he had enjoyed it.

Also, on the few occasions that Zach had come to The Club, over the years, he and Sam had enjoyed each other's company. Sam was absolutely amazed at the amount of scotch that Zach could consume and still carry on a very coherent conversation, if not more coherent than some of the sober members. He would just laugh and smile that mustache smile of his and shake his head a little after Zach had his fifth scotch. Four drinks were not noticeable. The 'climbing' started at five when Zach would get a telling glow to his face. Then a permanent smile would come to his face accompanied by a whit that would go to the brink with people and then make them laugh at themselves, sometimes in relief that he was only kidding.

There was one episode, among many, in college where Jake used Zach's stare and whit to great effect when he started 'climbing' or when he was at the state where he would do almost anything to make people nervous. They were playing softball at a field along the Charles River against an MIT fraternity when Jake picked out one of the MIT players, the centerfielder, as a prime candidate. He told Zach to start giving him the piercing stare non-stop and Jake would do the rest. Zach's full head of black curly hair and black beard topped by those piercing blue eyes also added to the effect as he stared at the guy from the dugout to deep centerfield. The stare was so strong that it had the guy flustered at that distance. Jake for his part warned the guy, during inning changes, that Zach was an Acid head and a real freaked out guy and that if he started staring at you be careful because he was like a bull, he would fixate on only you. It only took two innings of this and the guy's face had changed like he was looking for the nearest exit when Jake told Zach, "Go". Zach ran out of the dugout headed for centerfield right in the middle of a pitch. The guy did not even take his glove dropping all extra weight as he headed for an exit with all he was worth, except there was no exit but fence all around. Zach chased that guy around until everyone, except the chasee, realized what was going on. Some were on the ground while others leaned up against the fence for support while they laughed. Well, that was a form of 'climbing'.

Carter always seemed to disappear around the Fourth of July, at least that's what Jake recalled when asked by Kate. Jake had seen Carter around The Club for the better part of the last seven years and never recalled having seen him at The

Club on that day in years past. Come to think of it Kate could not remember having seen him in the two years that she had gone there for the Fourth.

Three years earlier they had spent the Fourth in Tuxedo Park, New York at the house of a family who knew Kate's family. This experience had left its own memories. They had stayed in the 35 room house overlooking the lake that Fourth and Jake had to sleep alone in a bedroom on the top floor under the roof. He had to climb a long narrow staircase to get to it. To be proper he could not stay in the same room with Kate. He liked the family quite a bit, especially the lady of the house, Mrs. Jumel, who had one of those caring personalities that Jake gravitated to. She was a recovering alcoholic and she had a worldliness that put her far beyond her peers. She and Jake, in just a brief meeting, had a special respect and like for each other. She was a self-made woman.

The room was small and Victorian in its appointments, and would have been quaint and enjoyable for Jake if not for the ghost. Before sending him to the room Mrs. Jumel told him about the existence of a ghost in the house, '…just in case you happen to see her so you won't be startled,' was how she helped to preface it. 'See, what?' was Jake's quick reply accented with surprise and concern.

Mrs. Jumel laughed and then went on to briefly explain the 'ghost'. "She's been seen on the occasion of the Fourth of July several times over the years," she had said as she concluded.

"Where?" asked Jake with concern.

Mrs. Jumel could not help but smile with a subtle laugh at Jake's unease. "Well," she had said, "she's usually been seen in the study at the bottom of the stairway to the room you'll be in."

"Usually?"

"Well, yes……….she was once seen in the room that you are in. But that was back in the 40's."

"Oh, so she's been around for a while and in that room. That's just great."

"Yes, but she's friendly although a sad character. Your room is an old sewing room, or used to be back in the latter part of the 19th Century. She is dressed in a Victorian wedding dress. "

"Oh great."

"It just so happens that a young woman of the house by the name of Elisa was left at the altar and then vanished. No one ever knew what happened to her. It was a great tragedy and mystery at the time."

"Oh, no.............a ghost and an upset one."

"But a friendly one," Mrs. Jumel had promised with a smile.

That night, after the fireworks over the lake, while Jake was climbing the stairs he just kept muttering, "I do believe, I do believe in ghosts. I don't want to see you. You don't have to prove that you exist, I do believe." He sat upright in bed and repeated this several times that night before finally falling asleep. No ghost would appear and he was thankful.

That was an eventful Fourth of July to remain in one's memory and after telling Kate about the ghost, which she had known about, he was rewarded by a smile and a hug and the words, "You are such a child and I love you." How could she always take his concerns so lightly, 'oh but what the hell' he had thought.

This Fourth could have its own ghosts and one of them lived at the top of the stairs from the main hall in the Lugers' house, and this was now on Jake's mind. He was visualizing a fiery cross with her dancing around it out in the field with the fireworks display. He had a vivid imagination which was sometimes responsible for his over reaction or as Kate would say, 'part of the reason that you are such a child at times.'

That Saturday and Sunday passed in a relaxing manner for Kate and Jake. Alice was missing, or at least that's what they had assumed. She would disappear for days at a time and then when Jake thought the world was safe again she would show up just to push him out of balance.

Rodney was at The Club both Saturday and Sunday playing tennis aggressively and getting covered in red clay as usual. Carter and Margaret were at the house for an hour on Saturday to pick up some items to take to Margaret's. Other than this and a brief conversation with Margaret while Carter took some folded blankets out to her car Jake, Kate and Oliver spent a relaxed weekend mostly alone. Margaret let Kate know that both she and Carter would be at The Club for the Fourth of July barbeque, which was a first.

On Sunday Jake finished an article he had been working on while Kate plowed through a pile of studies she had taken out of the library at Sarah Lawrence that Friday.

***

Monday and the Fourth was on the morrow and things seemed to be at peace. This made Jake nervous compared to an unsettled atmosphere where you knew that something bad was going to happen. He thought about it as the difference between being in the middle of a stampede of bulls and seeing where the bulls were coming from as opposed to being on the other side of a little hill in complete calm knowing that at any moment a stampede was destined to come right over the little hill at him without a sound until it was upon him and trampling him. He had a vivid imagination.

Monday morning July 4, 1977 brought Zach zooming up to the house in his Aqua colored 1968 Mustang Fastback with the 302V8 under the hood. He and Jake used to race it up to school and back and forth on Storrow Drive in Boston. The car handled beautifully and had a fluid look to it that made it appealing to the eye as well.

It was 10:00 in the morning when Zach arrived, an hour after he said he would get there. He came in and pulled a bottle of Ballantine's scotch out of a brown bag and explained, "Sorry I was late, had a helluva a time finding this bottle. I went to three liquor stores, the second being closed. Can you believe that on the 4th."

"You went to three liquor stores for that?"

"Yeah, they always said that it was premium in those magazine ads so I had to try it."

"Two peas in a pod," said Kate with a laugh while looking at the two of them, "and I'm driving."

"No problem," agreed Zach.

***

Zach hadn't met Alice yet, he had only heard about her and was curious enough that he was going to knock on her door. It was now 11 o'clock and they were finally about to leave for The Club.

Jake hadn't seen Alice but he wasn't taking any chances, one never knew about her and the 'stampede' could start with Zach knocking on the door.

As Zach headed for the stairs he smiled and said, "I've got to see this, cat, doves and all."

"I wouldn't, really, if she is in there she may be in a type of hibernation, I wouldn't tempt fate, really," said Jake with a concerned voice as he watched Zack head up the stairs.

"Hibernation?!" questioned Kate just before she laughed.

Turning to look at Kate behind him Jake just smiled. "You never know."

"Now I've gotta knock," said Zach as he headed up.

"Oh, Christ, here we go," said Jake shaking his head and looking back at Kate who just stood with an impatient smile on her face.

Zach knocked lightly at first and then progressively a little harder until he heard the flutter of wings, which did not sit well with him and he came back down the stairs.

"Hell, I'm not that curious, it sounds like bats in there. Glad I don't have to live here."

"Why do you think I have the knife under my pillow...., Jesus."

"Are you two done?" asked Kate as she headed for the door.

As they left with Oliver leading and Jake trailing, Jake said more to himself, "Thank God she's not here," just before he shut and locked the door. Jake knew if she was there she would have answered the door with that demonic grin and sparkle in the eye which would have sent Zach dangerously backwards at the top of a steep flight of stairs. She would have put the fear in him escalating his drinking. Jake remembered when they had been invited to a party in New Jersey that was being given by a known relation of the mob. The son of this known relation was a friend of Jake's and Zach's through a college buddy. The party was right out of a movie and when Zach saw a gun in a shoulder holster he went right to the bar and didn't leave until his eyes were glassy. He would only say to Jake, "Did you see that guy, he had a gun," after he came back to their table from the bar.

"Yeah, a couple of them do," said Jake with a knowing smile, and Zach had quickly drunk down the scotch that he had brought back from the bar.

He knew Zach would have the same response if he met Alice, so it was better that she wasn't home for all sorts of reasons including Zach's measured drinking.

***

The Club was decked out for the Fourth with real flag cloth bunting made out of wool, or tammy. It was probably the same bunting that had been out when he was a kid and when his father was a kid but with a few more small moth holes in it, collected over time.

Jake enjoyed the Fourth at The Club because some things had never changed since he was a kid. Such things as the appearance of the club building itself covered in white stucco, put on in the 1920's, with turn of the century American Craftsman Style window frames finished with green trim. The striped canvas awning over the brick patio was another as it made a distinctive fluttering sound in the late morning early afternoon breeze. Someone was playing chopsticks on the old standup piano in the corner of the patio as someone always seemed to do and Jake knew that there would be a frozen Milky Way available at the outside service counter just as there was when he was a kid. They cost a nickel when he was a kid. He remembered ordering them from George who wore a white waist coat and took care of the kids at The Club snack bar during the day and played in a Jazz band at night. George always looked down at Jake when he was small, maybe six, as he handed him the frozen prize and he would always say, "Be careful, don't break your teeth." He said this with a voice that reminded Jake of Louis Armstrong who Jake loved as a child. When his parents played Louis Armstrong Jake felt safe from everything that could possibly lurk in the shadows or the dark.

The Club held all of these memories and more every July 4th. It was on July 4th when he was six-years-old that he had finally climbed the ladder to the high dive without backing down and jumped off into the deep end and manhood. This was the true test. Every little boy at The Club looked at this as The Test. Jake was five years old and taking group swim lessons, starting with the rising of the sun, two or three times a week when he first looked up at the high dive as the test that would be before him. That hamburger that he had that Fourth after meeting the test, many years ago it seemed now, was the best that he had ever had. This was because it was the reward he gave himself for taking on the challenge of the high dive and meeting it. The simple things really were the best.

It was a good day and Sam had his barbeque set up on the patio. The Fourth of July barbeque had been started by George and had not changed over the years. The barbeque itself was made up of an oil barrel cut in half the long way. Then they cut the bottom off each half and welded them together at the open ends to make one long trough barbeque that made great burgers.

"Hey Jake ol' buddy," Jake heard Tim Ferguson's unmistakable voice booming as he turned to face it. Tim stood 6 feet, to Jake's 6'2", with sandy hair, light blue eyes and a slim athletic build. He was wearing an Aloha shirt with white flowers on a faded black background to go with his worn out Levi jeans.

"Jesus Tim, where the hell have you been? I thought you

were dead," said Jake with a smile reaching out to shake Tim's hand, as best he could with the half cast, while grabbing Tim's shoulder with the other hand.

"You don't wanna know. And, by-the-way, what the hell is that on your hand?"

"You don't wanna know," returned Jake. Then turning to Kate and Zach, who were now sitting at the table they had reached before Tim had called out, Jake said, "This is Tim Ferguson, we've known each other since we could crawl although I'm a year older." Then turning back to Tim he asked, "Grab a seat?" and smiled energetically, happy to see an old friend in a familiar place.

"I'll stay for a little while, and this one year older thing is relative," Tim qualified with a laugh.

"Everything's relative," said Jake as he smiled. Then turning slightly towards Zach and Kate in order to introduce them he said, "This is Zach a buddy from college, and Kate."

"Nice to meet you both, ...The Sahara."

"What?" asked Jake.

"The Sahara. I've been in Africa for the last three years."

"That's why I thought you were dead," said Jake.

"I know who you are," said Kate. "You sent Jake a postcard from Morocco years ago saying that you were heading across the Sahara and that was the last that he said he had heard from you."

"That's me."

"I thought that was a bit mad when Jake showed me the postcard, that's why I remember," added Kate.

"It was," followed Tim. "I tried to cross it through the Atlas Mountains with two Frenchmen and the bastards robbed me after getting into the Sahara."

"Were they wearing blue and white striped soccer jerseys?," put in Zach who lifted the Ballantine bottle and put it on the table. "Want a snort?" he added.

Tim smiled. "Yeah, why not."

"So what happened?" asked Jake.

"Believe it or not I stayed with some nomads. I continued

on like an idiot after they robbed me and ran into the Tuaregs, and they took me in. I was gone for a year and a half until we crossed out of the interior and near civilization once again."

"Never trust a Frenchman," said Zach as, half rising out of his seat, he pushed the bottle over to Tim who smiled as he took one of the red plastic cups set in the middle of the table and the bottle with a single motion. Zach already had a full cup in hand.

"Don't mind if I do," said Tim addressing the bottle.

"So what are you up to now?" asked Jake.

"Harvard in the Fall. They like the Tuareg encounter. They think it makes me more interesting. I didn't tell them about the Frenchmen."

"You finally heading towards becoming an attorney?" queried Jake.

"No, not anymore. I'll give Harvard a shot year by year and see what comes of it."

"So you don't know what the hell you want to do," put in Zach.

"No, not really but I'm sure it will come to me," answered Tim with a laugh.

"Like the two Frenchmen," said Zach who smiled a Cheshire Cat smile and lifted his cup.

Tim touching his cup to Zach's responded with a smile and said, "It all leads someplace interesting."

"I'll drink to that," said Zach raising his cup and taking a sip.

"You'll drink to anything," Kate said as she smiled, "but I love you anyway."

"I see Rodney is still 'court diving'," said Tim nodding in the direction of Rodney walking across the field with Dick Baxter.

"Some things never change," said Jake after turning a little to his left in the direction of Tim's nod and seeing his older brother walking in his direction covered in red clay.

"By-the-way, what's that thing on his nose?" asked Tim looking at Jake's half cast and putting it together quickly, knowing the history of the two brothers.

"You don't wanna know," said Zach as he laughed and held up his cup again, this time to Jake and then took another sip.

"Man, he looks like a raccoon with rabies. How long ago did it happen?"

"Long enough," said Jake smiling somewhat embarrassed.

"Jesus, you got him right on the button," said Tim staring now at Rodney as he got closer.

"Ah Jesus, don't stare he'll notice you and stop," warned Jake with his back towards the field.

"Too late," said Tim still staring with his stare focusing closer, "Hi Mr. Luger, it's been awhile," said Tim getting up to shake Rodney's hand.

"Who, who?" said Rodney as he stopped just staring at Tim.

Dick Baxter sounding out of breath cut in, "He's having a little insulin thing, I need to get him something to eat."

"Grab him a burger with a lot of ketchup and relish on it and have him wash it down with an orange juice, he's not too bad off yet," said Jake.

"That's where we're headed," said Dick as they headed towards Sam with Dick holding up one finger to hasten the order as he walked Rodney over.

Sam knew immediately and loaded up a hamburger, and Jake could hear Dick Baxter say, "And orange juice."

"Juice is inside at the bar. Don't worry. I'll give him the burger first."

"Some things really never change," said Tim watching and listening in amazement.

"Everyone's used to it. It makes it easier for me."

"I guess," said Tim still watching Rodney but starting to turn back to everyone at the table.

"Did you ever tell them about the 10K in Central Park with you and V?" asked Tim with a smile.

"No," said Jake trying to end the conversation.

"It's too good, really," said Tim now laughing.

"I'd like to hear it," said Zach.

Kate looked on with curiosity and Oliver was sitting up alert at the sound of the word hamburger accompanied by all of the smells that were now around him.

"Well, Jake and V were entered into a 10K in Central Park by Rodney," said Tim then turning to Jake. "What, were you a freshman in college? Had to be, because I was finishing up at Hotchkiss and left the end of that year. Well anyway," Tim continued turning back to everyone, "Jake is just in college and V is just starting prep school, I think, and these guys are pretty good I have to say. They get into the city and they are in their track stuff and sweats and Rodney is in street clothes and dressed in those multi-colored pants."

"I've seen those," said Zach finishing with an exaggerated smile. "They're enough to make you come to a full stop."

"They are an attention getter," said Tim, "but that day wasn't good for gaining any attention. Rodney started to have an insulin reaction about 10 minutes before the race, halfway between the Central Park Zoo and the starting line."

"How can you remember that? You remember better than me," questioned Jake.

"Because I visualized the whole thing when you told me about it. It's just one of those things you see in your imagination and never lose it."

"Great," said Jake sarcastically.

"Now I want to hear this," said Kate.

"Well ol' Rodney, over there porking on a burger," said Tim looking over towards Rodney with Dick by his side as he chewed big open mouth chews on big bites he was taking from his burger as the juices dripped down his white and 'red clay' Lacoste shirt, "went into insulin shock right there in the Park dressed like a neon sign with these two guys in their running shorts," Tim said as he started laughing at his mind's picture.

Jake starting to smile on the verge of a laugh adds, "Now I want to hear it."

"Well, they figure they have to get something in his system real fast but they don't have any money on them. Only Rodney has a wallet and the type of insulin reaction that he's having is one of the irritable type."

"Oh, Christ. I remember," put in Jake.

"So V holds Rodney while Jake tries to get his wallet out of the back of his multi-colored trousers and all of sudden Rodney starts screaming , 'HELP, HELP......,'" says Tim as he starts laughing now with Jake joining in remembering the scene. "So, here they are, two muggers dressed as runners trying to take this poor drunk's wallet and the guy is dressed like a clown so he really stands out," said Tim as he laughs even more before finishing, "and he really put up a fight till they got the wallet."

"I thought we had had it for sure," added Jake with a laugh.

"So what happened?" asked Zach.

"I took off for the zoo with the money, passing the polar bear, and the seal clapping me on and barking at me as I passed. I got an orange juice and loaded it with sugar and started running back. The damned race was about to start. By the time I got back V still had hold of him and just looked like a guy holding up a drunk. We got it into him and he was starting to come around enough where we could leave him with the remainder of the drink knowing he would come out of it quickly. Then we ran to the start line and made it to the tail end just as the gun went off."

"How'd you do?" asked Zach.

"Well, I was nicely warmed up," said Jake with a smile. "We rabbited out into the lead and there were a couple of thousand runners. I'd never seen that many before. We were on the grass going around them and around trees to get up front."

"How'd you guys end up?" asked Zach.

"We both finished in the top 25. There weren't a lot of great runners in the race. Some guy from the NYAC won, he was good. I stayed in his pack for a while but I had to dial back."

"Ah come on; all you Lugers were good," said Tim as he smiled.

"Yeah, we were, and knock on wood," said Jake rapping his closed fist twice on top of the table, "V and Jack still are besides the other sports they do. I guess that was one legacy of the Rodney Olympic debacle. We all, including Tom and Brian, became pretty good in one form or another until injuries took us out one by one," then clearly thinking of the past Jake continued, "Christ, Rodney, I remember that crazy bastard showed up at one of my high school cross-country races and he started running along side me screaming. He really scared hell out of the course official and the starter," shaking his head, "and a freshman on the team who didn't know my Dad said, 'you have one crazy father', Jesus".

"All's well that ends well," summed up Tim. "Has he gotten over that Olympics deal yet?"

"Look at him, what do you think?" said Jake as he nodded and pointed his half cast towards Rodney finishing his burger, with part of it on his shirt.

"Well, he never liked you anyway," said Tim laughing and purposely staring at Jake's half cast.

"No kidding," said Jake.

"I hear he's renting the place out."

"Yup, and he has a couple of crazies in the house," put in Zach after swallowing another sip of scotch.

"They're not that bad," added Kate.

"Jake sleeps with a KA-BAR under his pillow," said Zach with a smile.

"Jesus, how bad are these people?"

"Well the girl is something out of the Exorcist. I'm waiting for her head to rotate and throw out projectile vomit," said Jake.

"That's disgusting," said Kate shaking her head subtly.

"Ah, it's true," Jake retorted.

"I've never seen her but I heard bats in her room this morning," noted Zach.

"Bats?" questioned Tim.

"Doves, they're doves," said Kate.

"Just as bad," finished Jake, then adding, "Then there's Carter. You know Carter. I think, he's had The Wise Owl for years."

"I briefly knew one of his daughters in prep-school, used to call her legs, it was the first year they went coed. Was she beautiful and smart!" reminisced Tim.

"Never met his daughters but ever since the dove woman moved in he's been seeing Japs all over the place apparently."

"I knew he was in the war and all and figured that's   why he drank but I didn't know he was hallucinating," said Tim.

"Well, that's what it's gotta be because I don't see the Japanese Imperial Army leaving any traces around the house and I've heard him blurt it out that he sees them. Sam was the first to let me know that he was seeing them," explained Jake.

Zach just laughed. "Jesus, that bad?"

"Yeah, sorta," said Jake.

"Well, I've never seen him hallucinating," said Kate in his defense.

Jake turning more toward Kate, "Well what about the 'I killed her' message that he's sent loud and clear a couple of times recently? I mean the way he said it on the phone to Bea put the fear of God on the face of that girl working on the commercial. You know, the one who flipped out and ran out of the house. He's seeing something."

"Well, I don't know what that is, and the girl got the full house experience," said Kate.

"He killed some woman?" asked Tim.

"I don't know what he killed but I know he killed some things along the way, not like he wanted to."

"Well, that's part of it wouldn't you say," defended Kate.

"Speak of the devil," said Jake looking at the entrance to The Club's patio.

Tim and Kate facing Jake and Zach turned to see Carter coming onto the patio with Margaret.

"Don't look now but it looks like they're headed this way," said Zach.

"Well, it looks like my brother's in the locker room cleaning up so they won't drag him over this way too."

"I like Carter," put in Kate.

"I think we all do, including Oliver," said Jake as Oliver came to a sitting position staring at where Carter and Margaret stopped to talk with someone.

Oliver was sitting for no more than a couple of seconds when he was off in the direction of Carter in the '150 pound Newfoundland barreling towards you' mode.

"Jesus Oliver," said Jake startled.

"He'll stop in time," said Kate.

"I didn't notice him sitting there," said Tim who was just as startled.

"That's Oliver," said Zach smiling. "You didn't see him rise up at the word 'hamburger? He's a bear."

"I see that," said Tim, "Great looking dog. Hey, maybe we can just ask Carter."

"Ask him what?" said Jake.

"If he killed a woman and who."

"Oh that's good," said Jake.

Zach laughed and Kate said, "It's probably nothing really."

"Oh Christ, don't ask him Tim, he'll start seeing Japs all over place."

Tim smiled. "Jesus, I'm not that stupid."

"Hey boys..........and young lady," said Carter now standing behind Tim with Oliver at his side. They hadn't paid attention to the fact that he was on the move again towards them.

Tim jumped, "Jeez, Mr. Mills you scared the Jap oughta me, I mean the crap oughta me."

Jake just gave Tim a nervous look.

Zach just smiled and Kate shook her head subtly.

"I thought I saw Margaret with you a minute ago," Jake came back.

"You did that, she just went to get an orange juice at the bar."

"Mr. Mills, I hear you're at the Lugers'."

"Carter. It's Carter, Tim"

"Jesus, you remember me?"

"I do, my daughter liked you so I kept an eye on you." Carter smiled and then looked back nervously looking for Margaret.

Jake smiled at Tim and ran his index finger across his throat while Carter was looking the other way. Tim just smiled back sheepishly.

"Carter, are you staying for the fireworks?" asked Tim.

Carter, turning back to them now as Margaret was visible making her way in their direction with two glasses, thought for a second and answered, "Well, I guess so."

Tim smiled at Jake and then it dawned on Jake: Carter's version of Swish-Bangs. As he looked at Carter with Oliver sitting next to him, his tongue out breathing contently with that 'Newfy smile' on his face, at least he thought it was a smile although Kate doubted it, Jake suffered a sudden shock wave. The big black cuddly dog and older mild looking man now across from him could both be turned into uncontrollable flesh and blood panic in a matter of hours. They really did not know what was coming, as Jake was reminded of Kate's earlier warning.

"I've never seen you here before for the fireworks Carter, is there a reason?" asked Jake hoping it might dawn on Carter what he may be headed for.

"No, I just never came. Ah, Margaret," he said as he turned his attention to Margaret now at the table. "How about this table right here?" asked Carter indicating the table next to the one where the boys and Kate were seated.

"Fine. Kate I brought you an orange juice without the grenadine. They are even better than they were the other day," said Margaret as she handed one of the glasses to Kate.

As Zach, Tim and Jake pushed back their chairs and stood Jake made introductions, "Tim this is Margaret. Margaret you know Zach. Tim..."

"Tim Ferguson,..........I know your parents," Margaret came in.

With Tim looking confused Margaret laughed. "I've come to know them in your absence, welcome back. I saw a picture of you taken before you left for Africa and you haven't changed," reassured Margaret.

Carter pulled out the chair closest to Kate at the next table for Margaret. After she sat, Zach, Tim and Jake took their seats again while Oliver's head went back and forth between the two groups in reaction to their movement, in case they were offering some food.

"How's the hand doing?" offered Margaret as everyone was now seated.

"Ok, I guess."

"Don't worry about it, you were defending yourself and you delayed doing so," said Margaret to Jake smiling conspiratorially at Kate as she did so.

"Too bad you didn't break that limey's goddamned nose," followed Carter followed by Margaret giving him a feigned look of disapproval.

"You have Englishmen running around that house too?" questioned Tim with a humorous smile.

"Just one and he's gone," said Jake smiling at Tim not to go there.

"And an annoying guy at that," put in Zach toning his thoughts down in deference to Margaret's presence.

"That guy wouldn't know a Jap from an Eskimo," muttered Carter to himself but loud enough to be heard.

Margaret just moved her hand to Carter's arm and patted it.

Tim looked at Jake with eyebrows lifted and said softly, "Fireworks."

Carter's edginess seemed to be present below the surface all day and every day these days since Alice's arrival.

"Maybe we should get some of Sam's burgers before the line gets too long," noted Jake to change the subject and the mood.

By evening Carter was feeling no pain along with Zach and the conversation at Jake's table went from baseball, as

Zach knew too many baseball statistics through his love for the game, to politics briefly. Then it went to old friends and stories of mishap and accidental adventure and back to the Luger house again.

The Baxters had joined the table with Carter and Margaret. Rodney, it appeared, was nursing an insulin shock hangover at the bar.

By 9 p.m. the fireworks were set up in the field and ready to go and the two tables, with everyone present, had a front row seat. Tim's staying 'for a little while' turned into the entire day up to this point.

With the first swish-bang there was a clattering under Carter's table and the cry of Dick Baxter, "Jesus, what the hell, we have a whale blowing....?" He finished as his chair went backwards, taking him with it, followed by a dark black shadow, like a bear, pelting out from under the table and crashing through several other seated people as he headed for the exit from the patio.

"Oh crap," muttered Jake to Kate over the noise of the second bang. "Not again, I thought he'd be over that."

"Well, how would you know, I told you it might happen," said Kate noting the conversation that morning when she had mentioned to Jake that Oliver had never been exposed to fireworks since Mexico and the little car experience was why they had left him home in the past. Jake had just replied, "Nah, that was a long time ago, he's grown out of that stuff." Kate had just smiled.

"No, oh JAP!" added Tim smiling in the break in noise from the two initial bursts.

"Oh Christ," muttered Jake to himself as he glanced over at Carter whose eyes were changing. Jake had seen that look before like he did not know where he was but did and it was not a good place. Jake thought how strange a dichotomy and then a cluster of rockets went up and burst two and three at a time.

Carter was up, his chair was flung back. He went into a crouch and mouthed, "Christ, take cover will you," with only part of it being heard between more booms. Then he was under the table.

"Uh-oh," muttered Jake as Margaret looked under the table with concern. She had been close to this before so she wasn't panicking. It came with the package.

The table moved and a couple of people moved aside to the right of Carter's table like people trying to escape a quick rising incoming tide. Then a shadow shot out in front of the planters with the red geraniums. And by the light of the next salvo Carter could be seen in a crouch moving off towards the larger oak tree shading the driveway and into the shadow of its large trunk and on to the parking lot beyond and away from the incoming fire.

"Christ," was all that Tim could add.

Through the explosions Margaret could be heard shouting, "Stay here, I'll go find him."

"I'll help," offered Jake.

Getting closer to Jake so he could hear better Margaret said warmly, "No, that's ok, you're a sweetheart but he reacts better to my voice alone. I just need to get to him and hold him." As an afterthought she added, "I shouldn't have brought him to this."

Jake just smiled as she excused herself loudly enough to be heard and moved off in the direction that Carter had last been seen heading in.

"I need to find Oliver," shouted Jake to everyone.

Zach just raised his cup to Jake and smiled. Tim just shook his head from side to side with a big grin and Kate just nodded to Jake in agreement.

***

Jake found Oliver that night in the back parking lot and it took a while to find a black dog at night. Thank God for the moon which was just a couple of days past being full. Oliver's tail and backside were sticking out from behind the front of a car parked nose first into the chain link fence at the furthest spot in the lot. Jake yelled, "Oliver" as loud as he could and a brief break in the bangs allowed it to be heard, so Oliver wouldn't flinch when he touched him.

He got to Oliver and backed him out from in front of the car and turned him around and sat next to him and held him as he shook and for some reason tears came to Jake's eyes, "I'm sorry buddy."

Margaret found Carter too. He was next to a tree through a passageway in the old chain link fence establishing the border between The Club and several acres of land that the town had left green. He was holding onto the base of the tree looking down shaking and crying softly. Margaret was cautious, she had learned to be. "Carter, it's me, it's okay," she yelled between rockets going off and going up to replace those that had just exploded. He looked up with a bewildered look and she knelt then sat beside him and held him with his head against her chest like a child, effectively covering his ears as he shook. She just held him and cried lightly but enough where she felt a tear or two fall on her hands cradling his head. The anger that he felt at times through the years during his waking hours was giving way more and more to the fear that he had always had in his dreams since the end of the war.

Chapter 9

The Neighborhood
and
Dr. Bob

The Fourth of July had been more than everyone had bargained for except Tim who seemed excited by the whole scene. This may have been attributed to the fact that he was still with the Tuaregs in his mind and was in a state of re-acclimating to the relatively calm atmosphere back in New Jersey, USA.

Oliver would never again be subjected to explosives or anything remotely similar or for that matter anything that went SWISH. Oliver had a couple of fears, this being the major fear. He also had a propensity to bark defensively at the statue of Mr. Goodwrench whenever Kate took her Opel to the garage for major work, but the other major fear was unexplainable and it resided downtown. Whenever Oliver was walked downtown and he was walked by this particular store, which had been a shoe store when Jake was a child, he would make a dash for the street and oncoming traffic saved only by the restraint of his leash.

No one could figure it out, it was just a quirk. The store-front had been built in 1933 and the door was recessed in-wards by about ten feet to allow for more window space and the entrance walkway was black, silver flecked, buffed con-crete. It upset Oliver like Alice upset Carter. Everyone had their own demons and Oliver saw something that no one else could see, so did Carter.

The Fourth of July 1977 would be the last Fourth of July where Carter would be out where he could hear fireworks, if Margaret could help it. Although it would be a daunting, if not almost impossible, task every year. Margaret was becoming adept at protecting Carter from what he did not need to experience and Carter was becoming edgier when he was around the Luger neighborhood, where Alice roamed.

Bob Wholefield lived next door to the Lugers in the corner house. Bob was an eccentric research doctor and no one really knew him to see him. The only part of Bob that people ever saw regularly were his two beautiful teenage daughters and equally beautiful wife, that is until Carter ran into him by chance a few days after the Fourth.

Bob was an eccentric who never stepped out of his house unless it was to get into the car to have his wife drive him some-place or to work in his garden; and the garden was shielded from the road and the adjoining houses by a tall wooden fence.

Bob was tall and thin, in his late 50's and a bit on the gawky side, although not clumsy. He looked more like a recent release from a prisoner of war camp than a healthy doctor.

To add to this appearance Dr. Bob, as people called him, strangely enough, because they did not know him but they knew of his research, wore tattered clothing and a war surplus hat when he worked in the garden. The hat was actually a 'field cap' of unknown national origin to which the good doctor had added a strip of cloth extending from the back lower rim of the hat down to his shoulders as a sun guard for his neck. This was much like what the Japanese troops did with their field caps during the war.

This day Dr. Bob decided he needed the use of an imple-
ment that he had recently misplaced and for the first time
ventured out of his backyard and headed towards the Lugers'
where no one was home except Carter. Carter was sitting on
the back steps of the side veranda alone and having a scotch
while he contemplated the large green leaves of the now
flowerless magnolia. Everything was calm with Carter, for the
moment.

"Hello!" hailed Dr. Bob from the other side of the Victorian wire fence and waste high hedge waving his hand at the
same time and trying to get the attention of Carter who was
looking in the other direction.

"Hello, do you mind if I come over?" the doctor called out
again, failing to get Carter's attention but coming through the
small gate in the fence anyway.

Turning, Carter tried to focus and when he did he went
back again in time. It was an American dressed like a Jap.
Carter flinched and looked behind and from side to side of the
doctor to see if there were any more before he answered. To
Carter, Dr. Bob looked like a Marine who had gone 'Asiatic'
from battle fatigue or from being in the Pacific too long.

"You okay bud?" yelled Carter with a little nervousness in
his voice.

"Yes but I need a spade," Dr. Bob yelled back as he got
closer, "would you happen to have one?"

"Jesus, no, I lost my 1910," answered Carter concerned
about the Marine who had been outside the wire and who'd
gone 'Asiatic'.

"What was that? 1910?"

"My M-1910 entrenching tool. You want a drink? I've got
some Johnny Walker."

Johnny Walker at 2:00 in the afternoon struck Dr. Bob just
right as Johnny Walker, it turned out, is what the good Doctor
would allow himself to enjoy as his only weakness, besides
black coffee. So, with a smile, he said, "I don't mind if I do."

And with that Dr. Bob and Carter Mills met sitting side-by-side on the three steps leading up the side veranda of the Luger house. After shaking hands and exchanging first names Carter had grabbed an extra glass tumbler from the small portable bar in the den and now they sat with the bottle between them.

Lifting his glass Carter said, "Here's to you, here's to me and to hell with you and to hell with me."

"I'll drink to that," agreed Dr. Bob smiling, and they had their first drink together with nothing more than an exchange of first names and a toast. There was a perceived commonality between the two. They met in the eccentric middle world as though they were part of the same fraternal order.

"Bob, how long you been here?"

"Oh, I don't know now, maybe 15 years."

"Jesus Christ, that's a lifetime, how'd that happen?" asked Carter with his eyes opening bigger in surprise as the core of him thought that he was talking to a fellow Marine who had lost his mind from being in the Pacific too long.

"I don't know, come to think about it. They brought me in for a major task concerning making operations more efficient. I've been in enough of those too."

"How many operations have you been in?" Carter asked in amazement.

"Scores!"

Carter just swallowed hard and poured them both another drink. Carter knew he was in New Jersey but part of him was not. Part of him was talking to a fellow Marine who had been in too many amphibious operations and yet had survived. It was baffling to Carter, he'd only been in three and he didn't know how he had survived.

"Are you going to get a rest?" asked Carter.

"A rest is for the weary not for me."

Carter now knew that Bob had really gone 'Asiatic' if he wanted to stay active.

"I haven't seen you before. Where'd you come from?" asked Carter.

"I've been on the other side of the fence, digging holes

mostly trying to get away from those bastards who keep fir-ing stuff at me," said Dr. Bob with a look of concern on his face, "But I misplaced my spade and I need to make a hole deeper."

"I know how that is, Christ, you can never make a hole deep enough. I think someone stole my tool," said Carter.

"Some people are always doing that to me and then I'll run into what I was looking for a month later sometimes, so they probably moved it back just to get me."

"They're sneaky bastards," commented Carter as he took a sip from his glass tumbler thinking about the enemy that haunted him.

"I'll drink to that," agreed Dr. Bob taking a drink from his tumbler and thinking about the little men, 'some people,' who moved things on him so he'd bust his nuts trying to find them. It drove him insane. It was the only thing that got to him and it would seem that the missing items would show up again once he'd had a chance to go a little crazy. As brilliant as he was he was also a little delusional which helped to make him eccentric and he actually believed that the only explanation for missing things was that they were moved on purpose. And the only type of person who would do that in his house would have to be an unidentifiable character and he'd have to be small like a Gnome because he never saw them. The good doctor and Carter had more in common than they knew. They were each having one of the sanest stress free conversations they'd had in a while.

"I bet they wear funny caps," said Dr. Bob thinking of gnomes and elves.

"Ha-ha-ha. Funny ain't the word for it, downright scary, sorta like the one you're wearing," said Carter with a smile just before taking a sip of scotch from his tumbler.

"I was wondering where I got this," said the doctor taking his cap off and examining it with his scotch free hand.

"They don't give up either. They're fanatical, the little bas-tards."

"Do I know that, they just don't stop coming and I've tried

to stop them believe me," noted the doctor.

Carter never felt so relaxed as he did now talking about the Japs he saw in his dreams and now saw around the Lugers' on occasion. His dreams were starting to take on a reality during the day. What Carter did not fully realize was that the enemy in his dreams were appearing during waking hours. They were not so scary now that he got to talk about them with someone who knew and it was different than talking with Sam. With Sam the enemy was still scary but not supposed to be around, and as they were around talking with Sam would make him feel okay for a while and then they would return. Bob saw them and could deal with it and it wasn't so bad so maybe he could deal with it in the same way. He had gone 'Asiatic' but maybe that wasn't so bad.

"You can't stop them, they keep coming and they will always keep coming," added Carter.

"I guess you're right. Maybe I can dig a hole deep enough so one will fall in and never get out again," the doctor seriously commented as the scotch started to take affect.

"Forget it, they'll always climb out and come at you again."

"Hell!"

"Yeah, we're fucked," stated Carter. The scotch was having its normal effect on Carter but Dr. Bob was having a different effect on Carter. Carter had one foot in and one foot out of reality and was sharing it with someone in the same position so his fears were more real than ever but he could deal with them next to this 'Marine' who'd gone 'Asiatic'. It was all less frightening.

"Well, what the hell, how about another Red?"

"Here you go," said Carter as he leaned over and poured Dr. Bob another scotch then topped his off.

"Where the hell do they come from anyway?" thought Dr. Bob out loud.

"I'd say Hell but then again they are just their own evolution."

"That makes sense," agreed Dr. Bob and then he drained

half his tumbler. "I bet they took your '1910'."

"No, doubt they did. I don't even remember what it looks like now. Sorry I can't help you out with it."

"No problem. They'd just take it from me too."

And with this they just both started laughing like two school yard kids laughing at a dumb joke and the laughter gained momentum so they couldn't stop as though someone had opened the floodgates. Dr. Wholefield had been under great stress for months which had increased over the past month and Carter had been stressed for years which had increased since Alice moved in. And now, for some reason, the pressure valve finally opened as the two men howled like hyenas visualizing their own sources of stress in a harmless humorous state.

When Dr. Bob finally left he did so with cap on and as he passed through the outer fence, with a slight stumble, he turned, and for some reason, saluted Carter who in return saluted casually and admonished, "Be careful Bob and don't let the little bastards get you."

Dr. Bob just smiled and headed off in the direction of his house. It was now after five and the two men had talked, unknowingly, about two different subjects as though both were the same. As a result, they were both calmed and looking forward to the next day and the next.........and possibly the next.

The neighborhood was quiet for what was left of the day and Carter was relaxed taking a long alcohol induced dream free nap on the sofa in the living room. It was quiet when Jake and Kate came home separately about an hour apart and it was even quiet when Rodney showed up at 7 p.m. and left again at 7:30 for dinner at The Club. But this all changed when Alice appeared at a little past 8:00 that evening.

From the main hall came a terrific screeching like a baby howling or to Carter, in his non-dream state, the start of a Banzai charge.

"Holy Christ, LOAD AND LOCK, LOAD AND LOCK," yelled Carter as he hit the floor flat alongside the sofa and looked out. He vaguely remembered something about a Marine who had gone 'Asiatic' and then had gone outside the wire. "Christ, Bob," he muttered then thinking to himself, 'the poor bastard's probably dead'.

The howling came back followed by a bark then another bark and the reality dawned on Carter, it was Oliver in trouble.

Cautiously getting up and walking through the den to the main hall Carter stopped short. There was Oliver and a white cat circling each other and a figure in the shadows giving off a demonic giggle. As she came out of the shadows, moving back towards the mud entrance to get to the front door to open it, Carter stopped. He froze in his tracks and reversed two steps back into the shadow of the den away from the Jap with the grenade who was heading away from him.

As Alice entered the mud room the two doves lifted off her shoulder and flew to Henry's antlers in the den sending Carter in retreat into the living room, and through the pass- through to the kitchen and up the back staircase.

As Alice opened the front door, to give either Oliver or the cat an escape, the doves took the opportunity and flew from their perch in the den, through the open door and onto a perch in the large oak on the front lawn. The cat followed and was out the door. Oliver sat and licked his side briefly then headed to the cool floor of the kitchen.

Oliver had smelled food and had also sensed Carter in the living room and had headed downstairs to investigate only to run into Alice and her menagerie while Jake wrote and Kate read.

Jake started for the stairs, after the second howl, with his KA-BAR knife at his side, in its scabbard, thinking someone was being killed. Near the bottom of the second flight of stairs he ran head long into Carter coming up.

"Christ, make a hole, the bastards are coming," yelled Carter, eyes wide as he pushed past Jake leaving a vapor trail of scotch as he headed for the second floor and the safety of his room.

"What the hell.....?" was all that Jake got out as he looked after Carter heading up.

Jake half crouched in the shadows at the foot of the stairs between the kitchen and the main hall in the now semi-dark house as the sun was setting. Most of the light seemed to be coming from the open front door. As he started to move forward to see what was going on he felt a cold nose on his right hand and turned to see Oliver looking up at him quietly.

"Hey boy, you ok? What were you barking at?" Then looking up from rubbing Oliver's head he saw Alice framed by the fading light, going out through the front door as she stepped out onto the front porch.

"Come here now you little she-devil," she intoned with command in her voice.

Jake kept his distance in the shadows watching Alice cautiously as he scratched Oliver's head while Oliver looked up at him tongue panting.

"Come here, I say," she demanded loudly with stern authority and loudly enough that the immediate neighbors would all now hear Alice. And Jake could tell through the character of the voice that she was escalating.

"Uh-oh," muttered Jake while still scratching Oliver about the ears.

"YOU DAMNED BITCH, I SAID GET OVER HERE." She had escalated. "WHEN I GET YOU I WILL MAKE YOU PAY TO SATAN YOU LITTLE PARIAH. I AM THE DEVIL NOW AND YOU WILL PAY TO ME!"

"This'll go over well," muttered Jake.

Jake could hear steps behind him and turning he could see Kate making the turn to the last flight of stairs.

"What is all the shouting about?"

"Well, now you get to see Miss Demon."

"I SAY GET OVER HERE YOU LITTLE FORNICATING SHAPE-SHIFTER, I KNOW WHO YOU ARE."

"And I know who you are and if you don't go back into the Luger cave you came out of I'll call the goddamned police from hell," came a voice out of the darkness and down the street sounding very much like George Hurley, who had been at the 'pool party'.

"SATAN IS ON YOU GEORGE, I KNOW WHO YOU ARE."

"Jesus!" came the voice out to the dark. "Poor Luger………".

Alice just started giggling loudly and out of all proportion 'like she was possessed', thought Jake.

"I bet her head is spinning around right now and the pea soup will be next," said Jake quietly to Kate.

"She's just a little nutty," said Kate as she turned to head back up the stairs. "Come on Oliver, let's go."

As Kate and Oliver headed up Jake nervously watched as the doves fluttered down under the eve of the porch and landed on Alice's shoulder as she turned to head in. And at the same moment the white cat bounded up the porch stairs to her side as she walked in giggling self-assuredly to herself.

Jake patted his 12" long knife on the hilt, and part of the scabbard sticking out of his pocket, and then headed up behind Kate.

Someone would hear about this and the neighborhood would really be abuzz by tomorrow. '…just a little nutty'?, thought Jake, hearing Kate's interpretation in his ear as he topped the first flight of stairs and turned onto the last flight.

As he entered the room Kate was already on the bed reading and Oliver was licking his left shoulder which Jake had never seen him do before. But he only thought about it for a millisecond before looking at Kate and asking, "How can you read after that?"

"Easily, I get on our bed, make sure that the pillows are comfy and pick up my book". She was reading 'All the President's Men'.

"Maybe, 'In Cold Blood' would be more appropriate."

Kate just looked sideways at Jake for a second and smirked then went back to reading.

"Well she put the fear of God, or should I say the devil, into Carter. He came screeching by me when I was walking down the last flight of steps."

"Screeching?"

"Yeah, that's the way it looked to me, in somewhat of a desperate panic to escape...'screeching'."

"He's just smart enough to stay away from her," said Kate in support of Carter and not looking up from her book.

"You saw him at The Club on the Fourth!"

"That's just shell shock, like your English teacher in high school who had that twitch from the war."

"This is more than a twitch and old Milton had a handle on it, he understood why he had it and just dealt with it. This is different."

Putting down the book and looking at Jake Kate asked, "How do you mean different?"

"Carter is seeing things."

"He drinks a lot."

"That's a symptom not a cause. Come on, you're the one who's supposed to understand this stuff, you studied it for Chrissakes."

"I think you're over-blowing it, like Alice."

"Alice is scary and that's just a reflex of self-preservation, a natural instinct on my part. Maybe you're just dull to the normal reaction to these things as you look at them through a text book."

"There's some of that, I agree. But Carter is not delusional according to Jaspers, but your brother may be."

"Well, I know he is and always has been.........who's Jaspers?"

"Karl, he developed the guidelines to determine if a person is delusional or not. Rodney fits perfectly."

"Well we know that but Carter, he sees things."

"Well, that may be a bit different and I don't know if he really sees things."

"He sees Japs!"

"Who?," Kate asked, now looking confused.

"He sees Japs, the bastards that killed his buddy in the Pacific....during the war."

Kate finally remembering, "Oh, what you were talking about on the Fourth! Well, I don't know about that."

"Well, he let everyone who was working on that commercial know when he walked across the walkway above where they were shooting. And he let them all know that there was no doubt that he was seeing them."

"Then it's the alcohol."

"The chicken or the egg?" muttered Jake.

"What?"

"Which came first, the chicken or the egg?"

"It's not as simple as that."

"Maybe it is. We have no idea what he saw and felt in the war. We may think we have an idea but I am coming to realize that we have no idea and you being one of the brightest people that I know should understand that. Christ, you study this stuff."

"I know. You say that but combat fatigue is something that I've only touched on. Most studies coming out of the government are only meant to determine how much the average man can take exposed to a combat environment until he collapses or has a sudden break with reality. At least that's all that I've seen and the break is then dealt with like any other mental break."

"Well maybe they need to look more closely at this one whoever the powers may be because Carter is in pain and think how many Carters there are out there. You'd think that they are at least owed that."

"I can't argue with that. Working with New York State I know how deficient the resources are for mental health."

"And resources for Vets?"

"I really don't know, but what little I do I'd have to say that it's worse."

"The better part of a bottle of scotch a day is the easier cheaper way I guess," stated Jake sarcastically.

"I still don't think Carter is as bad as you think, I think most of it comes from the drinking."

"It's a circle isn't it."

"The best you can do is to be patient with him."

"That's not a problem. Carter has a gruff personality but one that you can't help but be attracted to. There is something about that guy."

"There is and sometimes he talks with me the way I wish my own father had."

"Sorry about that one," said Jake confirming that he felt some of her childhood pain and the distance she had with her father.

"Do you think Oliver needs a walk?" Jake asked changing the subject.

"No, he should be okay," said Kate going back to her book.

***

The next day was Saturday, just less than a week after the Fourth, and there was the feeling of a buzz in the neighborhood, or, maybe it was just Jake.

He knew that George Hurley probably had his shorts in a knot but when Alice launched his name the way she did Jake knew that he would keep it to himself.

On top of this Oliver was not okay. That afternoon Jake noticed a large bulge on Oliver's left shoulder where he had been trying to lick himself the previous night, now it connected.

He and Kate and Oliver were sitting on the side veranda. While Kate read, sitting in the wicker love seat, Jake felt around the lump on Oliver's shoulder. He also listened to the neighborhood for any telltale disturbance that might have been created from the night before but most people kept it in tight to the chest until it affected them. And Mr. Hurley would surely keep it quiet, the demon woman had his name.

Oliver yelped.

"What are you doing?" asked Kate looking up from her book.

"I think he has an infection….. damn," said Jake still feeling around the lump and looking at Oliver with concern.

"Better call Rolm," said Kate referring to their   veterinarian.

"Yeah, maybe we can get him in today. Maybe Oliver did this just to get one of those big bones Rolm's wife always gives him," said Jake smiling up at Kate.

"You're just stupid…….. and I love you," said Kate as she turned back to her book.

"The neighborhood's quiet."

Not looking up from her book Kate just said, "What did you expect?"

"Well, with a little neighborhood exhibition of the Exorcist on our front porch last night I was expecting something."

"No pea soup, huh," said Kate with her face still in her book.

"Very funny. She put the fear of God, or should I say the Devil, in George Hurley last night, you heard that."

"She just got his name right, that's all, she probably has a good memory, and the Devil humor isn't funny," said Kate now looking up from her book.

"Nothing phases you."

"I've seen worse," said Kate and then she returned to her book.

"And you want to work with this for a living?"

Looking up again, "Sure, I love you don't I."

"That's it," Jake said as he quickly ran over and started tickling Kate until she begged him to stop as Oliver started barking loudly and wildly.

She had to catch her breath and Oliver was bouncing around by the time he stopped. Oliver barked whenever Jake did this or whenever Kate was in the bathtub as he was frightened she might drown. It was different to take a bath and have a big black dog stand at the edge of the tub and bark at you until you were done. She'd throw a little water on him once and awhile just to really get him nervous. Water safety was embedded in the boy's DNA.

They both took Oliver up the hill to Dr. Rolm's late that day and after shaving Oliver's shoulder the verdict was obvious.

"Do you have any cats in the neighborhood Jake?"

"Sure do."

"Well, that's the culprit, see those puncture marks, the big guy's been clawed. I'm going to irrigate the wound then I want you to take this blue stuff I'm going to give you and squirt one dropper full every morning into the top opening of the wound. It should drain itself and heal up pretty well in a week. Don't let him play with cats," finished the doctor as he pushed back and got up from the low stool on wheels next to Oliver's shoulder after putting a large dropper full of blue solution down the top hole.

"What is that stuff?"

"One of the greatest miracles of man. It was developed during the war by the German army to clean wounds. Great stuff."

"I've never seen it before."

"They never cleared it for use on humans, amazing isn't it. But it's like a miracle solution."

"Too cost efficient I guess."

Rolm laughed. "Let me know how it goes."

"Will do doc. Thanks."

Jake met Kate in the waiting room and Oliver was spoiled by the doctor's wife/receptionist Claudia with another giant sized bone biscuit before they left. He also got another lesson in German from Claudia who was originally from Ludwigs- hafen, Germany. Oliver had bits and pieces of three languages going through his head which could be humorous with a 150 pound dog.

'The she-cat had wounded the friendly bear,' was the only thought Jake had as they headed home.

Chapter 10

The Boys Are Home

Sunday, July 10th

That Sunday afternoon the Luger boys, both V and his younger brother Jack, came home from the Cape without letting anyone know. They said that the Cape was expecting a heat wave and that they had decided to come home to stay cool. They were actually curious about their father's house guests and, besides, The Barn where Jack worked had a kitchen fire so he was out of work. V had been giving sailing lessons on the Cape, based on his own schedule, so he could leave to come home whenever he wanted to.

Their rooms where two large connected rooms on the second floor at the end of the hallway coming off the walkway above and looking down on the main hall, and right down the hall from Alice's front room.

Jake, working on the third floor, was informed of their arrival by the sudden rising of Oliver to a full sitting position for two seconds to listen before he was up on all fours. Then he was out the bedroom door in a mad dash downstairs, nails against wood announcing his quick departure.

"Ah what now?" was all that Jake muttered as he turned from staring at his Remington typewriter bathed in the light from the porthole window in front of him. The window allowed light from the heavens to shine down on the typewriter as if to say 'come on' as he tried to make an article materialize while Kate was in Manhattan for the day.

Heading downstairs to check on Oliver Jake could hear the energetic voices of his two nephews as they put their packs down and laughed, and talked to Oliver.

"What happened to you boy?" was V's voice as Jake was heading down the second flight of stairs to the hallway to the kitchen.

"Looks like he got stabbed," commented Jack as Jake hit the ground floor just off the kitchen. Jack was almost the spitting image of his older brother but just slightly shorter at 5'11" with a dusting of freckles over the bridge of his nose and on either side of it.

"Alice's cat!" said Jake. "What the hell brings you both home so early?"

"They're expecting a bad heat wave on the Cape and besides, Jack tried to burn The Barn down," said V now looking at Jake. "That little nut cat did this?"

"Yup," Jake answered V, then looking to Jack he asked, "You burned what?"

Jack started laughing, "Nothing, The Barn's kitchen hood caught fire and V's trying to blame me."

"Good to see you both, it's been a little strange around here," said Jake now scratching Oliver's head.

"I was telling Jack about the party and demon lady; we sorta had to come home to see what was happening."

"Came to watch the show, huh," said Jake now crouching in front of Oliver and checking his wound.

Jack laughed again with his infectious laugh, anticipating that it all might be humorous.

"If her head spins around I don't want to miss it," followed V.

"God V," commented Jack with disgust, and a little fear

written across his face as his humor changed.

"You need to tell Kate that V. I've been trying to tell her about Alice but she won't believe me," said Jake followed by a laugh. "You missed it last night," continued Jake shaking his head, "the whole neighborhood got to experience Miss Satan."

"What'd she do?" grinned V.

"Well, it started with Oliver getting clawed and ended with the princess of darkness letting ol' George Hurley know that she knew who he was. This was at high volume for the whole neighborhood to hear. Also at full volume, she called her cat a bitch and a shape-shifter."

"Jesus," said V.

"You've got to be kidding... and Mr. Hurley...." put in Jack.

Turning his head toward Jack, V said, "No, I told you, she's for real," looking back at Jake, "Man, and I missed it. George Hurley huh, that's funny. He was at the pool that night."

"Yeah and she remembered, calling him by his first name."

"No kidding," commented V.

"No, and it shut him up. Also, when I came down the backstairs to initially check out what was going on I ran into Carter heading up in a hurry with panic on his face. She did something to scare the hell out of him."

"Jeez, I don't know if I want to stay," commented Jack with concern on his face.

"Ah, it's nothing really," said V taking humor in his younger brother's concern.

"So, is Oliver going to be okay?" asked Jack.

"He'll be fine. I've just got to keep him away from those claws."

"We can give the cat a new home," V guaranteed with a smile as Carter stepped into the kitchen from the pass- through from the living room.

"Hi boys."

"Were you in the living room for the past five or ten

minutes?" Jake asked concerned that Carter had heard himself mentioned.

"No, came in from the porch," said Carter not questioning the question. "Had a few drinks with Bob."

"Who's Bob?" asked V.

"Bob the Asiatic. He just came through the fence again."

"Asiatic?" asked Jake.

"What happened to Oliver's side?" asked Carter not even registering the question about Bob's description.

"The cat," put in V.

"Oh," said Carter not really putting it together as the cat was always with Alice and when he saw Alice he only saw a scary Jap and nothing else.

Trying to join the conversation Jack asked the obvious, "Mr. Mills, are you going to play tennis?"

"It's Carter, no, why?"

"Well, because…," V tagged his younger brother in the arm to stop him from saying more.

"Because they have a tournament at The Club this weekend," finished V.

"No, I don't think so, it's been a long time, I'll see you boys later," said Carter as he crossed through the kitchen and headed for the stairs dressed in his tennis whites.

"What was that about?" whispered Jack after Carter started up the stairs.

"Haven't you ever noticed when you have seen Mr. Mills what he's dressed in?"

"Never thought about it but usually tennis whites, ………..Jeez that's different," finished Jack.

"He's different Jack," said V.

"So, what are you up to? Going to The Club for awhile or what?" asked Jake.

"Yeah, then we had a plan to follow Alice tonight if she goes out for one of those walks of hers."

"What walks?" asked Jake.

"The ones where she disappears and then shows up with some strange item the next day or a couple of days later....Well, I don't know if they're walks," continued V, "I just noticed her go out a couple of times at night, before I left for the Cape, and twice I saw her come back with something,... I thought."

"Like what?" asked Jack.

"I don't know but I'd bet one was another one of those big candles with the gold cap on top from the church because Mrs. Campbell threw one in the pool the night of the 'big party'." And then he chuckled. "I did notice something on her window sill two days after taking one of those walks," V continued with a bit more seriousness in his voice, "It was the holy veil that they put over the communion chalice."

"You're kidding, from the church?" asked Jack.

"No I'm not and she has a big robe like the one that Reverend McGee wears, and a giant cross. I think she's hitting the church."

"I'd be careful with that one. Who knows what she's up to. She gives me the creeps and only sleeping with that knife near my bed makes me feel better," added Jake.

"Knife?" questioned Jack in a surprised tone.

"So you don't keep it under the pillow anymore unck?" asked V with a big smile.

"Wise guy, no, it's too big." And he and V laughed.

"I don't think that's funny," said Jack with concern, "Is she that nutty? I'm just down the hall from her for godsakes."

"Don't worry, you'll hear her coming in plenty of time. She mumbles and giggles to herself and talks to the cat who follows her all over the place," said Jake smiling at Jack.

"Great," said Jack then turning to V, "Glad you talked me into coming home."

"We'll see tonight," said V.

Nothing happened that night, they watched for Alice as discretely as possible by taking turns sitting at the end of the hallway fifty feet or so down from Alice's room and staring at her door. There was no movement and there was no Alice. She had left for the day and night to places unknown. Other than an occasional giggle and some mumblings Alice was   as quiet as a ghost when in her room so it was fair to assume that she was in the room when she was not.

The boys saw her finally come in the next day, early in the evening. She was like a wisp. They were in the driveway playing one-on-one basketball when they noticed her coming down the driveway, or when Jack noticed her. Playing with the backboard and net up against the garage, which had been an old barracks building at Camp Merritt, New Jersey during WWI, they had their backs to her when she came home. Only Jack turning sideways to guard against V's move with the ball enabled them to catch her coming in.

Jack got a good view, and she was once again dressed in red with tight red leather slacks. Jack could see that she was grinning to herself, not noticing the two of them, as she walked down the front portion of the driveway and then turned right to walk up the steps of the front porch. She walked out of his view as he stopped, and V went by with the ball and dumped a basket.

"What the hell Jack, seen a ghost?" said V after collecting the ball he just dropped into the basket unchallenged.

"No, ...maybe,... her grin is nuts."

Stopping and looking at Jack as Jack turned back around to face his older brother V asked, "She's here?"

"Yeah, couldn't be anyone else. I just got the chills."

V laughed. "You and Jake, but she is nuts, has to be after what I saw at that pool party. Tonight we see what goes."

"Yeah, at a distance," put in Jack with some trepidation in his voice.

Back at their 'covert' watch position that night it was V who saw her leave her room at just before 10 p.m. He was sitting in the shadows but she looked in his direction and gave a demonic smile that included the frightening glint of her light hazel eyes for total effect. V felt the shivers go up the back of his spine as the hackles raised up on his neck. "Jeez," he muttered silently to himself.

As she descended the staircase V quietly moved back into Jack's room, where Jack was reading, and got his attention punctuating it by nodding his head.

The boys were dressed in dark clothing and although it wasn't a moonless night it was dark enough.

They waited until they heard the front door open and then close. Then they dashed downstairs not to lose sight of where she was headed, although they had an idea of where that was.

They dashed out the back door through the kitchen and ran up the side of the house so they were below the front door with a complete view of the street out front. They could see Alice on the other side headed down the hill towards St. Paul's.

As she turned the bend in the street and dropped down to the right, out of view, V and Jack ran low across the street. They ran like they were in a spy movie, although she wouldn't be able to see their movement from where she was even if they had run standing up straight flailing their arms trying to gain attention.

They crept down the hundred-year-old flag stones, hugging the tree line along that side of the road. In their stealth they tripped occasionally on the irregular height and depth of the large grey stone squares. The stones had moved out of sync with each other due to root growth and weather over the previous hundred years. This made it difficult to follow someone in a low crouch at night, but they still tried to maintain their stealth.

"Goddamnit," muttered V tripping over one uplifted edge which sent him reeling down the incline of the hill out of balance, just catching himself before falling into a noisy heap.

"Slow down will ya," whispered Jack coming up from behind, "I think we know where she's headed."

As they cleared the turn of the descending road they could see Alice in the immediate distance headed for St. Paul's. She was on the grass of the church lawn and seemed to be headed for the front door out by the main road. Seeing this, the boys kept low until she turned the corner then at V's direction, with a tap of Jack's shoulder, they ran up the adjoining street to get around the church from the other side.

It was a large building but they were on the opposite corner in time to see Alice tugging at the main door to the church, which again was locked.

They heard her mumble something that sounded like a profanity then start to go back the way she had come. Once again, as she turned the corner, V tapped Jack and said, "Let's go," and they started to run to the door she had just left.

V, reaching the door first with Jack still behind, held his hand up to let Jack know that he needed to stop where V was standing at the door, and quietly. As Jack came to a stop V crept to the corner of the building, just past the front door, and tentatively peered around the corner. He could see Alice tugging on the side door in the manner she had on previous, nights unknown to V. She tugged and V heard her say, "Bastards, how dare you," and then she giggled a mischievous giggle as though she knew something no one else did, and she did to an extent.

V watched her head to the other corner, then stop and look back in his direction as though she felt something. V pulled his head back and just muttered, "Shit."

"What?" asked Jack, now at his side.

"She looked right at me but I know she didn't see me, let's give it a minute or two. She's headed for the back and there is no exit from there except to head up the hill."

They let a minute pass then V tentatively peered around the corner and not seeing Alice tapped Jack on the arm. Then he headed around the corner and past the locked door that Alice had been tugging on.

When Jack caught up, V, just short of the next corner and looking at Jack, put his finger up to his lips, as though he really had to tell Jack to be quiet. Then he crept to the edge of the corner and peered around expecting to see Alice too close to be comfortable, but there was nothing.

"Christ," muttered V, "What the hell?"

"What?" responded Jack.

Turning back to Jack, V said, "She's gone, holly crap. Did you see her go up the hill? I sure didn't."

"Maybe she is from hell," whispered Jack with a half smile on his face.

"Or a magician," returned V.

Cautiously, V stepped from around the corner and to the back of the church looking closely at the corners of the church in back and the hill leading up from it just in case she was hiding in a shadow. He could again feel the hackles on the back of his neck go up as he thought of the look that she had cast in his direction before leaving the house. It was as though she knew he was there and knew that he would follow, and dared him to do so.

Jack followed as V walked along the back of the church and past the old wooden grate. They really didn't take notice of the grate as it was part of an immoveable piece of the building and part of their memory since early childhood. It just was and therefore did not stand out as it had to Alice the day that she had tested it and found the secret passageway. They could not know that she was walking slowly in a darker environment then they, almost parallel to where they were as they reached the halfway point across the back of the church.

Stopping and turning to Jack, V said, "I don't get it Jack. How the hell could she just disappear?"

"You tell me, you're so sure that she's just a nut and that's all,…….. maybe there's more to it."

"I don't know but it's freaky," said V. "Let's just go up the hill and around and check the place out."

They spent the next twenty-five minutes or so walking up the hill and then around the church and saw nothing. It only served to shake them up a little more as there was no way that she just vanished into mid-air like that. They took a seat on the steps at the front doors to the church, just below the stone owl on the side of the belfry. They sat there in mutual quiet both thinking of where she may have gone when they heard it.

"I-I-I-I umph," came from above them very softly as though muffled so that they could not really triangulate where from above it was coming, if from above at all.

They just looked at each other quietly and then they heard it again, "I-I-I-I umph," somewhat muffled but definitely coming from above them.

"What the hell," said V as they both looked straight up.

Then it came again, this time louder, "I-I-I-I umph," and they turned and looked right up at the belfry waiting to hear whatever it was again.

"I-I-I-I umph," it came again, this time followed by a full throated scream. "I-I-I-I umph," and another scream.

Jack was up and gone followed by V. They ran up the side of St. Paul's to the back of the church, just below the hill, where Jack stopped. He was breathing heavily, mostly from adrenaline, as he turned to see V stopping right behind him partly out of breath as well.

"What the hell...... was that?" asked Jack looking in the direction of the bell tower.

"It sounded...... half human," said V looking not at Jack but turned around facing the tower and looking at it.

"It sounded half man...... half woman," countered Jack still partly out of breath.

"It didn't sound good," added V catching his breath but now fully alert from the adrenaline.

V was looking at Jack as they listened again and heard it in the near distance.

"Do you think....."

"Don't say it," finished V.

"It's like the devil............... or something from hell," said Jack with his eyes wide open.

"It can only.........be her," said V finally calming down to a reality. "She's got us going."

"V, it doesn't sound human."

"Yeah, well it has to be her at the top level of the church.......... in the bell tower maybe. But how the hell did she get in?"

"I don't know.......... and I don't think I wanna hang around and find out," said Jack. "If it is her.......... she's more than just nutty, if it's not her it's just as bad."

"Well, it all is pretty strange and anyway..." V stopped mid-sentence as they were interrupted by a louder scream from hell as delivered through Alice. She put her mouth right up against the wooden slats of the belfry and let it rip adding a modulation up and down which gave it the character of something otherworldly.

Both boys were looking in the direction of the church when she let loose. V, standing just below jack finished, "That's enough for me let's get outta here."

With that they were both running up the hill and ran until they made the sidewalk. They walked home from there with Jack looking back occasionally to see if the 'she-devil' had magically appeared and was following them.

Twenty minutes after they returned to the two bedrooms on the second floor one could see, from the top of the hill where they had been standing, the grate on the back of the church move. It moved then stopped, then moved again coming off the back of the wall and resting to the side of the opening now showing itself briefly as a dark figure moved out of its interior carrying an item which was difficult to see. The figure exited the opening and put the item on the ground then lifted the grate back in place leaving the back of the church looking just as it had when the boys had left quickly twenty minutes earlier.

They did not bother to put out a lookout that night to see when Alice returned or if she did and with what. They'd had enough for one night.

She did return but it wasn't until after midnight as she had walked the streets of the neighborhood quietly looking into the lit windows of all the neighbors within a half mile radius of the Lugers'. She did this while holding a scepter-like crosier topped by a dove, which she had taken from the church, and quietly chanting, "I see with the eye of a bird, I see into your private souls from the night sky." As she said this she dipped the scepter. She carried out this ritual at each house she passed as though she were conferring knighthood.

From his deep sleep that night V heard a demonic giggle

which came from the hallway and became part of a soon to evolve nightmare. Shortly after this giggle, at one o'clock in the morning; a deep, escalating, partly muted, grunting giggle started to come through Alice's door as she gave herself an orgasm while holding the scepter. She was in 'exquisite joy'.

V's nightmare was minor in comparison to the true picture.

The house finally went quiet after a few more giggles, which were barely loud enough to reach the hallway let alone the boys' rooms. V's dreams would eventually return to normal as Alice fell asleep in the dark with both eyes open, scepter and cat at her side.

Chapter 11

Rodney Gets a Girlfriend

Tuesday, July 12th

The next morning brought a loud scream of surprise and a scream not yet heard in the Luger house. It was the scream of a tall slim brunette by the name of 'Birdie'. She had run smack into two white doves exiting the door at the top of the stairs in their rush to fly down across the main hall and into the den to lit atop Henry's antlers.

The scream was one of surprise. The gaping open mouth of the tall attractive woman followed immediately after as Birdie's eyes fell on the bird lady and then she froze in her tracks. The woman with the birds was in a sheer white semi see-through dressing gown from the 40's with a large cross, one only sees in church, held firmly between her breasts. This sight was not what, in the end, froze poor unknowing Birdie to that spot on the floor. It was the stare of this woman as though she were reaching deep into her soul and the words that followed immediately upon eye contact, "You are in my church and you are not welcome," that truly froze Birdie.

Poor Birdie was only trying to retrace her steps from the

previous night in order to find the kitchen and some much needed coffee. She had come in with Rodney an hour before Alice came in from her voyeuristic tour of the neighborhood. She never heard the demonic giggle coming from the hall nor the muted grunting as she was in an alcohol induced sleep by that time.

Alice retreated back into her room and let out a loud audible giggle just as the door closed. Birdie came unstuck from the spot on the floor where Alice had left her and started to back track down the elevated walkway above the main hall.

She backtracked stepping backwards staring at Alice's door to protect herself in the event that this crazy person decided to all of sudden come out again. She backtracked halfway down the hall back towards the section of elevated hallway that turned right and headed to the master bedroom before she started to turn quietly and slowly to face the direction of her walk. She turned slowly with her eyes on the floor protecting herself from a misstep when she felt a presence as she started to look up at the end of her turn. There in front of her stood an older man in dirty tennis whites with glazed over eyes and smelling of scotch. It was 7:30 in the morning.

"Have you seen any Japs?" the figure asked, not seeing a woman in the man's heavy blue colored, terry cloth robe but another haggard soul like himself in a Navy hospital robe and lost in the boondocks.

With this Birdie was gone, quickly to her right down the perpendicular short hall and into the master bedroom throwing the door shut behind her. Then, wide eyed, she got on the bed next to the sleeping Rodney. She sat looking at the wall as she pulled her knees up to her chest and wrapped her arms around them contemplating where the hell she was for a minute before Rodney started to move. It was dark after all when she followed Rodney into the house. She seemed to be in an asylum of sorts. Was this a grand joke?

Turning over in bed blurry eyed, Rodney focused on the movement in the bed next to him. As he focused his dark blue corduroy navy surplus hospital robe, with the caduceus   and

USN insignia embroidered on the chest pocket, came into clear view. What? Who? Who was in his robe and then as Birdie turned towards his movement while she looked at the walls he remembered. It had been awhile since he had a woman in his bed.

"Where are we Rod?" asked Birdie with some hesitation as she continued to look at the walls and the color of the room that she was in, now lit by the early morning sun. It was blood red. Then looking back at Rodney and having momentarily forgotten about the bandage still running up the bridge of his nose, now two weeks after the 'incident', she flinched with a gasp nearer to a shriek.

Rodney hesitated as his mind was trying to process everything from the night before and bring it back to this woman in the present who had just shrieked at the sight of him, which he barely noticed.

Rodney had known Birdie, a freelance yoga instructor, for only a week having met her in Mellon's bar on the East side of Manhattan. It was in this same bar that they had the conversation the night before that had sealed their fate. As they had been drinking rather heavily they had wisely hailed a cab instead of taking Rodney's 1969 Porsche 911E, which was garaged in the city. They had talked the cabby into crossing the George Washington Bridge. And Birdie had paid the exorbitant fare when they had arrived in front of the white stucco Victorian called the Lugers'. "Home," Rodney had mumbled when the cab stopped.

"You have strange people walking around," and looking up at the ceiling which was blood red as well, "and your room is red!" exclaimed Birdie.

Rodney following her stare, looked up and said, "Yeah, Helen liked............I thought the color was vibrant."

"No wonder you had a divorce, this color is unnerving," said Birdie, then looking down at Rodney, "and who is that woman with the birds............. and the drunk tennis player?"

"The who?" Rodney questioned, still trying to clear his

head.

"The woman in the room at the front of the house, the scary one, who is she?" Birdie asked still unsettled over the encounter.

"Oh, you mean, ah..........Alice.., that's right. She rents a room."

"You had to think of her name, are you sure this is home?," commented Birdie lifting her eyebrows with nervous concern. "And the mad tennis player?"

"That's probably Carter, he's okay."

"He's someplace........but...."

"Bird's? What was that about birds?" cut in Rodney with lack of concern and not fully paying attention.

"Nothing, but that woman.........Alice, seems to be a little fanatical, she actually gives me the shivers like a bad horror movie."

"Whaddaya mean?" mumbled Rodney.

"She seems to be a little religious."

"Oh yeah.... yeah..........God, it's Tuesday, we'll be late," said Rodney not really taking in what Birdie was telling him.

"I'm not going to be late, I'm fine. My time is mine but this is someone's church," said Birdie as she shook involuntarily.

"Half day for me, I guess...............I'll take a day today, it's been some time since I have," mumbled Rodney more speaking to himself than to Birdie as he looked at the rumpled bedspread and blanket in front of him. Then looking at Birdie, "Someone's what?"

"Church."

"That's down the hill. Let's get some coffee."

"I'm afraid to step out of this room."

"Ah, it's okay but let me make a call here first and leave a message on the floor at work."

While he was making the call on the bedside phone Birdie found the large Victorian bathroom attached to the master bedroom. It was large enough to be its own living space. She let the open ends of the blue robe fall to either side of her while she made herself comfortable on the toilet from the same time period. It had an elevated water tank and a label in blue on the back of the bowl "Crapper" for John, even though it was actually Thomas. While Birdie was making herself comfortable Alice was in the bathroom at the end of the hall near the boy's room.

Alice was using the boys' bathroom and they had no idea. They had never thought about her needing a bathroom and besides, she had left nothing behind in the bathroom every time that she used it. Also, they had only been home a couple of days so it was a surprise when Jack, half awake, stumbled into the bathroom through the adjoining door from V's room. This startled Alice's white cat, who blew by Jack with a howl. The turning of the door knob, before Jack opened the door had already drawn Alice's attention and alerted her. She was naked with her back towards jack. When the door fully opened and the cat inflated into a terrified ball of white fur and claws she turned her head staring right at Jack with eyes that burned straight through him. Later he would swear that she pivoted her head. The sight was so shocking to Jack, not expecting to find anyone in the bathroom let along a howling cat and something out of a demonic movie, that he howled as well, "WHOA....WHOA...WHOAAAAA," and was out into V's room a second later, slamming the bathroom door closed behind him. He then shot into his own room and closed the door between his room and V's for added protection.

In his sleep the howl of the cat changed the course of V's dream as he started to come awake. The WHOA from jack sounded like a cross between someone trying to stop a horse and call out from a distance as a warning against an unstoppable force like a howling horse, which made no sense, then he was awake. Whatever it was it was loud enough to be heard on the entire floor and it brought V out of full sleep.

Alice was finishing her ablutions and left by the hallway door returning to her room by the time V was up and in Jack's room asking him what the hell happened.

"I swear V I'll never appreciate the appearance of a naked woman ever again."

"What are you talking about?"

"Demon Alice was in our bathroom, holy God, her eyes burned right through me and that damned cat almost made me pee myself."

V just started laughing. "Well, I guess she had to use some bathroom," he admitted and then continued to laugh.

"It's not funny."

"Oh yes it is."

"I swear, I think her head rotated when she looked at me."

"No pea soup?"

"Real funny."

While V and Jack were talking on the other side of the hall from the master bathroom Birdie, who had heard the howling cat and the 'WHOA.....WHOA.....WHOAAAAA', was getting more fearful by the second. It was loud enough that it came to her clearly although muted, which made it sound more sinister and supernatural than it was. Rodney, as usual, was totally oblivious to it as he left a message on the office 'automatic receptionist' machine and then dialed in a three digit code to access a general message for the syndicate members.

Carter heard it as part of a nightmare as he finally went to bed after running into Birdie in the U.S. Navy hospital robe. He had been up all night unable to sleep having a nightmare in real time while still awake, a living nightmare. Now he was having one in his sleep and the cry of Jack transformed itself into a muffled call for help directed to Carter but he was paralyzed to help. He needed to help but he could not and not only could he not help the person calling out but he could not move himself out of harms way which was slowly and methodically coming towards him in the form of several Japanese soldiers with rifles and fixed bayonets. They were sticking their bayonets into every dead body that they passed and they were inching towards him as he tried to move but could not budge. When they were upon him, laying amongst other bodies on a small wooden bridge, his eyes met those of one of the soldiers. The soldier smiled with glee and delight and Alice's eyes as he lunged his rifle, with its bayonet, into Carter. Carter hollered out as he came up out of bed sweating and breathing heavily.

The holler was blood curdling. It was the holler of someone being killed and this Birdie heard loudly muffled through the wall to her left almost opposite that of the direction of the first muffled noise. She froze right there on the "John J. Crapper" pulling herself in for protection, short of becoming a ball, using her yoga techniques to consolidate her mass and make smaller her being.

Jake and Kate and Oliver were up and they had just been listening to the goings on below them, just imagining what might be happening until Carter's scream came to them. At the end of the scream Oliver had finally barked several times knowing that it was Carter.

Jake had calmed him down by stroking the back of his head but when Carter let out that delayed and audible whimper, after the scream, Oliver had had enough. He was down the stairs and headed towards Carter's room with a bark.

Birdie hearing the barking looked above her head in the direction of the bark, then hearing the whimper again coming from her left she looked left. This was followed by another bark and the noise of something large coming down stairs. Now looking straight ahead she had had enough.

Alice was already leaving by the front door when Rodney finally hung up the phone to his office and headed into the master bathroom to find Birdie curled up on top of the Crapper. All of her appendages were pulled in tightly so that nothing stuck out and it was all wrapped in his dark blue corduroy war surplus hospital bathrobe. Rodney was briefly impressed by her balance but the concern in her eyes had him confused. He had just not heard anything or if he had it did not register like most things that did not directly concern him.

"What do you have here?" blurted out Birdie nervously.

Rodney once again not truly listening looked at her. Then he followed the pipe from the back of the toilet up to the tank several feet up behind Birdie, with his eyes, and then settled back down on the toilet with Birdie perched on top and answered, "A real Crapper".

"You're nuts."

Now finally listening he jumped to explain, "No, No, the toilet, it is an original John J. Crapper, it's Victorian, check out the writing under the seat."

The desperation created by the fact that he might lose something again shook Rodney to a temporary state of alertness.

Calming down, Birdie dropped her feet to the cold tile floor then stood and looked, for the first time, at the toilet behind her seeing that it was unusual and attractive. As she bent to look under the seat Rodney prodded, "Right behind the rim in blue on the white ceramic," trying to get her mind away from recent events as she tried to do the same.

As her eyes fell on CRAPPER she laughed involuntarily as unacceptable fear started to give way to acceptable reality.

***

The boys were dressed and in the kitchen by the time that Birdie had collected herself and was ready to head downstairs with Rodney for that long overdue coffee.

With Rodney now in another robe closely following behind her Birdie, still in the U.S. Navy robe, stopped abruptly before opening the door that led out to the hall. The hall where she had met the horror movie figure and the drunk tennis player muttering something about 'caps, nightcaps, ball caps, tennis caps' possibilities that her mind had quickly wandered through in that split second meeting. Abruptly stopping in front of Rodney had caused Rodney to bump into her and bang his nose with a painful grunt. Not realizing that Rodney had just bumped into her with painful consequences she asked, "What was that scream before with the dog barking? Do you have a dog?"

"No, my little brother does," said Rodney thinking more about the pain running through his nose at that moment as his eyes teared up from it while he touched his nose trying to ease the pain.

"Little brother? How old?"

"Twenty-three," said Rodney now holding his hand just over the nose, that his little brother had broken, in the belief that this would continue to relieve the pain and protect it from further harm.

"That's not little," she said as she turned back to the door and slowly opened it peering out in the direction of Alice's closed door. The only occupant of the room at that moment was a white cat preening itself in the middle of the bed. The two doves were missing.

Halfway down the hall she turned to Rodney again as he protectively covered his nose and continued the conversation which Rodney was not really paying attention to, "And he lives here, with his dog?"

"Who?" returned Rodney.

"Your 'little brother', are you listening to me?" she questioned now stopped right in front of Rodney and facing him.

"My brother, yes, he rents a room on the third floor with his dog and girlfriend."

"How many rooms are you renting?"

"Not many," replied Rodney hesitantly. It wasn't that he didn't know, it just didn't occupy his mind much.

Taking over the lead Rodney, in order to preempt any further harm to his nose, started down the hallway above the main hall with Birdie following wearing oversized slippers to go with her oversized blue robe. Rodney actually had on one of Helen's old white terry cloth robes with Hamilton Princess, Bermuda stitched in gold across the left breast. He could not get himself to throw it out. It was too tight on him as he walked along in old topsiders covered in paint with a bandaged nose and Birdie following wrapped in a bathrobe much too large for her frame even though she was tall.

The way they were dressed they looked like Mutt and Jeff, except that they were both tall. It was a comical sight to anyone who might have watched them descend the staircase.

At the ground floor Rodney started for the hallway that led to the kitchen and was to the left across the main hall when Birdie heard the flutter of wings and a 'coo'. When she turned in the direction of the sound she thought, in the dim light of the den, that she saw two white doves perched on top of the head of a deer. She froze for just a second and when she turned back in the direction that Rodney had been heading she saw him enter the hallway to the kitchen. She immediately picked up her pace and forgot what she saw in order to catch up and not be left behind and alone in this house she found herself in. She was now on edge.

As she entered the hallway she heard more voices and laughing. The laughing had been preceded by V exclaiming, "Where did you get that bathrobe, you look like Gandhi just after a fight." After which he and Jack started laughing un-controllably.

As Birdie entered the kitchen, tentatively, she saw Rodney looking down at himself dressed in a robe, too tight to be normal, completed by paint covered ratty old topsiders and laughing himself although his nose hurt as he laughed.

With her entry Jack and V, facing the entrance to the kitchen from the hallway, stopped laughing. Rodney then turned to see what it was almost forgetting that Birdie was directly behind him.

"Oh, oh…, this is Birdie, a friend of mine."

V stepped forward and nodded and extended his hand. "I'm Rodney, Jr.," he said with self gratifying humor that only he and Jack understood.

Jack did the same after V and just said, "Jack."

Birdie stood a bit stunned. Then, "These are yours?" she asked looking at Rodney trying to process everything that was happening to her starting again with the chance meeting with Alice.

V answered for him, "I hope so."

Jack just smiled.

Rodney not really paying attention started to walk over to the kitchen double sink and looking down into the right hand

sink, typically just used for rinsing, he saw what he was looking for. Bending over and reaching down into the basket of the
drain catch he came up with a cigar butt that had probably
gone through a rinse or two and had dried out again.

Rodney looked at it for a second as Birdie watched him.
Then he reached for a box of wooden matches on the shelf
above the sink and without thinking about anyone else started to light the tortured butt which was crumpled in on itself
besides everything else that it had gone through.

From behind him came laughter and V's voice, "I told you
so, you owe me five bucks Jack." And they continued to laugh
as Rodney puffed hard to try to get the butt going again.
Rodney was an unsophisticated 'aficionado' of any cigar
whether it was a butt from a drain or a 16-year-old White Owl
that he had given to Jake as a little kid when V was born. Jake,
just barely walking himself, had saved it in a box as little kids
will do and had given it to Rodney, a year earlier, to give to V.
But Rodney had decided to smoke it instead, even as it un-
raveled on him dropping fiery pieces of material that were no
longer strands of tobacco but simply the equivalent of flecks of
cardboard. He had almost set himself on fire, the sight of which
almost made up for the loss of the memento that Jake had saved
for his nephew.

As the boys were laughing and looking at Rodney a voice
came from behind them and it was the shocked voice of Birdie, "That's disgusting." And the boys laughed even more.

Not listening as usual Rodney continued to puff and got it
going as he grunted to himself with both pleasure and the
acknowledgement of those around him laughing.

"Put that out right now or I'm leaving," boomed Birdie.

That got Rodney's attention and the butt went back into the
sink with a hiss as it landed in a bowl half filled with water,
and the boys laughed again.

"That's enough Rod, how about some coffee," said Birdie
and then turning to the boys, "I'm sorry boys, your father
didn't tell me about his family."

The boys just smiled at her and then Jake came through

the kitchen doorway followed by Oliver and Kate.

"And the kitchen gets smaller," said V smiling.

"What's up?" asked Jake looking around.

"He lit the drain butt," was V's response.

"Alright," said Jake still sporting his half cast and laughing.

Birdie's eyes darted subconsciously from the new arrival's half cast to Rodney's bandaged nose as Rodney headed to the coffee maker and the cupboard above it which held the coffee. Although she did not consciously think about it the connection was made.

"I'm Jake," said Jake extending his casted hand to the woman in blue then turning back halfway and looking down at Oliver, "and this is Oliver, the big black one on all fours and that over there is Kate on two." He finished by looking over at Kate and smiling at her just before he turned back to Birdie and smiled again.

"You must be 'little brother'," commented Birdie smiling with some self-conscious embarrassment now that Kate was present and as well dressed as she was to head into the city. She also could not help but see the wound on the left shoulder of the big black dog, which would all go into her subconscious as something not necessarily important now.

"I guess I am," confirmed Jake hating this title which came out of the mouth of anyone who knew his older brother before meeting him. If they were around Rodney for some time before meeting Jake they would greet him coldly as his older brother had time to add the brush strokes of a horrible picture of his younger brother stroke by stroke. It was almost a gauge indicating how long someone knew his older brother before meeting him. It was measured by the degree of coldness that he would receive at his introduction.

Looking over at his older brother trying to figure out how much coffee to put in the automatic drip coffee maker Jake noted, "Where did you get that robe, you look like Gandhi," and the boys laughed in unison.

"How much coffee do I put into this thing?" asked Rodney

showing once again that he wasn't listening.

"Here, let me do that," said Birdie as she started to walk over to help him.

"Was that Carter this morning seeing another Jap?" asked V of Jake as Birdie passed him to help Rodney, her ears tweaking at the question.

Stopping and turning Birdie interjected, "Jap? I thought he said cap, if you mean the tennis player."

V laughed. "You got it, the tennis player. Did he say Jap to you?"

"He desperately said, 'have you seen any caps?' which I found odd."

V and Jake laughed together.

"He probably said Japs as in Japanese soldier," explained Jake. "He must've had a helluva nightmare because that scream got Oliver's attention."

"That's what I heard!" said Birdie now looking at the two of them while Rodney continued to make a mess of the coffee.

"Oliver ran down to him. He was asleep when I went in to get Oliver just before we came down," said Jake to   everyone as Birdie again noticed Oliver's wound.

"I think he was drunk this morning," commented Birdie as though it were a revelation and the boys, including Jake, laughed again.

"He's a good man who drinks a bit too much at times but he's harmless. I've gotta go," said Kate who had been listening to the Luger clan not saying a word as she did so. She kissed Jake on the cheek, patted Oliver on the head and headed towards the back door from where she'd then head to the left side of the garage where she had the Opel parked.

As she passed Birdie on the way out she just said, "It was nice to meet you, don't let these men tell you stories, they like to exaggerate."

Birdie smiled. "It was nice meeting you as well, I hope we meet again."

"I'm sure we will," returned Kate as she stepped into the mudroom on her way out the backdoor and Birdie turned and went to Rodney's side to help him with the coffee.

Chapter 12

Birdie Comes to Stay Awhile

Friday, July 15th

Birdie came back for more that Friday evening. Her arrival was announced by Rodney stalling his Porsche 911E as he made the turn into the driveway coming from the city with both Birdie and her suitcase onboard. Jake heard this from the top floor as he sat in front of the Remington trying to think while looking out the porthole window, which faced the front of the house. The stall broke his concentration, and he just shook his head. Then he winced as Rodney started the car in gear and it jumped to a stall after which Rodney just let it coast down the driveway to the garage. The man had this wonderful car but yet he could not drive it and he was destroying it as he learned to do so. This fact hit Jake in the gut as he had driven Formula Fords over two summers during college when he could get enough extra cash besides what he was saving for school at the time. He could only afford a 'lapping day' here and there but it was enough to secure his appreciation for a good chassis, a working gear box and a suspension in top form even for a Formula Ford and even though he was just running laps.

With the sound of the back kitchen door opening Oliver stood up. He could hear it but Jake could not. He did not move but just listened as he knew that it wasn't Kate. Oliver knew the sound of the Opel and 'Kate never stalled it'. Even Oliver could appreciate that or at least that's what Jake, in tune with Oliver, thought at that moment with a sarcastic laugh at the expense of his older brother. Not only did she not stall the standard shift in the Opel D that she drove but she was an excellent driver. Jake smiled at the thought that she could also time and tune the Opel after Zach had shown her how. Rodney on the other hand would never check the oil and would on occasion forget to put gas in the car, running out twice in recent memory.

Another noise came from the second floor. It was a mumbling sound and it was no doubt Carter talking with himself as he entered his room. With this, Oliver was out the door and heading down the one flight of stairs before heading on to Carter's room. Carter must have walked in the front door at the same moment that the back door was opened.

Before Jake could look back to the typewriter he heard Kate's Opel pull smoothly into the driveway. 'It's becoming a full house,' thought Jake as he pushed himself up out of the wooden captains' chair that he had brought home from college.

The boys were home too, as he heard them laughing in their adjoined rooms as he headed downstairs to meet Kate. Alice would be the last ingredient and one never knew if she was in the house or not until you ran right into her or heard that demonic giggle. It was strange: she wasn't a presence until she was square in your face. It was rather unnerving.

Rodney had been at Birdie's on the Upper East Side on the evening of the 13th when at 9:27 Ravenswood 3, or the biggest generator in the City of New York and better known as "Big Allis", shut down. Nine minutes later the city went black for the next 25 hours.

Birdie and Rodney had been in bed together with the

lights on when they went off all of a sudden. Birdie had blamed
Rodney and Rodney knowingly said that it was probably a
circuit breaker in the building and it would be on in no time.

Two hours later, with the lights still off, they had decided
to go out to where the lights were but there were none. And
when they saw windows being smashed and looting going on
they headed back to the apartment as fast as they could and
walked the six flights up. There they stayed until the next day
but without power they could not retrieve the Porsche nor take
the subway so they stayed another night with the lights coming
back on that evening. When they left the city on this Friday
evening Birdie had a large bag packed with the intention of
staying in New Jersey for a few days more than the weekend.
The bag was so big that Rodney had put an outward dent in
the front trunk hood of the Porsche as he smashed it down on
the soft bag. This was even after removing some items from the
bag and spreading them around in the front trunk, without
telling Birdie.

They were in the kitchen looking haggard as Jake entered
on his way to meet Kate. Birdie was sitting at the kitchen table
while Rodney went to the refrigerator to find something to
drink.

"You both look tired, how was the blackout?" asked Jake
smiling.

"The city was mad," said Birdie.

"They were looting stores," said Rodney still looking
through the refrigerator and not turning around.

At that moment Kate walked in and Oliver came down the
last few steps behind Jake, into the kitchen and up to Kate
wagging his tail.

Setting her briefcase down Kate knelt and wrapped her
arms around Oliver, "Oh, good to see you boy." And seeing
that she was among company and, on top of that, refugees from
NYC, she looked only at Birdie and said, "You look like you
could use a drink. We saw the glow of the city disappear from
the horizon Wednesday night as we sat on the side

porch, it was eerie."

"It was madness in the dark, they went crazy," Birdie confided to another woman.

"I'll get you a drink other than juice if you'd like," said Kate understanding the woman better than Rodney did.

"A scotch neat would do," said Birdie as Rodney stopped looking in the refrigerator and got the message.

"I'll get it," said Rodney turning around and once again revealing his taped nose which still caught Kate off-guard.

"Thank you. It must've been some night with broken windows and broken whatever else," said Kate with a smile.

"Jake," said Kate looking over at Jake and standing but still bending over and rubbing Oliver's head, "maybe we could order some Chinese and make it easy on everyone tonight."

"Sounds like a plan. I'll check with V and Jack and see if they're interested." Still looking at Kate, "What about Alice?" he asked with a big grin on his face while lifting his right hand in a 'stop and think' motion for emphasis, forgetting that it sported a half-cast.

Kate just looked at him with a look of absurd disbelief, then thinking about it said, "You could ask Carter."

"He mentioned something this morning about going out with Margaret someplace."

"Okay, and this is my treat, the trust fund can pay for more than my work," said Kate with a confirming smile. She also knew that Rodney would never offer and Jake was getting paid by the story, and that was another story.

***

Kate, Birdie and Rodney were out on the side veranda where they had moved some extra chairs and a couple of collapsible TV tray tables. They had also just stacked some dishes from the kitchen on the veranda's coffee table when Jake and the boys came through the front door. They were carrying several bags of Chinese food from Dr. Wing's "Once Chinese", whatever that meant to those buying Chinese food.

Oliver was up and met them halfway having smelled the food from around the house before it was even through the front door.

"Come on Oliver, back," said Jake holding the three bags he had up high as Oliver backed up with his eyes on the bags.

Kate called Oliver over to her side again on the far side of the love seat. She sat here so she could keep Oliver at bay with her right hand touching him now and again being careful of his left shoulder. Jake had a brief memory flash of another type of food in a cup and of the day Oliver had joined he and Kate in the front seat of the Opel. A 150 pound dog, once he had decided to go for it, was impossible to stop when it came to certain foods in a cup, especially food with extreme food odors such as Dr. Wing's.

While Kate and Jake sat on the love seat and Rodney and Birdie sat in the wicker chairs across from them the boys sat in chairs they had brought out from around the dining room table. The bag of food had been put on a large rectangular glass topped coffee table between the love seat and the wicker chairs. And as Jake pulled the little white cardboard containers out, one-by-one, he described what he was pulling out. As he pulled the last container out of the bag he looked up at Birdie, directly across from him, and asked, "Birdie, what is your pleasure?"

"Sweet and Sour pork sounds good."

"With chopsticks?" asked Jake as he handed her a plate.

"There is no other way," she confirmed with a smile.

As everyone started to serve themselves V looked over at Birdie, who had already been served, while she was wrestling her first piece of pork to her mouth with unsteady chopsticks and asked, "So, I hear the city was a riot."

Holding the piece in midair and watching it until it fell back on the plate Birdie looked up and said, "It was horrible, store windows were broken and items from the windows were strewn on the street."

"Anyone killed?" asked V.

"Jeez," said Jack.

"Well, I wanna know. Son of Sam was probably running around in the dark too," he came back.

"Nice dinner talk," put in Kate.

"Well, he likes girls with long brown hair."

"That's just great, if you notice both Kate and Birdie have long brown hair," said Jake waving his half-cast from Birdie to Kate.

"Precisely," said V, "I wouldn't go out in New York with that hair, or I'd get it cut if I were you."

Rodney looked at Birdie's hair around his taped nose as though he were seeing it for the first time. "He's right," said Rodney.

"Jesus," said Jake, "are you trying to scare them."

"No, they just over exaggerate like you," said Kate as she reached over and kissed Jake on the check as he bent his head to put a piece of broccoli in his mouth. The kiss made him smile and almost drop the piece of broccoli.

"No, it's true, the guy goes after women with long brown hair and they think he lives in the suburbs," continued V.

"Oh, great," said Jack.

"Don't worry Jack he only goes after women with long brown hair and their boyfriends, you and I are safe."

Kate just smirked but Birdie looked over at Rodney, looking right at his taped nose and looking a little worried. But Rodney did not notice as he shoveled white rice into his mouth right from the plate, as he held it up to his lower lip.

"Ah, Jeez Dad," said V.

"What?" he said with his mouth full of rice and more as a statement as the boys laughed.

"Do you think he could be in a place like this?" asked Birdie.

"Who?" asked Rodney with his mouth open and full now showing everyone what he had combined with the rice all highlighted by his nose.

"Ah Jeez Dad," said V as they all laughed again.

"What?" he questioned tilting his head back to keep the food from falling out. And the boys and Jake laughed again as

Kate just shook her head and Birdie looked concerned.

"Do you think Son of Sam could be here in a town like this?" Birdie tried again.

"Nah," said Rodney hesitating as though not sure, with a mouth still full of food and what was now a dirty bandage running up his nose like a medieval nose guard. The man just kept banging his nose every time he had an insulin reaction and he had had a lot of them since the night of the 'confrontation'.

"I wouldn't be so sure," said V. "There are some strange people walking around this town and who says it has to be a man or one person. But it does seem that it could be a religious person or someone into the devil. "

"Oh God," said Kate partially rolling her eyes, "here we go".

"I'm just saying, you don't know".

Birdie not concentrating now absentmindedly tried to pick up a large piece of pork and had it just below her chin when the sound of the front door opening was heard along with a distinctive throat clearing. With this Oliver was up and off squeezing between the wicker chair and the flower box forcing Birdie to dump the red covered pork chunk on her white blouse. This was accompanied by some of the sauce from her plate as she was knocked over into it while holding it with one hand above her lap and midway up her chest for easy access. Her entire front was splashed in red.

As she set the plate down and assessed the damage a mumbling voice could be heard coming through the den. "Asiatic Bob, that you?" Preceded by Oliver, wagging his tail, Carter walked to the French doors dressed in slacks and a button down blue oxford shirt, something different. Behind him came Margaret.

Carter's eyes appeared a little glazed and as he happened into the threshold of the French doors, leading out to the side veranda, he had expected to see his new friend Bob. But instead he saw blood red on this woman who looked remotely familiar. At that same moment he saw chopsticks picking pieces off of her 'blood' soaked shirt. It was Rodney trying for his rare attempt at humor by picking bits of food off of Birdie's blouse. He was also not eating fast enough to take care of the large amount of insulin that he had taken way too early. On top of this Birdie was not in good humor with all the Son of Sam talk.

Carter did not see Rodney picking bits of food off of Birdie. He saw a young woman who was bleeding with a Japanese soldier sticking her with his eating utensils to make sure that she was dead.

"OH CHRIST. OH CHRIST………. I KILLED HER. IT…. WAS ME. I DID IT. MY GOD. HER LONG BROWN HAIR…………. IT'S GONE FOREVER. I KILLED HER I SAY. I KILLED HER," intoned Carter.

Everyone froze in place except Oliver who still looked up at Carter wagging his tail expecting something good, and Margaret who came around him and looked at him to get his attention.

"It's ok Carter, look at me. It's okay," she said softly.

"But I killed her, I killed them both," he said looking at Margaret but looking off in the distance at the same time.

"It's okay Carter, let me take you upstairs," she said. Then turning Carter around to go back the way they had come she looked back at everyone and said, "Sorry about that, he's been a little off lately." And they headed through the den to the living room with Oliver following, his tail down as now he felt something was wrong.

As they left, everyone else was till frozen in place until Birdie came unstuck. She was fueled not only by this little event but as well by the subconscious visual of a dog with stab marks on his shoulder, a taped nose and someone in a cast. "OH..MY..GOD, IS THAT HIM? My God, my God, we can't stay here. I knew something was wrong with him." As she finished her face took on a look of fear, panic and desperation all in one.

Everyone still frozen averted their eyes from the last place Carter and Margaret had been to the blouse of now hysterical

Birdie, covered in sweet and sour sauce.

"Well, I guess that about sums it up," said V.

With this Birdie was up and off through the den and up the stairs to the master bed room and was heard to say, "It's him, it's him, Son.......of ....Saaaam."

"You'd better head up," said Jake to Rodney who froze dumb faced and somewhat lost as the insulin was starting to win. Immediately recognizing what was going on Jake took a serving spoon and dipped it into the sweet red sauce and fed it to Rodney who was now hovering. "Now go," said Jake and Rodney was off through the den to follow her upstairs. "The food and sauce should kick in by the time he gets to her," Jake noted to no one in particular.

"Good job V," said Jake turning to V.

"Well, you didn't help, you're just as bad," said Kate as Jack sat there quietly. "And you too Jack," she added now looking over at Jack.

"Me, what did I do?"

"They like to hear you laugh that's what you do. You encourage them to do these things by saying nothing."

"I thought V was talking about Alice as Son of Sam," said Jack looking confused. And then Jake and V started laughing.

"What?" asked Jack.

Kate just shook her head at all three of them, but then unable to hold it back as she visualized what had just happened she smiled just a little so that they could barely see it.

The rest of the night would proceed relatively uneventful. Oliver returned twenty minutes later, which meant that Carter had probably calmed down. Jake thought once again of Rodney's hovering near insulin Looney Tunes and filled another plate with as much of the starchy and sugary items as he could, and headed off to the master bedroom.

Birdie told him to come in when he knocked as Rodney was still hovering a little and was slow at the uptake. Birdie had no idea why. Her feeling was that Rodney was hiding the real truth about Carter and this put her more on edge.

"I need to feed him some of this Birdie, it'll pick him up.

You do know that he's a diabetic?" asked Jake.

"Yes but....I don't understand."

"He hasn't eaten enough and the insulin is having an affect on him, it's making him lethargic right now."

"I didn't know."

"No problem."

Jake watched as Rodney worked on the plate while staring ahead. He left when he saw that the additional food was taking care of the insulin. Birdie would start to compromise with herself about Son of Sam being a resident at the Lugers' as she started to understand part of Rodney's behavior and attributed more of his behavior to insulin than was actually attributable.

By Sunday the house was calm having experienced an easy and relaxing Saturday, although Carter had been back to fighting on the phone with Bea that Saturday night. It was about something that she had forgotten to order for the store and he had been screaming a lot of 'God damn it Beas', which Birdie had heard. Birdie's ears had perked up when she heard this and she was put on her guard but Carter's voice was less intimidating than it had been the previous night.

Alice was nowhere to be seen on Saturday but that changed Sunday morning.

Rodney was up early this Sunday morning, earlier than normal as he had promised George Hurley a ride to JFK airport. George's wife was now on the Cape visiting Helen, Rodney's ex-wife, and George was left to his own devices. He had to catch an early flight to Texas to take care of a family emergency. As the only direct flight that he could get that early was out of JFK that is where he needed to be. He had been contacted by his Texas family only that Saturday night. As he could not put his normal limo service in place he called Rodney. Rodney would do it but he needed some money for the car and tolls. George would wind up paying Rodney the same amount that he paid his limo service minus the tip, so it worked out for both. Rodney was not one to simply do favors, money was always involved.

At 6:30 this Sunday morning Jake could hear the tortured Porsche struggle to back out of the driveway and then have it's gear ground as Rodney moved down the street to the Hurley's. Mostly still asleep Jake just winced as the car, now in his dreams, called out for his help. As Jake fell back into a deep sleep he dreamed of a Porsche being brutalized. It was being brutalized over the roadway under the apartments after crossing the George Washington Bridge. And then it got beat up at the start of the Cross Bronx Expressway before turning off to go past Yankee Stadium and head to the Tri-Borough Bridge. He faded away in his sleep now in the passenger seat of the Porsche unable to talk to his older brother behind the wheel in order to tell him what he was doing wrong. It was a frustrating dream as he was not even noticed in the right hand seat as he tried fruitlessly to prevent harm coming to the car.

Birdie was busy getting cozy again after Rodney slipped out of bed and she was falling back into a deep sleep as George was getting into the Porsche. Rodney figured he'd be home again within an hour and a half this early on Sunday.

George Hurley, a large man having played linebacker in the Top Ten as a younger man, squeezed into the right hand seat after Rodney had put his short trip bag into the front baggage compartment.

As he closed the door and settled in, Rodney put the car in gear and moved to the end of the block before turning right and then right again to get onto Lydecker Street and then to head up the hill to the George Washington Bridge.

"So Rodney, you still have 'Grimhild' living in your house?" asked George with a smile already knowing the answer.

"Who?" returned Rodney partly paying attention to driving and partly paying attention to George and not really paying attention to either.

"Oh nobody," said George with a laugh, "just someone out of Norse mythology, my little joke. Nice nose by-the-way. Will that thing ever heal? It's nasty," he said not really expecting an answer as he tried to settle into the seat as best he could so he could start to contemplate his family emergency.

Rodney just grunted in return to the nose comment not questioning the 'Norse mythology'.

As they drove onto the George Washington Bridge, clear of traffic, Birdie finally found deep sleep back at the house. She was deep in sleep but it was a restless sleep and strangely partly in black & white and partly in color. She heard a voice that sounded like Rodney's son V but it wasn't quite him and it was whispering, 'it's a woman not a man and she is in league with the devil, beware'.

Birdie found herself in a room with a presence and she could not get out of the room. She heard a demonic giggle, a guttural giggle and she tried to wake herself but she couldn't and the more she tried to move and shake herself awake the more deeply guttural and demonic the giggle became.

As Birdie broke the hold of her dream she started to wake but the giggle did not go away with the coming of full consciousness, instead it grew in intensity and clarity. As her eyes opened they automatically fell on the large overstuffed chair off to the left of the bed next to the bedroom window looking out on the side yard. There was movement in the chair and as Birdie's eyes focused and her mind became alert she started to feel her vulnerability, as she lay on the bed completely naked this warm morning.

She felt vulnerable and became too frightened to move as she focused on the woman whose 'church' this was reclining in the chair with the bedroom door having been left wide open upon her entry.

Alice was reclined wearing nothing but her semi-sheer white dressing gown which lay open to either side of her while she moved her left hand between her legs and held the church scepter-like crosier in her right hand, which to Birdie looked like an ax. She was smiling with pleasure as she said, "I am the devil," then she giggled demonically with a grunt and a turn of her head, then a look back at Birdie now paralyzed and frozen to the sheets with fear. "Ah, your hair is long and dark like THE MOTHER OF ALL," and she groaned and moved her head up with her eyes closed as she had an orgasm followed by decreasing tremors. As she finished her head came back down and her eyes set on the frozen Birdie and glared with joy as she giggled, reminding Birdie of the Exorcist and bringing her fully alive from her previously frozen state.

At just before seven that morning the Luger household, as it was, was awoken by an earth shattering scream. Oliver was up as Jake came out of his dream before the Porsche ran into a bridge girder after hitting someone or something that let out a loud scream. Kate was up bleary eyed after a late night of reading.

Jack was up before V and in his room within seconds, "What the hell was that?"

V leaning on his elbow in bed was still processing the noise and coming awake when he muttered jokingly, "Maybe it's Son of Sam."

"Funny," said Jack with concern, "I've never heard anything like that, not even in a movie, not even the church scream."

"Ah, Jeez, it's probably Carter scaring Birdie, I'll check."

Carter had been in a fitful sleep and the scream strangely enough calmed him and he fell into a deep sleep.

Before V was up Alice's door closed quietly behind her and Birdie was up and standing naked in one spot screaming again repetitively now that Alice had left.

As V came out of his room there was Jake, barefoot in torn jeans and a grey t-shirt, "What the hell V?" he questioned, the screams having already stopped.

"I don't know, it's coming from Dad's room and the door is open, I'll follow you," V said with a smile.

"You're brave."

"I'm smart," corrected V with a smile.

At that moment Jack came out in a bathrobe, just in time for another scream which froze all three of them to the spot in the hall where they were each standing.

"Oh, nice, you decided to join us," said V to Jack.

"No, I'm staying here."

They still hadn't moved when Kate came down the last of the steps to the second floor with Oliver behind her. Kate was dressed in her gardening clothes of old jeans and a polo shirt.

"Hasn't anyone gone in there yet?" Kate asked the obvious more as a scolding to the three Lugers, as another scream came from the room.

With that scream Kate was off towards the room with Oliver, Jake, V and now Jack following.

When Kate reached the door she saw Birdie just standing next to the bed naked, hunched over and using her arms to cover her breasts and her hands to cover and protect herself between her legs as though she had been violated. She was just staring at the overstuffed chair by the window in fear and not screaming now as she sensed Kate's presence.

Kate grabbed a bathrobe from the wooden chair at the foot of the bed and walked over trying to calm Birdie, "Birdie, it's me Kate. It's okay, it's okay, I'm here," she said in a calm soothing voice as she wrapped Birdie in the robe.

Everyone was now in the room.

"I don't think we need an audience," admonished Kate as she held the robe around Birdie who started to calm down.

"It was Son of Sam, she's a demon woman, it's Son of Sam in this house, it's Son of Sam," repeated Birdie.

V turning to Jack said, "I told you."

"You told him what?" asked Kate as it was heard clear as a bell.

"Son of Sam, I told him it was probably Son of Sam," said V and he smiled.

"Out, all three of you and you too Oliver," she said finishing by looking down at Oliver who could tell by her tone that he needed to go.

As the three of them left, with Jake calling Oliver to back up Kate's command, Birdie whispered to Kate as she stared off into the distance, "She was rubbing herself. She's a devil, she was going to kill me. She had an ax."

"Come sit down Birdie," said Kate. And as Birdie sat on the bed Kate opened the blinds more to let the morning sun flood in and change the mood.

Kate returning to the bed sat and said, "Tell me what happened, you're okay now and the boys are outside your door so no one can hurt you."

And perfectly timed Oliver barked outside the door as he saw the white cat outside of Alice's door wanting to get in. The boys turning in the direction of Oliver's bark saw the door open a crack for the cat to enter then close again. They just looked at each other, putting it all together.

"Christ," was all that Jake said.

"No, apparently an active member of the Exorcist cast," said V as he smiled.

"I have no idea what she did but I tell you, I'm locking my door," whispered Jake while they were still in the hall not too far from Alice's door.

"I think maybe I should head back up to the Cape," added Jack with a humorous smile, "This is getting too weird for me."

"We'll let Kate take care of it, anyone want any coffee?" asked Jake.

"Sounds good," said both V and Jack one right after the other. The thought of getting off the floor and into the kitchen sounded like the perfect out from the immediate situation.

Kate calmed Birdie but Birdie was having no more of the Lugers'. As far as she was concerned she had slept three different nights in a house with two mad people, one of whom could be the Son of Sam if not both working together. That was it, she could not pack fast enough.

Kate tried to get her to wait until Rodney returned but that wasn't going to happen, she wanted a ride to the nearest bus back into Manhattan.

As it was Sunday, and the bus schedules were sketchy, Kate drove Birdie and her hurriedly packed bag to Fort Lee and one of the many buses crossing the bridge.

While Kate was driving Birdie to the bus Rodney was

stuck in unexpected traffic on the Van Wyck Expressway not even a third of the way home. Birdie would be across the George Washington Bridge and back in Manhattan long before Rodney neared the bridge trying to return to New Jersey. Alice was in her room or at least the boys thought so. Her birds were not on Henry's 'perch' but this did not necessarily mean that she was not home. Although it usually seemed to be the case, recently, that she was out when they were not visible either flying or perched someplace in the open, usually atop the antlers.

Chapter 13

After Birdie's Flight

Sunday, July 17th

Kate was back at the house, still well before Rodney who had now been gone two hours.

She explained to Jake what Birdie had told her.

"See, I told you, she's demonic," said Jake.

"Well, she's something and you'd better tell Rodney. Birdie said she had an ax but I think she may have imagined a great deal of it thanks to you and V."

"Whaddaya mean thanks to V and me?"

"V fed her imagination and you and Jack backed it. One thing seems to be certain, Alice was in the room staring at her in bed, everything else is up for debate," said Kate.

"I don't think there's any debate when it comes to Alice, distance is the best approach..........and a knife under the pillow. And by-the-way, Jack and I were made just as nervous about that talk of long brown hair. Blame Carter he's the one who '...killed her' ," Jake finished as he smiled.

Kate just smiled. "You are a child and you've watched too much Hitchcock."

Jake just smiled again.

A half hour later, while brushing Oliver on the third floor, Jake heard the tortured Porsche return. He could almost hear the car breath a sigh of relief at being finished for the moment when it again stalled at the head of the driveway as Rodney forgot to down shift.

"Ah well, here we go," sighed Jake to Kate who was reading on the bed with a cup of coffee and an English muffin at her side on the bed stand. A nice Sunday breakfast was not the order of this day as Jake got up to head downstairs and talk with Rodney about Birdie's departure.

Oliver sensing something decided to stay with Kate who noticed. "Ah smart dog," she said and laughed as Jake headed down the stairs.

Rodney was actually checking his blood sugar at the kitchen table when Jake walked in. He did not check his blood sugar as consistently as he should but he was this morning as his schedule was thrown off.

"How was the ride?" Jake asked with a smile knowing how the car probably got beat up on the New York roads.

"Ah, okay, the VanWyck backed up for a long time. Thought with it being Sunday I'd be home faster," said Rodney as he got up and headed to the refrigerator to get some insulin.

Jake just sat and waited while Rodney injected himself in the fat just above his right hip then lowering his shirt, "Is Birdie up yet?"

"Oh, yeah," said Jake, "a while ago."

"Where is she?"

"Back in Manhattan."

"Oh, ok," said Rodney putting the cap on the needle to dispose of it. "What?" he asked as it connected.

"Kate took her to the bus into New York"

"What?"

"Kate took her to the bus, she was a little frightened."

"Frightened of what?"

"Well, she woke up to find Alice sitting in the chair across from her," said Jake waving his half cast to illustrate 'across from'.

"That's ridiculous."

"Hey, I'm just repeating what I heard."

"Why would Alice do that, she pays her rent on time."

'A non sequitur', was the thought that came to Jake's mind. Their father used to say that surrounded by other words depending on the situation when one of them said something that made no sense or was not connected in any way to the discussion at hand. Rodney was a living example of the Non Sequitur.

"I don't know; someone who pays their rent wouldn't just go into someone else's room and sit in a chair and look at them naked on the bed, makes no sense," said Jake in sarcastic follow-up shaking his head subtly at his older brother, as his back was turned, while he put the insulin back in the refrigerator.

"No, it doesn't," Rodney said turning to face Jake sitting in one of the kitchen table chairs, then thinking, "Naked?"

"Yeah apparently she was naked and Alice was looking at her and touching herself."

"Ah, nah, that's just too much," said Rodney now back at the refrigerator looking for something quick to eat; 'short of opening a can' thought Jake.

"Suit yourself but Birdie's back in the city."

"She probably just got homesick, I'll call her later. Have you seen any bananas around?"

"Look above you, on the top of the fridge," directed Jake.

"Oh, okay, good," said Rodney reaching for a bunch of bananas and ripping one off.

"Let me ask you, do you find Alice a bit strange?"

With his mouth overfilled with too large of a bite of banana Rodney tried to answer before getting the banana in his mouth to a manageable amount before he did so. "Whaddaya mean?"

"Jeez, finish chewing a bit first."

Rodney just laughed as he hurriedly swallowed the last of

the large chunk of banana he had bitten off.

"Did you happen to notice that she has a large cross in her room somewhat reminiscent of the one we would see in St. Paul's every Sunday."

"No, not really. And so, she's religious," Rodney said with a smaller amount of food in his mouth and now going after another banana from the bunch on top of the refrigerator before he had finished the first.

"Did you happen to notice the robe that she wears, similar to the one Reverend McGee used to wear with a big cross on it?"

"No, not really," said Rodney looking at Jake past his bandaged nose and chewing.

"The doves, have you noticed the doves?"

"Is that what they are? The one's on the deer antlers?" Everyone knew who Henry was except Rodney and Henry belonged to Rodney. He had been a gift to Rodney from their late uncle who Jake had been named after.

"That's right, they're hers."

"No, I saw them sitting in the tree outside her window when she moved in, they probably just flew in through the open French doors."

"Whatever you say but be prepared when you call Birdie, and you may want to do that sooner rather than later," said Jake.

"I will, I will," Rodney finished as the footsteps of several people bounced down the last flight of the back steps and into the hallway between the kitchen and the main entrance hall.

Led by V, Jack and Sally came into the kitchen. When V and Jack saw their father stuffing down his second banana just below his bandaged nose, and having experienced what they had that morning, they just couldn't help themselves and started laughing.

The whole joke of it hit Jake too and he started laughing. Sally smiled but looked dumbfounded and Rodney just smiled and laughed in short laughs, in simpatico with the three other Lugers, not realizing everything that they were really laughing about.

"What is it with all of you? You laugh at the slightest thing," said Sally smiling. This only fueled them more. They could not stop laughing now about this comment and everything that had happened over the weekend while their father, and brother, continued to stuff more banana into his mouth below that ridiculous looking bandage.

"I'm going to have to have brunch alone. I can't go out with you hyenas," said Sally, which just served to throw more gas on it as their laughter increased even more.

Oliver could be heard coming down the stairs, now that there was laughter.

"The big O is going to join us," indicated Jake through the laughter as he could hear Oliver's 150 pound frame hopping down the steps.

Oliver was in the kitchen in the next moment having squeezed by Sally in the doorway, who simply said, "Excuse me," as she looked down at him and got out of his way.

At 150 pounds, and big and black with expectant eyes and tail wagging, Oliver walked into the middle of the kitchen. As he did so he just perpetuated the laughter with his shaved and wounded shoulder standing out as the Luger clan gathered in the kitchen. Kate would be next, to complete the circle.

It wasn't more than thirty seconds before Kate showed up behind Sally to view the spectacle of four men who just could not stop laughing.

"It sounds like an asylum down here. It can't be that funny, whatever it is."

"Oh yes it can," said V through laughter.

Sally shaking her head said, "They won't stop, maybe we should go to brunch and leave them behind."

"Not a bad idea," agreed Kate.

As they started to calm down a bit Sally just had to say it, "You might set off Alice and her cat." And they went off again.

"It's better just not to say anything, they'll run out of steam soon," said Kate.

"Rodney, did Jake tell you about Birdie?" asked Kate. Now V was up against the wall holding his stomach he was laughing so hard and Jake was having a hard time catching his breath.

"Oh God," said Kate turning to Sally. "Let's leave them to it, we're not getting anywhere," continued Kate as she touched Sally on the shoulder and started to head to the den with Sally following, the laughter fading in the background behind them.

"It's like they're drunk," said Sally now alongside Kate as they walked towards the French doors and the side veranda.

"Worse than that, they're having an idiot episode," said Kate with a smile as Sally laughed, and they stepped onto the veranda.

"Don't you start," admonished Kate.

"No, don't worry. When will they stop?" asked Sally as they both started to take a seat on the wicker love seat to look out at the yard.

"When they can't breath anymore," said Kate as Oliver came out to the veranda after them.

"Couldn't take it anymore, huh boy," said Sally, and Kate smiled.

Jake was the first one to escape a few minutes later, out of breath.

Still laughing to himself he walked out on the veranda.

"You're not going to bring that out here are you?" asked Kate.

"I can't anymore my stomach's hurting."

"My pride would be hurting," said Kate with an appreciative smile.

"Maybe we can make it to brunch anyway," said Sally.

"If they ever stop," said Jake.

"Did you tell him about Birdie?" asked Kate.

"Sure did, but he didn't believe the Alice part."

"Afraid of losing the rent?"

"I don't even think he thinks it out that clearly. His thinking is 'that doesn't make sense, why would somebody do that?' "

"You mean it doesn't make sense in his head therefore it isn't. Wait till he wakes up to find her sitting in that over-stuffed chair grinning at him early in the morning," said Kate.

Jake shivering said, "I'd be up and gone."

"She's just a little off, that's all."

"I'd say," said Sally, "I saw her at the pool, it was a little scary with that big cross and long candle and all."

"See", said Jake looking at Kate, "another sane person here."

"You make it seem as though she's supernatural and part of the Devil, and all of the negative spirituality that goes with it. She's just a young woman with different ideas," Kate finished just as they heard a flutter of wings and Jake, sitting in the chair opposite the love seat, looked up.

Just landing on Henry's antlers were the two doves.

"Oh, Christ, she's out," whispered Jake looking somber faced at Kate and Sally who had heard the wings fluttering as well.

Oliver, who had laid down in the same place he always did to Kate's right, sat up abruptly with ears perked. He remembered that the fluttering had come before the cat had clawed him, Pavlov.

"Stay you little fornicator," Jake could hear Alice say as she stood outside her door talking down at her cat. Jake, now sitting in one of the wicker chairs and facing the opening to the veranda, could clearly hear all of the sounds coming from the house.

"Uh-oh," cringed Jake, "she's coming down the stairs."

Oliver, hearing her coming down, stayed right where he was and actually moved up closer to Kate.

"What is wrong with the two of you," Kate said with humor in her voice as she looked at Jake while putting her arm around Oliver.

Sally just sat there listening for what might happen behind her on the other side of the wall.

Alice walked into the den with Jake sitting rigidly in the

wicker chair bathed by the morning sunlight as though he were waiting for the executioner to pull the lever. As he was facing the French doors and the den he got a glimpse of Alice. "Jesus," he whispered more to himself.

At least Alice was dressed and not in red leather this time but black leather pants and a purple top. It reminded Jake of the funeral bunting that he had seen outside the town's fire department when one of their old members had died at age ninety-two. 'Funeral colors, God' thought Jake.

He just froze in his seat as Sally listened and Kate watched him from the love seat with curiosity and a smile to see what would happen next.

Alice paid no attention to Jake as she took something out of her right 'watch pocket' as the other pockets were too tight. Jake watched as she put something on her right shoulder, which he could not see as she was facing the fireplace and Henry, where the birds were perched. As she did so she made bird noises.

As the two doves flew to her shoulder and to the mix of sunflower and millet seeds that she had laid there she turned one quarter turn to her left, and looked directly at Jake with piercing eyes and giggled. She then turned left again and headed back to the stairs and her room.

Jake remained frozen until she was well up the stairs as Kate continued to watch him with curiosity waiting for him to say something.

"Whad she do?" asked Sally first.

"Fed the birds," said Jake now looking at Sally.

"See, not so bad," said Kate.

"Yeah, well you didn't see the look that she gave me," Jake said still hearing laughter coming from the kitchen.

Jake heard her door close and almost as fast as it had closed it opened again and then closed again as Alice headed down the stairs once more.

"Uh-oh, here she comes again. What the hell did she forget, she got the birds?" said Jake staring ahead again.

As Alice made the turn in the main hall to head for the

front door she stopped, turned her head, with her eyes landing on Jake, and smiled before turning to head for the door
again. Jake could swear that she rotated her head.

"Jeez."

"What?" asked Kate with a laugh.

"She just left."

"So you both can calm down," she said to Jake.

And turning to Oliver and hugging him she added, "Don't
follow his lead, he sees things."

"Oh funny, I tell you, she's dangerous, wait and see........,"
said Jake just as Alice came even with the porch they were on
heading towards the downhill from the same side of the street
as the house. She was close enough to hear if anyone was
talking loud enough.

He watched her until she was almost out of sight at the crest
of the hill before turning back to Kate and Sally. "Great, she
probably heard that."

"And what?" asked Kate with a laugh.

"Who knows, she may turn her sights on us with it's 'her
church' in mind."

"She is creepy," added Sally.

"Well, she's gone for the day," said Kate.

The laughing had stopped and the boys voices, along with
Rodney's, were in the hall heading towards the veranda when
Rodney, barely audible, said to the boys, "I guess I should call
Birdie." And he quietly headed up the stairs Alice had just
descended.

"Good, now maybe we can go to brunch; finally," said Sally hearing the voices without the uncontrolled laughter.

V was the first out on the veranda with a big smile.

"Have you seen Alice yet?" V asked all.

"Just did, she left down the hill."

"Oh good," said V relieved, "I didn't feel like running into
her."

"Did she see you," asked V.

"Yeah, she looked right into my eyes after collecting her
birds from Henry. She called her cat a 'little fornicator'."

V started to laugh.

"Oh no you don't, this girl wants to go to brunch and if you start that again she'll go hungry," said Kate.

"Okay, okay," said V, "do you two wanna come?"

"It would be nice but no, I think we're fine," said Kate.

"Yeah and I've really got to finish this article," added Jake.

"Where's your dad?" asked Kate.

"Went to call Birdie," said Jack.

"Good," said Kate.

"Well, have a good time and try to keep the laughter on an even keel," added Kate as Sally got up and they started to head out.

"Yeah," said V with a smile before he followed Jack and Sally out through the den.

The rest of Sunday was quiet and Birdie would not soon be back, if ever.

Chapter 14

The New Dynamic

Saturday, July 23rd

It was just less than a week after Birdie's departure on the following Saturday that Rodney, in a by-the-way manner, let Jake know that there would be a new tenant and that she would be coming in the next day.

"Where is she staying Rodney?" asked Jake with some concern as they stood in the kitchen while Rodney looked around in the refrigerator.

"Oh, in the train room," said Rodney subconsciously trying to disguise the room's location.

"In the train room? Do you mean the room across the hall from us where the train that belonged to me was going to go, years ago, for Jack to play with?"

"Yes, and they were my trains and I had a right to sell them," said Rodney not turning from looking in the refrigerator.

"No they weren't and no you didn't. That American Flyer number 2-9-3 New York, New Haven and Hartford Railroad Company engine from the fifties was mine. Dad bought it for me when I was born and the other two belonged to Tom and Brian."

"You're wrong. All of them belonged to me, always did."

"Where do you get this stuff from that you make up?"

"It's just the truth that's all," said Rodney turning to look at his 'baby brother' while starting to get angry without a drink in him.

"Well, that's done and calling it a train room is a misnomer."

"I really don't care," said Rodney turning his attention back to the refrigerator.

"Apparently. Now what about this person moving in?"

"She's a student at NYU staying for summer school I think she said; a stage student."

"You mean theater."

"Whatever, she'll be here tomorrow," said Rodney still looking inside of the refrigerator.

"How did you find her? I'm sort of afraid to hear."

"I put an ad on one of their bulletin boards."

"Gee, no one out of the ordinary has called here in the past couple of weeks that I know of."

"They were calling my office number."

"How many when you say 'they'?"

"I don't know, about ten," said Rodney trying to think while still looking around the refrigerator forgetting now what he was looking for.

"They must've loved that on your floor. What about the other nine?"

"No one wanted to pay what I was asking until she called."

"Who's 'she' who called?"

"Aidall or something like that."

"Oh, good. Did you tell her about Carter reliving WWII, Alice playing the Exorcist and the birds flying around the house? Did you tell her about us at the end of the hall?" asked Jake more frustrated with his older brother's inability to properly pronounce the names of people and places because he did not pay attention.

"I don't know what there is to tell. I just described the house and where it was and she agreed. A friend of hers is driving her out tomorrow," said Rodney as he gave up looking in the refrigerator and closed the door.

"Well, I can't wait until someone tells Alice that another mortal is moving into 'her church'."

"What's that mean?" asked Rodney now looking at Jake but not fully paying attention as he was still thinking about what it was that he had come to the kitchen to get in the first place.

"Nothing, really. We'll see, but I'm sure that you won't see it even if you bump into it."

"I don't know what you're talking about," said Rodney as he opened the refrigerator again and pulled out an opened can of Chef Boyardee and grunted a laugh as he did so.

"Great lunch," said Jake looking at Rodney holding the can and pulling a fork out of the dish dryer next to the sink.

"What?" asked Rodney as he turned with the fork already dipping into the half full can.

"Nothing," said Jake. "I'll talk with you later," he added as he turned to head up the stairs to the third floor.

***

Well, Rodney did get the day right and Adelia showed up the next day at around 3:00 in the afternoon.

Jake, Kate and Zach had just returned 30 minutes earlier from brunch at Kitty Hawk's in the city and were on the veranda when the front doorbell rang.

"Oh God, are the doves on Henry? I forgot to check," said Jake knowing who was at the door as the bell was never rung.

Zach with scotch in hand laughed. "This should be good."

"It's not funny, you don't have to sleep here."

"Don't worry, I didn't see the doves," said Kate.

They could all hear Rodney clear his throat as he crossed the main hall to answer the door.

"Aidall?" asked Rodney after opening the door.

Jake grimaced when he heard him knowing that he had just badly mispronounced the girl's name even though he himself didn't know what it was.

They couldn't hear her reply but they heard Rodney say, "Oh Adelia, ok."

"You think he'd say that he was sorry for butchering the poor girl's name," commented Jake.

Zach just smiled and Kate said, "It's just the way he is."

"Yeah, I don't know how we're related."

"Should we go out and meet her and see if she needs any help? She is going to be our neighbor for better or for worse."

"Yeah," said Jake as he got up and Zach and Kate followed in suit.

Adelia was just stepping into the main hall wearing a day pack and carrying a large suitcase that she put down in order to shake Rodney's hand as Jake, Kate and Zach entered from the den. Rodney was dressed in his now 'pink' tennis whites, which must have impressed his new tenant along with the smaller protective bandage now on his mostly healed nose.

Adelia turned and smiled at the three of them and then, with her right hand now free, turned back to Rodney to shake his hand.

Adelia was striking and Zach was awestruck as he lowered his glass from chest level to his side. She was 5'10" slim and shapely, and athletically built but yet feminine in all respects.

Her hair was long and black two thirds of the way down her back and her eyes were a piercing blue even more stunning than Sally's which was amazing. In a word they were penetrating, so much so that they pulled you in and were just short of being overbearing. Her skin was clear and milk white with just a touch of rose to give her a healthy vibrant appearance.

With the protective tape on his nose more than obvious Rodney said, "This is Aidella", not bothering to introduce the three of them.

Jake hearing the butchered name again and realizing   that

Adelia was now just putting up with it said, "Adelia, I'm happy to meet you." As he said this Jake extended his left hand with a smile holding back the half casted right hand, "I'm Jake and this is Kate, and the one with his mouth open is Zach."

She smiled. "Nice to meet you all." The semi-bandaged nose and half cast hand connected in her subconscious but went no further.

"We're right across the hall from you," said Kate. "Oh, and this is Oliver," added Kate looking down and rubbing Oliver's head as he had been quietly by her side since they walked in from Manhattan.

"He's beautiful, is he a Great Pyrenees?"

"No, he's a Newfy," said Zach finally getting his tongue.

"A Newfoundland," added Kate seeing Adelia's confusion.

"Oh, he's beautiful," she said concentrating her gaze on his left side which still looked shaved although the hair had grown enough so it wasn't just white skin.

Noticing this Jake said, "Cat."

"What?"

"A cat scratched him."

"Do you have a cat?"

"No," answered Jake.

"Oh good. I'm allergic and they also frighten me when they sneak around," said Adelia with a warm smile.

"How about doves?" said Zach smiling with a grin.

"What?" asked Adelia now looking at Zach.

"Oh, nothing," said Jake. "Can we help you carry anything up?"

"That would be great. I have a friend here too to help, she drove me."

"The more the merrier," said Zach as he smiled.

Rodney, who had been standing there looking impatient finally said, "Good, that's settled, do you have the check for the deposit and one month?"

Jake rolled his eyes.

"Oh, yes, I almost forgot," said Adelia removing her day pack. Setting it on the floor she knelt over it and retrieved a small beaded purse that looked to Jake as though it had once been owned by a flapper from the twenties. She pulled out a folded check, put everything back in the pack, and stood to hand Rodney the check.

Instead of just taking the check, thanking her and talking to her about the house he looked closely at the once folded piece of paper to make sure that it was the correct amount. Then, satisfied, he looked up and said, "Ok, well I see that you're taken care off, I left a key on the kitchen table for you. Gotta get to The Club." And with this Rodney was off through the kitchen and out the back door where he was going to start to torture his Porsche once more, forgetting that his new tenant had a car in the driveway. But they soon heard about it as Rodney's voice came up from the bottom of the driveway and in through the front door, "CAN YOU MOVE THAT CAR, I HAVE TO GO............. OKAY GOOD."

He must have said the last part when he saw Adelia's friend move to get behind the wheel.

He was fast getting to his car. They were all still in the main hall just restarting the conversation. And they had just started talking about the location of the room with Adelia while in anticipation of meeting her friend when Rodney had yelled out from the bottom of the driveway.

"Real class," muttered Jake so Kate could hear.

Kate nudged Jake's foot with her own and then smiled at him. He got the message.

They headed out to the front porch leaving Adelia's bag in the main hallway. They were in time to see Rodney stall the Porsche directly in line with the porch before getting it out of the driveway and headed in the opposite direction of the hill leading to St. Paul's. As he left, Adelia's friend pulled back in and stopped even with the porch.

They all met Joan seconds later. She had driven Adelia in her green Mercedes station wagon. It was a sleek style and they were all impressed as none of them had ever seen a Mercedes station wagon before. Her father's connections with the car company had made it the first of its model in the United States. Joan also seemed not to be concerned about money when it came up a couple of times while they moved Adelia to the third floor that day. Unlike Adelia, Joan was very plain in most ways but she seemed to have a strength about her that Jake could not quite put his finger on.

There seemed to be an uneasy tension between the two friends as they worked to get Adelia settled. It was strange. One could tell that they were good friends but Joan seemed to be a bit commanding and angry at times and then reticent at others while Adelia was complacent at times but yet apprehensive at other times. It was as though they had suffered the death of a mutual friend and were trying to come to terms with it.

Jake had retrieved Adelia's key from the kitchen and showed her the idiosyncrasies of the shared bathroom between the two rooms.

They had asked her if she wanted to have dinner out with them that night but she had declined in a way that made one feel wonderful for simply having asked. She was going to have dinner with Joan and asked if they could suggest a restaurant close by, which they did. Zach was heart-struck.

Monday, July 25th

It was not until the next late afternoon that Adelia started to get acquainted with the other inhabitants of the Lugers'.

Jake was writing at just past five in the afternoon when he heard the boys below him. Hearing them he decided to get up and head across the hall to see Adelia, who was cleaning her room and straightening it out as best she could.

"Adelia, sorry to bother you," said Jake having first knocked on the front of the open door.

"Oh no, that's fine. We're neighbors, right!?"

"That we are. My two nephews are home and it might be a good time to introduce you and I think you'll like them. You'll also notice that we're all relatively close in age."

Oliver followed them as they went down the steps to the two adjoined rooms. Jake knocked on V's door just to the right of the steps and the door opened immediately as though he were waiting. He opened it while looking behind himself in the direction of the adjoining room and answering Jack. "LA," said V looking in Jack's direction then turning his face toward Jake at the door.

"LA what?" asked Jake.

"LA in the Series against the Yankees."

"If it is LA the Yankees will take them in six," said Jake.

"They'll sweep in four with Munson, Reggie, Nettles, Rivers and Guidry," guaranteed V.

"Oh, nice to add one pitcher in there."

V smiled. "Got to." Then his eyes caught Adelia and he was struck.

Jake turned to the side as he said, "V this is Adelia. Adelia this is V for short or fifth in the line of Rodney Lugers."

V frowned. "Just V without explanation is fine."

Smiling, Adelia extended her hand and said, "Too bad it wouldn't be the Brooklyn Dodgers."

V looked at Jake and smiled as he extended his hand to Adelia. "I like her."

"Hey Jack get in here and meet our new neighbor, she's a Dodgers fan," shouted V and he smiled.

"I didn't say that," said Adelia as she shook V's hand.

Just as Jack showed up behind V, Carter came around the corner from the direction of his room in his tennis whites and mumbling to himself.

"Uh-oh," said Jack just as Carter came up to them.

As he passed with a large receipt in his hand he mumbled, "...goddamned Bea, goddamned dress, goddamnit, goddamnit."

He did not even recognize Jake and this young woman in the hall talking with V as he walked right past and headed down the stairs to the kitchen and the phone.

Adelia just stood there listening as he continued to mumble while he headed down the stairs to the kitchen.

"Don't mind him," said Jake, "He mumbles a lot and Bea's his partner in a store they own, or he owns really."

"Yeah and he sees Japs too," added V smiling.

"What?" asked Adelia.

"Oh nothing," said Jake. "But get used to seeing him in tennis whites, even sometimes when it's freezing out. It's his favorite wardrobe."

"And don't speak Japanese around him if you know it," put in V.

Jake just frowned at him and changing the subject, "So, are you a Yankee fan?"

"Grew up with three older brothers in Connecticut who were addicted to baseball and they dragged me along. Luckily they were Yankee fans and not Red Sox fans."

"Hey, I've got a Mantle signed ball, ya wanna see it," said V.

"I'd love to," said Adelia with an enthusiastic smile.

From the kitchen came, " GODDAMNIT BEA, I TOLD YOU NOT TO BUY THAT DRESS TOO!"

V smiled at Adelia about what they were hearing and said, "At least he's not talking to Japs. Come on in."

And Adelia walked in followed by Jake with no question about what 'Japs' meant.

"Where'd you get this?" asked Adelia now looking at the ball through its protective capsule.

"Me," said Jake, Adelia turning to look at him. "I got it when I was just a little kid and he lived close by. I went to his house with two of my older brothers to get their ball signed. We were met at the screen door by a tall woman, at least she was to me at the time. When we told her what we wanted she told us to wait then returned a few seconds later, opened that squeaky screen door, handed us a ball and told us that we could copy the signature off of it. My brothers just looked at each other and handed the ball back. We had only one good ball to try to get signed because the other two were so worn they were covered in electrical tape. I still remember walking off that porch because my two older brothers were so dejected that it left an impression."

"So, how did you get the ball?" asked Adelia, now interested even more.

"A neighbor by the name of Rogers heard the story somehow and he gave me his ball."

"You're kidding?"

"No, amazing really. He had no kids so he felt for us and as my brothers weren't around I got the ball, that's why I gave it to V. Someone was nice enough to pass it on to me to enjoy so I gave it to V a couple of years ago and he'll do the same."

"Yeah, like give it to me," said Jack.

"I don't think so," said V with a smile.

"Jack, you got my draft card with all the Rangers signatures on it," and shaking his head and smiling he added, "except Giacomin who was afraid of defacing a draft card, which was pretty funny."

"Well, I'm a Ranger fan and a Giants fan as well," added Adelia.

"Great neighbor," said V with an oversized smile.

They talked for a short time and Adelia, it turned out, really knew her sports. They became so lost in it that they forgot to mention the fifth tenant in the house. Jake was actually trying to figure out a way of warning her without scaring her. So it was easy to have it slip away as they talked about other things although they could hear Carter now and again when he said 'BEA', as it was louder than the rest of what he had to say. It also helped that Oliver remained calm through Carter's tirade on the phone as he was familiar with it.

They were in the room for twenty minutes, or more, when Adelia said she had to get back upstairs to work on her room and said her good-byes while Jake and Oliver stayed behind.

Adelia left the room, by the same door that V had sat outside of to watch for Alice's leaving the house two weeks earlier, and she could hear the energetic conversation in the room fade when she stepped out into the hallway. As she closed the door behind her she heard Carter's voice grow louder from the kitchen and it didn't bother her having had it explained. But just as she pulled the door shut she felt a presence and saw movement out of the corner of her eye. It was down the hallway, which was now bright with the fading light of a late afternoon at the end of July.

The movement stopped as Adelia started to turn to look in its direction while hearing from the kitchen, "SEND THE GODDAMNED THINGS BACK!" As she turned, her eyes settled on a young woman in tight black leather pants and a black linen shirt to match. Her light hazel eyes were piercing and angry in appearance like a storm as they cut right through Adelia. They cut right through to the core of her being in an unsettling manner. Her stare froze on Alice for a brief moment unable to move until Alice ended it with what sounded to Adelia like a demonic giggle out of a bad horror movie. Alice then turned, turning the key in her door and entered her room. Adelia not being able to break her stare heard the flutter of what she thought were bat wings and then the door closed behind this woman in black. The event gave Adelia the shivers but she shook it off like she used to shake of getting hit in the shoulder by one of her brother's fast balls. Then she headed back up to the third floor leaving the now muffled laughter of the Lugers behind along with Carter's yelling.

Later that evening, while Kate was reading, Jake offered to show Adelia the yard and point out certain aspects of the neighborhood. He also offered to point out the different directions that she should walk in, in order to get to different sections of the downtown area depending on what she needed. She accepted the invitation with calm enthusiasm.

It was a beautiful night and Jake was able to get a better feel for Adelia. She was somewhat protective and did not stray too far from the protective shell that she had around herself. She was nice and congenial and easygoing, but protective.

Jake walked around the neighborhood with her pointing out where different people lived and what they were like and who they were just to give her a feel for everything. Then he walked her down the hill to St. Paul's and pointed out the two different avenues to get to the different sections of the town. While looking at the church he was reminded that he was thankful that Adelia had not run into Alice or at least not that he knew of. He decided not to tell her about Alice, just yet, even knowing that Alice had been home but had not apparently shown herself. He thought she might not appear to Adelia for a while. Maybe Alice was purposely keeping her distance for some reason, he thought.

They topped the hill coming back to the house under a waxing moon. It was just less than three quarters full and softly highlighted the Victorian neighborhood lined with old trees making the beauty of the place quite apparent. Neither one of them needed to comment while they shared it as they walked back towards the house.

As they stepped onto the front porch the door opened and there stood Alice in her red leather regalia eyes fixed on Adelia. Jake and Adelia froze as Alice squeezed by the right shoulder of Adelia who was just at the top of the front steps. As she passed Adelia she whispered loud enough for both of them to hear, "You are in my church and you are not welcome," then she giggled and skipped down the steps headed for the main street.

Adelia got the shivers again as Jake commented, "Oh don't worry about her, She's a kidder, although she does live here too."

"Well, she gives me the chills," said Adelia looking now at Jake.

"She gives you the chills!? Have you seen her before?"

"Earlier when I left your nephew's room, she was at the door at the end of the hall and she just looked at me and gave me that giggle."

"Great, well, I meant to tell you about her. She's a bit eccentric but harmless, somewhat like Carter," said Jake, but thinking that his KA-BAR knife was still next to his bed.

"It reminds me of the Exorcist."

"You too…..You see, that's what I see and V sees but Kate doesn't," said Jake, then thinking twice about having said it.

"Should I lock my door?"

"No, no. I meant that she reminds us of the Exorcist in a humorous way, I don't think her head is going to spin around or anything," said Jake with a smile.

"Well, I'm in theater and something tells me that there is something frighteningly real about her," said Adelia thinking as they still stood outside the front door. "And, by-the-way, what are Japs?"

"What?" asked Jake hoping that the question would go away.

"Japs! V mentioned it with regard to the man in tennis whites."

"Oh, Carter. He sees Japanese soldiers that aren't there once and awhile, it's really harmless."

"Why does he wear tennis whites all the time?"

"No one seems to know."

With a nervous smile Adelia asked, "Anything else I need to know?"

"Well, not really. Oh yeah, Alice has a white cat and I know you don't like cats but it rarely comes out of her room and she has two doves that occasionally perch on the deer head in the den."

With this Adelia laughed. "I thought they were bats when I first heard them."

They both laughed and the tension was broken. And the cat and the 'you are in my church' warning were forgotten, for the meantime.

Jake forgetting for a moment, as they were laughing, went for the front door with his right hand and bashed his half cast into the door frame right on the pinky jamming the knuckle with jarring pain. "Oh, Christ!" Then remembering Adelia was there, "Sorry, a little bit of pain," he said with tears in his eyes it hurt that much.

"How did that happen?" asked Adelia as Jake opened the door with his left hand.

"Long story and I don't want to bore you. I just sorta bumped into something."

"Oh,"said Adelia getting a quick flashback of Rodney's nose but not quite putting it together. "Were you in an accident with your brother?"

"Something like that, but we're okay."

Adelia just smiled as Jake stepped aside and let her in through the mud room and into the main hall.

Chapter 15

V Stakes Out The Church

Tuesday, July 26th

It was the next night, Tuesday night, that V decided to follow Alice to see if she would go to the church again so he could find out what she was really up to. He especially wanted to find out now, after hearing the story of her warning to Adelia. She was more than just creepy.

The moon was bright but thankfully not full when Alice left the house at around 9:00 in the evening. This time she was dressed in blue jeans and a white blouse, which was different. V stood back in the shadows of the garage watching for her to leave. He had waited only a half hour when she came off the front porch and headed for the street. Jack would stay home this time as V thought he could work better alone and, besides, she made Jack too nervous.

He knew where she was headed, or thought he did. He was only interested in her this night if she was headed to the church. So he waited until she had passed out of view in front of the house and headed for the hill before he ran to the corner of the house by the front stairs. He watched her until   she slipped below the crest of the hill. Then he slowly crossed the street to the right to get on the same flagstone sidewalk that she was on closest to the direction of the church, which was to the right below the hill.

He waited until the count of ten before cresting the hill himself and as he did he could see the form of Alice bear right, hugging the tree-line next to the flagstone walk. She was definitely headed for the church, so once again there was no rush. He again gave himself until the slow count of ten, 'one-Mississippi, 2-Mississippi, 3-Mississippi, 4.........' and then started to walk down the sidewalk in the direction of the church. As he cleared the tree-line he saw Alice, her white blouse lit like a neon sign in the moonlight, heading for the front of the church as she had that night that he and Jack had followed her. As he had on that night, he turned right up the adjoining street and ran to the far end of the church and around the far side until he had reached the front corner. At the corner he cautiously peered around and there was Alice tugging at the front door as she had that night with Jack and she again mumbled something out of frustration that sounded like a profanity. It was almost like a repeat of that first night that they had followed her.

As she turned the corner V stepped out and dashed for the front door. This was getting to be too familiar.

Again, V crept to the corner of the building just past the front door and tentatively peered around the corner. There was Alice, tugging on the side door in the manner she had on the night that V and Jack had followed her, as well as on the previous nights unknown to V. She tugged and V heard her say again, "Bastards, how dare you," and then she giggled a mischievous giggle as though she knew something no one else did, just as she had that first night that V had followed her. 'It was creepy', was all that V could think.

As she started out for the next corner V pulled his head back while remembering that the last time he had followed her she had stopped and looked back, although, luckily, she had not seen him. As things seemed to be repeating themselves, just as they had happened that night, he held back until he knew she would clear the corner after stopping to look back.

This night Alice did not stop to look back. She dashed around the corner going straight to the grate. Having had a great deal of practice over weeks she removed it adeptly, and quickly walked in replacing it behind her almost as though in one fluid movement.

When V thought he had given her enough time for that stop he had experienced the first time, along with enough time to have her go safely around the corner, he peered around his corner. Then seeing that it was clear he moved quickly to the far corner and then tentatively peered around it.

"Crap," he muttered. She was gone again. "Where the hell..........?"

His mind ran: Was she in the church? It had to be her creating that demonic sound the night that he and Jack had followed her. To confirm this V tracked back to the front of the church, sat on the front steps and waited just as he and Jack had. After ten minutes nothing, then, "I-I-I-I umph," followed by a pause then, "I-I-I-I umph" again.

"Jesus," muttered V as he looked up past the stone owl at the slats to the vents of the belfry knowing that this is where it had to come from, although the sound was playing tricks and was hard to triangulate.

"I-I-I-I umph," came again, this time followed by that full throated scream which had so unsettled Jack that first night and set V off following his mad dash back up the hill. "I-I-I-I umph," and another scream.

It was still unnerving even as V realized that it could only be Alice. It was unnerving in that the sound seemed to float above the church while sounding half human or 'half man and half woman', as Jack had said.

She had to be getting into the church someplace at the back of the building. But V just could not think where even though the back grate might be an obvious choice by   anyone not so intimately familiar with the outside of the church as was V. V did not notice the grate, as he had been passing it for most of his life so far. It was a part of the accepted scenery to him and nothing out of the ordinary.

There was only one way to try to figure out this mystery so V headed up the hill behind the church. He headed for a place near the hill's highest point. He headed for a spot which he knew would give him the best vantage point to view the entire back of the church but yet keep him concealed from anyone who might glance up the hill from down below. He would wait the entire night if need be.

While V was climbing back up the hill, and almost halfway to the top, Alice was climbing down the ladder past the initials 'R.L. 4/8/51' now covered over with the 'Devil's Trap'. As she did so she giggled deeply and uttered, "I fear no trap, I fear nothing," and she giggled again. This time, unlike in the past, she let out a primal scream, while on the ladder, which was loud enough that V, near the top of the hill under the waxing moon, thought he heard something. He stopped his climb briefly to listen again, but heard nothing and continued on.

There was nothing that Alice needed from the church this night. This night where she felt an exultancy she had never quite experienced before. She was in control of this church and her other church on the hill, even with the new addition.

She controlled this new woman like she controlled everything else thought Alice as she remembered the frozen expression that she had seen on Adelia's face at that first encounter when she was about to enter her room.

After entering the secret room behind the priest's closet, Alice immediately exited, pushed the stone wall section closed behind her and started to cross the secret room. Stopping halfway across the room she let out what would be a terrifying scream to anyone who could hear but to her the primeval scream was one of ecstasy, and control as she had never felt before. She lingered for a moment smiling at her self-stylized grandeur then proceeded across the room. For the first time in her many visits she started to investigate the walls with her flashlight wondering if there was more to the chamber and the passageway.

Just before entering the passageway, and to the left of the chamber, she noticed it. High up on the wall was a small cross etched into the stone but partially covered by the soot of time. As she crept closer, with curiosity, she could see a small set of initials under the cross which she could not make out. Leaning up against the wall to see the initials closer she pushed against it and felt a movement, as slight as it was, or at least she thought she did. Suddenly her feeling of exultant control was gone. She thought that she had known everything that there was to know about this church and this secret passageway, something that she thought no one else knew but she was wrong in both counts. Reverend McGee knew about the passageway as did the older parishioner but no one knew about what she was about to find.

She repeated her movement against the wall trying to pay attention to any discernable movement and there it was, the wall had a slight give to it. She pushed again with more force and felt the movement again. But she was not in the right place to gain maximum leverage to force more movement so she moved back a bit and laying her flashlight on the floor, pointing out towards the passageway, she pushed. Nothing.

She moved forward from where she had first pushed the wall and pushed again and there it was. Soot and over a century of dirt came down on her as the light filtered through it and another secret door moved without a sound other than the falling dirt.

It moved slightly and seemed to jam tight with the dirt of time. She stood and thought. Then she tried to push against the small portion of the wall that had started to protrude, from the opposite end that she had been pushing, trying to reverse what she had done. Again more dirt fell, darkening the light of the flashlight as the wall went back into place. She moved forward again to the point of the best leverage and pushed again. This time the door gave way with barely a sound while more soot and dirt came down on her. She swore, but this time under her breath as she was not really as sure of herself as she had been only moments earlier. The door seemed to be mounted on the same type of stone mechanism as the wall leading to the small room behind the priest's closet. It moved with a balanced ease as though with the help of a fulcrum and not at all representative of its actual weight.

As she stepped back from the settling dust and dirt, dusting herself off as she did so, she inadvertently kicked the back of the flashlight with her heel spinning it so that the light shown into the cavity behind the door.

Concentrating on the dirt that had soiled her white blouse, using the ambient light of the flashlight, Alice did not notice where that beam of light was falling until she finally looked up in the direction of the beam. She saw what looked like a familiar figure at the end of the beam of light as it filtered through the dirt filled air. As the dirt settled even more she could see that it was a wooden cross almost the same size as the one she had taken from this very church.

She was tentative, at first, after picking up the flashlight and moving across the threshold of the stone door which rose to about 6 feet. The door had moved enough towards its terminus to allow a third of the opening that it covered to be accessible. One adult at a time could pass through comfortably. The room was long more than it was deep. As she shined her light around the door she found a room maybe twenty feet long and ten feet deep. Spread on the floor was hay, which had long ago been trampled down and flattened. She quickly moved her flashlight back to the right hand far corner, the corner where her light had originally fallen and there it was, the wooden cross. As she walked closer she could see that something was carved into the wood where the cross arm of the cross intersected the vertical piece. She could see that the cross was finely fluted half the length from its center to the ends of the four tips. The edges had been planed down enough to take the 90 degree angle from them and soften them just short of rounding them.

Looking closely at the cross, and stepping onto a pile of left over masonry stone to do so, Alice could see the remnants of a familiar symbol in the unfluted center. It was similar to other crosses in the church, which would tell her that this was taken from the main church at some point in time.

Carved through the, mostly unrecognizable, symbol on the cross was the name 'LITTLE JIM' and under this was 1857 - June 1859.

At the moment Alice read this she started to lose her balance on the unsteady rock. She dropped her flashlight and fell forward as the pile of erratically shaped and broken stone that she was standing on tumbled down beneath her. Her legs went out from under her as she banged her knees on the pieces of stone masonry, and the stone floor, with her head crashing into the base of the wooden cross.

As she groped for the now extinguished flashlight with her right hand her left looked for a rock to steady itself on and found a smooth boulder. It oddly felt lighter than stone, thought Alice for a fraction of a second, as she searched for the light that had gone off when it dropped.

Finding the flashlight Alice shook it and moved the on/off switch back and forth and shook it again until the light returned.

Still leaning on the smooth boulder with her left hand Alice automatically shone the light on it, really without thinking because it felt different.

A loud scream came out of the secret Underground Railroad inner room. It was such a terrified scream that it made its way down the corridor, through the slats of the back grate and barely up the hill where V was now sitting.

V heard something, at least he thought he had. It was muted and he could not be sure but it sounded like a scream from the dead. It was different from the scream that sounded half man and half woman. This sound seemed, for a brief moment, to be a women's scream of surprise and fear similar to what one might hear in a horror movie, but still very faint.

It was just one muted and horrified scream out of the moonlit dark but enough to get V's adrenaline running again while making the small hairs on the back of his neck stand up. 'What was going on?' He would stay and watch.

Alice, having removed her hand quickly from the smooth boulder like object, found herself sitting on the stone floor frozen in fear with the flashlight shining unwaveringly on the small skull. It was the skull of a small child no more than two years old who had died more than a 100 years before.

This was not an adult but a child and it completely unnerved Alice to the point that her own scream scared her. Her world of control and dominance was turned upside down. She was looking at the remains of the child of Big Jim and Sarah. The boy had been their only child and their movement through the Underground Railroad, from Georgia up north to this point in New Jersey, had been trying on their young son who had always been sickly. He would die of exhaustion not short of love. He would die in the main room of the secret hiding space and be moved, by the priest, into the smaller secret room and covered with leftover masonry as the floor itself was stone. The Episcopal priest, Reverend Elijah Jackson, then took the wooden cross from the small chapel and carved the boy's name in it and the dates that he had lived between. Elijah Jackson took the better part of a day to get Big Jim and Sarah to leave the boy. It had almost broken them as Sarah wailed on the verge of hysteria.

'God would take care of young Jim,' Reverend Jackson had told them and no one would ever enter the space again, it had become the boy's tomb. The reverend standing on a short ladder, under the dim light of a torch, had chiseled a small cross into the stone just above the door and under this he had chiseled two letters barely visible. They were the letters FM for Free Man.

Alice, collecting herself, sat back for a moment or two and then remembered that she had seen something else in the far right-hand corner of the room. It was a lump on the floor when she had first moved the light over it before   concentrating on the cross. But now, after transferring the flashlight to her left hand for better control, she shined the light back in the direction of what she had seen just as a lump without definition.

As she regained her feet she focused the light on the object and headed for it, again, tentatively as the room had unnerved her. It had broken through the shell that Alice had surrounded herself with.

As she stepped closer the object revealed itself to be an old leather bag, not quite as big as a softball she thought. It appeared to be drawn closed at the top by a leather drawstring. She knelt beside the bag and as she wiped the dust from it she could see a simple drawing of a horse on one side with a small boy stick figure standing next to it. Laying the flashlight on the floor Alice delicately pulled the top of the bag open inadvertently breaking the old and dried drawstring. She started to pour the contents out onto the stone floor into the small circle of light created by the flashlight. A rock was the first item to fall out and as it fell out it dislodged a small feather which had stuck in the opening and held back other items. She eventually removed the entire contents: a piece of worn colored cloth of faded indigo blue as she had never seen before; a small carved wooden horse; the feather; the rock; and a small piece of wood which had a soft red and white color to it as it was cedar. She looked at the horse and could only think that it was the toy of the child she had stumbled upon.

Alice had found a Cherokee medicine bag from Georgia. It had belonged to the father of the boy Jim. The cloth was a piece from the child's swaddling clothes. The small stone had come from a creek near the spot where Little Jim had been born. The feather had fallen from a Wood Thrush that seemed to sing to Jim and Sarah every morning on the plantation in Georgia. The horse was carved by Jim for his son in the hope that he would someday be free. The piece of cedar was Cherokee. It had been put in the bag by the old Cherokee who had gifted it to Jim near the creek where Jim would get buckets of water out of the pools for those in the fields to drink. It was one's life.

The bag had been left behind for the boy, this much Alice understood and unlike other items in the church she returned this one to the spot where she had found it. She did not expect to find such things in a church and the fact that they had obviously been there for a great deal of time shook Alice's world. Her bravado in the face of the church and society around her had been knocked away and for some reason shaken to its core where she could no longer maintain it.

Big Jim had left his bag of tears behind for the boy he would never get to know and in some way even Alice understood this. It all seemed to alter her path in a way that she could not consciously understand or even perceive; it just happened.

After returning the bag to the spot where she had found it Alice, following the light of the flashlight without looking out of the scope of the cone of its light, left the safe room which had become a crypt for a small boy. She would never tell anyone of the small boy in the tomb even if she did tell someone, at some point, of the secret entrance to the church.

With flashlight in hand Alice could see how the stone to the left of the moveable wall had been cut on an angle on the inside to allow the wall to pivot out. She then pointed her light to the front of the moveable wall and put her shoulder against its edge, at the opening, and pushed. As the accumulated dirt of over a century was now gone from the top of the stone door it moved easily on its balanced fulcrum of stone, in the form of a small pedestal, and closed against a stone stop on the inside. The ingeniously designed door would seal itself again over time.

Before leaving the main room for the passageway out Alice slowly eased the flashlight in her left hand up until its light shone on the small cross etched into the stone. She found that she now viewed the cross in a new light, one that was framed by a respect that Alice had never really felt for anything. It was a childlike respect without really understanding why. At this moment she felt that she might never enter the church again, at least not by this entrance, which she felt only she was aware of.

V was still on the hill. Twenty minutes had passed since he had heard what he thought to be a muffled, somewhat ghostlike, scream seeming to come from inside the church.

Looking down on the church now for half an hour, he thought that he was starting to see things. It was movement that was not occurring which he knew happens when one stares long enough at one area, in the dark, expecting movement where there is none. Then in the middle of his picture of the back of the church, under the moonlit night, he thought he saw movement again. The grate on the back of the church seemed to move just a bit, and then it moved completely off its fitting as if floating, which completely rewoke V sending adrenaline coursing through his body. "What the hell...?" he muttered to himself as he continued to watch.

Then the grate was set to the side of the building and someone stepped out. It was Alice.

"I'll be damned," muttered V.

As he quietly watched, Alice put something on the ground to the left of the opening and then picked up the grate from where it was leaning on the right wall. Then she placed it back over the opening top end first. Then it looked like she was leaning her entire body into it after getting it into place.

V continued to watch as she picked up the item that she had laid down to the left of the now closed grate and as she did so a momentary light came on and was then extinguished.

"A flashlight," whispered V to himself.

Alice was taking the light now as she did not intend to return.

He continued to watch as she quietly walked off the property to the road avoiding the hill that he was on. She would not notice him at this distance as well as the fact that he was now partially concealed by a rise in the hill between where he was sitting and where the road and sidewalk where located.

Alice continued back up the hill towards the house on the sidewalk and V waited until she was gone behind the trees.

And just to make sure he waited to the count of 60 Mississippi before he headed down the hill towards the grate that he had never really paid any attention to until this night.

At the now revealed entrance he looked hard at the grate in the moonlight and then looked behind himself to make sure that she hadn't snuck up on him, just the thought gave him shivers. He tried to wiggle the frame and it was solid. He could see from the hill through the moonlight that Alice had seemed to put the grate back by first lifting the peak up into place then pushing the entire frame in. From the hill he could not see that it dropped into place once she did this.

Next, V stooped just a bit and put his shoulder into it as he pushed up and as he did so he felt the grate move as the bottom came loose from the stone frame. He then shifted his weight, took hold of the grate by the wooden slates and pulled out and down as it came out. "Damn, how in the hell did she figure this out?" he marveled.

Setting the grate to the side V looked behind himself and up the hill and out to the street to make sure that no one was watching and then he nervously stepped in and immediately stepped out again. It was too dark. It was almost pitch black and he had no idea what to expect. It was a little unnerving and Alice had a flashlight.

V once again looked around and then replaced the grate which was surprisingly easy to manage. He would have to return another time when he knew exactly where Alice was and preferably after she had left the church after another nighttime visit. He thought that this would be the safest way to explore what was inside not knowing that Alice had decided not to return, at least not in the near future.

As V turned to head for the sidewalk that Alice had just taken up the hill he wondered what could be behind these hidden walls in the church that he had been going to since he was a toddler. He thought of those summer Sundays when he was a child lining up to go into the small chapel from the lawn he was now on. It was part of Sunday school and V had fond memories of being among friends dressed in his Sunday best. The thought of these memories put a smile on his face as he then thought how amazing it was that for years he had stood across from that grate but yet had no idea that it was a secret entrance to the church. The more he thought the more excited he became about entering it in order to explore it. He also couldn't wait to see Jack's expression.

***

Jack was in his room reading a sailing book when V finally came in just before 11:00 in the evening.

"Where the hell have you been?" asked Jack coming up from the pillow he was leaning against and closing the book on his hand to keep the page he was on. "I heard queen Dracula come in a while ago," added Jack not knowing that V had followed her to the church.

"Queen Daracula?"

"Well, yeah, it sorta fits," Jack said with a smile. "I followed her to the church."

"Jeez, I sorta felt that you might have followed her. Strange, it made me a little nervous when I heard her come in and didn't hear that scary giggle you can hear when she enters her room. I figured something was up."

"Nothing's wrong really but I found out how she got into the church that night."

Jack sat up completely and closed the book.

"We can't tell anyone not even Jake for now."

"How?" asked Jack his eyes alight.

"You know that grate on the side of the church on the back near the chapel?"

"Yeah, what about it?" asked Jack.

"It comes off and there's a passageway on the other side."

"You're crappin' me!" said Jack with surprise as he was thinking that he must have walked past that grate a million times.

"No, and we're going in that way when we know where she is."

"Oh, no, I don't trust that. I run into her in there or anything like her and I'll crap myself."

"You like that word tonight."

"It fits."

"We'll we're both going to go and you know you want to," said V as he smiled.

Just down the hall Alice sat stroking her cat while she thought about what she had found and her face showed no real expression. The strange smile of demented delight that seemed to characterize her face when she was in thought was now gone. She could only hear the scream that she had emitted when she stumbled upon the skeleton of the child and she was frightened by her own scream.

There had been a disturbance in Alice's core and she did not understand it. That confused core that she had wrapped up tightly in false self-assuredness and dominance had been laid bare by the night's events. She found herself retreating within as she opened up to what was around her like a child looking at everything and listening to everything and taking it all in with a driving curiosity. This childlike curiosity appeared, in Alice's case, more subtle from the outside than it truly was.

The birds watched her from their perch on the curtain rod with a soft cooing which seemed to calm Alice this night. In past nights she would get excited by it and stick her head in between the birds and shake it until they stopped cooing and lifted their wings protectively. Then she would giggle with a guttural giggle frightening to anyone who could hear it.

In an instant Alice's world had been turned upside down by a seemingly minor event that had her looking inwards at herself for truly the first time in her young life.

Chapter 16

Adelia Confronts Alice

Thursday, July 28th

It was two days later, a day that Adelia had only one summer school class and one that she decided to skip. The city and the surrounding area had just gone through a nine day heat wave ending only six days earlier with a high of 104 degrees. It was a beautiful day although still hot and she decided that she would give it to herself with the house seemingly empty and quiet. Even the big black dog by the name of Oliver, who she thought was cute, was gone, spending the day with Kate.

She felt free again after having formed too close of an attachment with Joan whom she hadn't heard from since getting the ride to the house the day that she moved in.

Adelia took a brief walk around the neighborhood stopping to look at each Victorian she was to pass by. The gingerbread lattice work and the multi-colored adornment of the homes brought a smile to her face and intrigued her. She had never lived in the midst of these grand old ladies as she thought of them but she had always been attracted to them. There was something about their stated grandeur, accomplished with taste and an eye for a type of chaotic symmetry through functional form. As her German grandmother would say, it was 'gemutlich' or beyond cozy. She was happy to finally be alone and surrounded by these magnificent homes.

As Adelia started to return to the house she could only think of one simple thing and that was a warm cup of coffee with cream and sugar to top off the morning. The simple joys were hers to have this morning.

Her favorite coffee was waiting for her. It was a German blend that her grandmother would let her have a sip of now and again when she was a child.

She went straight to the coffee after coming into the kitchen from the back door of the Lugers'. As she opened the tin that she kept the coffee in she brought it up to her nose with the expectation of the robust fragrance that brought back protected memories. It gave her a feeling of aliveness that she could never explain to anyone else. As she slowly pulled in the strong aroma of the coffee as she inhaled she was rewarded once again with that magical feeling of childhood, strength and everything good. This was something that she would never tell another as it was hers and no one could possibly understand how the smell of coffee, a particular coffee, could be so important to her.

Adelia made coffee, as she recently discovered, 'cowboy style' in a nice diner mug she found in one of the cupboards. She would scoop out the coffee from the tin and put it directly into the cup or mug. Then she would pour the boiling water over the top, stir it once, let it sit and then stir it again a minute later to create a wonderful foam on top. She smiled as she stirred the old diner mug of coffee and thought of one of her first friends in New York remarking in amazement that she was making 'cowboy coffee' when making them both a cup in this manner. Harold was a fellow theatre student in the Tisch School of The Arts and he was from Texas. She smiled again as she realized that he would always be a good friend.

Adelia headed for the French doors on the side of the house and the side veranda. The love seat would be perfect to

sit on sideways, legs tucked under her while holding her cool-
ing mug of coffee cupped in both hands.

She curled up on the love seat with her coffee and simply
listened to the birds and took in the small detail in the yard.
She took in everything from the blades of grass to the different character of each outreaching branch from the grand old
magnolia in the back of the yard. It could not be better she
thought then a brief feeling of guilt, for the loneliness that she
thought Joan was feeling, entered her mind. It left her mind
almost as quickly as it had entered as though exhaling a breath
held too long. Adelia enjoyed companionship as much as she
appreciated her solitude and on occasion they would be in
conflict with each other. She was also confused and conflicted
about her relationship with Joan.

She was contemplating the subtle complexities of her
character and her life and why she enjoyed theater and acting
so much when behind her she heard a sudden flutter of wings
which made her turn her head briefly. As she saw nothing and
silence returned quickly she returned her gaze back to the lawn
once more as she took a sip of coffee and thought it odd, the
close flutter of wings. Maybe she was hearing the flutter of
wings coming to her through an open window in the house.
But she had heard that flutter before.

It wasn't more than a couple of seconds after she dis-
counted the noise as coming through the house from the outside when she felt a presence to her left. Then out of the corner of her eye part of a dark figure appeared and stood to the
side of the opening for the French doors.

Startled, Adelia turned and there was that woman with the
demonic giggle who had warned her about not being welcome. Adelia was shocked out of her reverie as her body became electric with fear. Here was this woman again but this
time in jeans and a white blouse and bare feet.

Alice was just staring at Adelia, not saying a word as
though she were surprised by an old acquaintance whom she
wasn't quite sure was now present. There was no demonic
smile or giggle.

"What do you want?!" Adelia said defensively as she unfolded her legs sitting straight and spilling some of her precious coffee as though it were water.

Alice said nothing but just looked at Adelia as though she was not quite sure that she was there at all.

"What! I don't give a damn if this is your church or whatever you think it is!" said Adelia louder while moving across the seat further away from Alice.

Alice just smiled. "I have no church. Why are you looking at me like that?"

"You scare me," said Adelia no longer being cautious about revealing her weakness.

"I won't hurt you."

"The fact that you say that scares me," said Adelia looking around for an exit, in case one would be needed.

As Adelia noticed the small gate through the fence with the hedge in front of it she moved even further away from Alice. She moved to the far side of the love seat realizing that she could jump over the porch rail to the yard below and out the gate. She could outrun this woman.

"Why are you moving away?" asked Alice as she moved further away from Adelia to the other side of the French doors giving Adelia more space but coming out of the doorway and barely onto the veranda.

"It's reflexive, and it seems the sensible thing to do, especially after you warned me not to be here."

"I didn't mean that," said Alice in a soft voice which no one who knew her would have recognized.

"What did you mean?" asked Adelia reflexively, now relaxing her guard a bit.

"I didn't mean to say that to you, you're different."

Now with curiosity in her voice Adelia asked, "Different in what way?"

"You are sure of yourself but you don't know it."

"That's a strange statement," said Adelia just as Alice's white cat walked up to Alice from the den and rubbed herself against Alice's ankle.

Looking down at her cat and giggling Alice looked up again with the start of a warm smile and said, "Oh, I don't think so. You walk like you know where you are going and you are beautiful," finished Alice with a smile.

Warming to Alice Adelia blushed, "I'm just thinking of a lot of things when I walk and really don't pay attention to it, sometimes winding up in the wrong place."

Alice smiling added, "I always get to where I'm going but sometimes I don't know where I'm going."

Just as Alice finished the two white doves flew from Henry's antlers landing on her right shoulder and startling Adelia, who finally made the connection hearing the now familiar flapping of wings once more. The bats had become doves.

Still startled, "Where did those doves come from?" asked Adelia.

"From Heaven," said Alice smiling and saying it in a way where it did not seem odd.

"A nice heavenly gift," said Adelia smiling back as she felt her earlier fear of this woman start to fade and get replaced with a strange sort of compassion.

"I bet you're an artist.......like those artists who can do a lot of artistic things."

Laughing, Adelia responded, "Yes, I guess you would call it that. I'm studying acting. Why did you think that?"

Moving closer now Alice smiled and said, "Because you have a gentleness about you. "

This connected as Adelia had just been contemplating the same thought.

"Can I sit?" followed Alice as Adelia was taking in what she had just heard.

"Yes, sure," said Adelia now not flinching nor moving as Alice took a seat. She sat more in the middle of the wicker love seat closer to Adelia than would be normal. Her two doves lifted off, as she settled into the seat, lighting on the lower support piece for the ornate gingerbread lattice which ran above the veranda and just below the roof's edge.

"It's in your eyes too!" remarked Alice now looking directly into Adelia's piercing blue eyes.

"My eyes always seem to be a topic for discussion," said Adelia not picking up on the momentary fixed trance Alice had on her eyes. Adelia was used to people gazing at them.

"You're eyes are like the sky on a crisp late summer's day," said Alice as her cat found her ankle again to rub against.

"Well, I've never heard that one," said Adelia glancing down at the cat and not picking up on the tone of Alice's voice, which was briefly that of a passionate admirer although the delivery was very clumsy as if from a child.

"They make me want to wrap my arms around them," followed Alice firmly and passionately.

"Well that would be difficult," said Adelia now feeling a little uncomfortable.

"It wouldn't be difficult at all," followed Alice as her two doves lifted off their roost under the roof and landed once more on Alice's shoulder.

Adelia's left hand reflexively felt behind herself for the end of the love seat. She was just actually short of being right up against the end of the seat.

"Why did you change your expression, it was so beautiful?....... But you are expressive," finished Alice before Adelia could say a word.

"I'm nervous again."

"But why?" asked Alice as she reached out with her left hand toward Adelia as the still doves turned slightly outward with the movement of her right shoulder.

"I wish you wouldn't do that."

"I just want to comfort you."

"No, damnit. You're just like Joan. Get away from me," said Adelia as she stood with shock on her face, still holding her coffee mug as she finally came to terms with her feelings towards Joan. A certain strength came over her.

"I promise I won't touch you."

"I've had enough," said Adelia as she walked past Alice and headed for the den.

As she crossed the den she could hear Alice giggle but it was somewhat different from the giggle that she had heard when she first ran into her. It was soft and not demented, it was almost nervous in nature. This thought was brief as Adelia was once again electric with alertness. Alice had just strongly reminded her of Joan and uncovered everything that Adelia had been hiding from herself.

Joan had been there when Adelia entered New York University at the end of a traumatic period at home after a summer when she lost her father abruptly to colon cancer. It had devastated her mother so much so that she had nothing left with which to comfort her only daughter. Her brothers tried to console her but they were in pain as well. What made this all the more impossible to bear was the fact that her boyfriend for all of her years in high school had left her for another girl. He had met her while visiting the campus of Colby College in Maine. He would attend Colby along with this new girl and he had only let Adelia know just before she left for school in New York.

Harold had been there when she arrived at NYU and his simple Texan common sense and friendship helped her but she was still missing the understanding of a woman until she met Joan. Joan was an older student, two years ahead of her, but still in the dorm with the younger students in the Tisch School. Joan had walked past Adelia's room one night when Adelia was still alone without her roommate and crying. Joan had heard the crying and instead of knocking had quietly opened the door to find this beautiful young woman sitting on her bed bent over with her head in her hands weeping. Her long black hair covered the side of her face except for the milky white sculpture of her cheekbone which had stopped Joan in her tracks for a moment of appreciation.

Realizing that Adelia had probably sensed her unannounced entry into the room and not caring, Joan asked in the softest voice possible but a voice with strength like a mother, "Are you okay?"

"No."

"Do you mind if I sit?"

"I don't care what you do.........I don't care what anyone does."

Joan sat and firmly but softly put her right hand and arm around Adelia's shoulder and her left hand at the base of Adelia's bent elbow, which was resting in her lap to help support her head. With this touch Adelia's floodgate let loose, floodgates she had been holding back for weeks. Her tears increased and she almost whaled, "How could they do this to me, how could they leave me?"

"I don't know why they would, but they do," said Joan not knowing who she was talking about.

With her free right hand Adelia automatically reached for Joan's hand at her left elbow and touched her hand in gratitude as a daughter would to a mother or a sister to a sister. Joan reacted by rubbing Adelia's right shoulder which was comforting for a moment before Adelia decided that she wanted to be alone.

"Thank....thank you....ah.."

"Joan," Joan filled in.

"Thank you Joan.......thank you. I think I need to be alone right now."

"I'm down the hall at the end in 02 if you need me," said Joan softly as she got up to leave.

"Okay," answered Adelia.

Joan bent before leaving and kissed Adelia on the top of her head. "It'll be okay, you'll see," she said then headed for the door closing it behind her as she left.

It wasn't but two days later, while taking a shower, that Adelia met Joan for the second time.

Adelia was in the large shower stall with tears camouflaged by the water running down her face when she heard the stall door being gently opened and the appropriately timed words, "It's okay, you are allowed to cry," coming from Joan as she entered the stall naked.

The words comforted Adelia and she accepted the gentle touch of kindness as Joan reached for the soap in the soap tray near the shower handles, just in front of her, lathered her hands and softly applied soap to Adelia's back.

Joan's touch was tender and considerate, something that Adelia had not experienced in months and with gratitude she started to again cry audibly. As she did so Joan returned the soap to the tray and gently moved her arms around Adelia's waist as she drew closer until her body was up against Adelia from behind.

"Cry, just cry, I have you," whispered Joan as she spread her hands flat against Adelia's upper ribs just below her breasts.

Adelia cried more as she moved her hands over Joan's arms and over her hands, wrapping herself in Joan's embrace.

She cried for a few moments and then, slowing, she turned around and faced Joan who stood almost at equal height if a half an inch shorter than Adelia. With her breasts against Joan's she closed her eyes and leaned over and kissed Joan briefly on the lips. Joan kissed her back and then moved her head to the side of Adelia's and held her as the water ran over Adelia before falling on her. Joan stroked her back and then her hands moved down, well below Adelia's waist, and caressed her gently from the back until she reacted.

Adelia felt a release as she felt warmth and, slowly, excitement. She opened her eyes and kissed Joan with more passion as she opened her mouth.

Joan stepped back an inch, just enough to enable her free hand to caress Adelia's breasts with care and affection as Adelia raised her head to the ceiling, closing her eyes and opening her mouth briefly to moan softly and thankfully.

As Adelia started to run away with Joan's touch and become lost in its sensuality Joan lowered her hand and started to caress Adelia from front and back softly until Adelia was moaning without reserve. The intensity increased as Adelia started to rub her own breasts pushing them up and running her hands over her nipples as she did so while Joan started to increase her tempo just slightly.

As Joan felt Adelia's orgasm coming on she moved her

right hand to her own body and started to caress herself with abandon. She felt her greatest arousal as Adelia's orgasm came with cries of joy followed by convulsing tremors as though it had been held back for far too long. As the crying out started to subside and the tremors got more rapid but decreased in intensity Joan just held Adelia.

Before they left the shower that day and just shortly after Adelia's tremors stopped, Joan caressed her again giving Adelia something that she had never had before. Adelia had found herself saying 'stop, stop' as the intensity became too much but Joan hadn't stopped until Adelia's final rapture.

In the ensuing months Joan had been a comfort to Adelia both emotionally and physically until the summer grew near and Adelia was brought back to the loss of her father and her childhood love. Summer coming again had allowed her to face these two events and to put them in there right place in her memory. She was healing and she wanted to be alone as Joan became more controlling.

When Adelia was accepted to a special summer program she knew that she would, at some point, need to find a place to live that was far enough away from Joan. Joan in the meantime had committed to an apartment in the city, for the two of them, without fear of affordability as she was the child of a wealthy family. Adelia had lived with her after she moved in knowing in her heart that it would only be temporary. In the end it was a good portion of the summer until she found the Lugers'.

When she had seen the ad for the room in an old Englewood house, after Rodney had placed it on one of the large bulletin boards at the entrance to the library, she knew that this would be the ideal world for her during the remaining part of the summer. She became excited about being surrounded by Victorian homes and her own thoughts. Rodney hadn't put much of a description on the ad but Adelia, having grown up in southern Connecticut, knew about the homes of Englewood.

Joan had been hurt more than upset, agreeing that what

was left of the summer would give Adelia time to herself. But Adelia could feel the underlying anxiety coming from Joan, an anxiety touched by an almost undetectable amount of anger below the surface.

Adelia was filled with these thoughts of Joan as she climbed the stairs to her third floor bedroom, completely forgetting about Alice by the time she entered her room.

It was hot and Adelia could still feel the 104 degrees plus the humidity of the heat wave, which had just passed a week earlier, as she kicked off her shoes and opened the window adjacent to her bed on the side of the house. There was a slight breeze that moved with delicate fingers across her room and through the hallway to Jake and Kate's room where the opposing window had been left open along with the door to the room.

The soft cool air felt 'delicious' to Adelia and without thinking about it she started to take her clothing off.

Fully naked she stood by the side of the bed for a moment and spread her legs apart and stretched her arms high and apart and let the breeze sweep into, over, and past her as subtle as it was. Adelia then lay naked on the bed, as she had done often as a young teenager in her locked room at home, to take what she called an 'air bath'.

As she lay there with the periodic movement of cool air softly touching her body Adelia started to escape to less confusing times several years before and before her father had died. She started to feel that she was once again back in her childhood room as that young teen of 14 or 15 and she smiled inside as she drew deeper and deeper into the safety of the past.

As though being brought out of a dream by noise that first incorporates itself into and then alters your dream before waking you, Adelia's eyes started to open with the feeling of a presence.

As she opened her eyes she looked at the ceiling, then she turned her head in the direction of the presence by the open door to her bedroom, and she was horrified.

Standing in the threshold of her door was a naked Alice with a pile of clothing behind her. She was standing there staring at Adelia and fondling her right breast with her right hand as she masturbated with the stubby fingers of her left hand.

Adelia sat up immediately as she finally realized what was happening and let out a scream that would wake the dead as far away as the church and she did not stop, she just kept screaming as Alice turned, grabbed the pile of clothing and stumbled down the stairs.

Adelia immediately came off the bed, ran to the door and slammed it. She then barricaded it with an antique decorative trunk left in the room years earlier and sitting next to the old couch Zach used to sleep on when he visited. Then she stepped back and stared at the door.

The scream scared Alice to her core as her own scream had done when she had stumbled upon the remains of Little Jim in the secret room in the church. She had found herself only to be rejected the first time that she acknowledged and acted on her true feelings, even as crudely as she had carried that out.

Alice was not the only one to be startled to the core by the scream. Carter was home and had been quiet in his room trying to sleep in a semi-drunken state as he was having a severe episode of remembering things that happened during the war as though they had just happened again. During the war Carter did not have the ability to dwell on violent loss as he tucked it away telling himself that he would deal with it later. Well, now in 1977 was later as it had been in every year following the war. Some episodes were worse than others and as he drank more over the years the memories evolved with the same sharp edges and depression attached as though they were within his power to change but he had done nothing. He was dealing with this guilt when he heard the screams coming from the third floor. Carter, though, did not hear Adelia. He heard Dorothy, the young girl of his dreams who he thought he had killed years before.

As the scream continued Carter came to his senses and

was up and out his door. He had moved faster than anyone would have thought he could move who knew him, if they had seen him. Carter was in the hall and at the foot of the stairs leading to the third floor when Alice descended the stairs naked and holding a mass of clothing in one hand.

As Alice stopped she looked down at Carter from two steps up from the floor where he stood and there was again silence as a door from the third floor was heard to slam shut.

Alice's eyes were panicked with the same intensity that Carter remembered every time that he saw Alice and to him he was confronting the creator of his worst nightmares. He did not see a naked woman distraught and holding her clothing in one hand. Carter saw everything that was destructive holding something dead in its hand and looking as though it had been caught.

Carter was shocked to come face to face with his seemingly undefeatable nemesis. But the panic in Alice's stare, which Carter took as the weakness of someone being caught with no way out, gave him the courage to correct his failures to the ones he loved.

"Stop, goddamn you," he bellowed up at Alice who had no response after what had just happened to her attempt to act on the reality of her new persona.

"Harper is not yours and you will not have Dorothy you son-of-a-bitch," screamed Carter as Alice now desperately looked for a way past.

As she started to squeeze past, Carter turned aside with fear in his eyes not wanting to be touched by this apparition as he intoned, "I damn you to hell you bastard, take your bloody trophy with you and die." Again he screamed, "Die," at the figure of Alice now moving down the hall towards her room.

"That's it, go, leave for good; destroy yourself," he finally yelled as Alice disappeared behind the door and threw it shut.

Carter just stood there and looked at the door and then started to cry. At first tears just started to roll down his face slowly then they came down in an uncontrollable flood as he started to shake. He leaned against the wall and cried and then looked up and cried again, "I'm sorry Dorothy, I failed you, ...I did. I will never stop loving you please hear me........Oh God please hear me..........."

Adelia, lost in her thoughts behind the closed door with the soft sounds of summer coming through the still opened window, never heard Carter.

***

No one saw Alice that night but then again it was rare to see her.

When everyone returned home Adelia was still in her room with the door shut. She simply stared at the trunk up against the door for the longest time contemplating what had happened that day and what her life had been like over the past year with Joan as her protector. She now did not see Joan in that light. She knew that she wanted her autonomy not even thinking of being loved by anyone. The thought of complete autonomy gave Adelia a feeling of security in the future yet to come. The sound of Kate eventually coming up the stairs with Oliver in the lead, as she could hear his paws and nails on the wooden stairs, gave her a feeling of immediate safety from Alice.

Adelia stayed on the third floor the rest of that day and left early the next for New York, taking the first commuter bus from downtown Englewood, across the bridge, and then the A train downtown.

Everyone was out of the house that Thursday the 28th of July and when they returned Alice was gone with her cat and everything else except the robe from the church along with the cross and candles. She also left her two doves perched on the curtain rod in her room.

No one realized that she had left until the doves started cooing loudly, getting Oliver to stand in front of the door and bark non-stop. The only time that Kate had seen Oliver do this was that time on The Cape when the toddler had started to wade into the water from Sunken Ship Beach or when she took a bath with Oliver present. Kate knew something was wrong and knocked on the door several times without an answer in return.

As Kate opened the door slowly the two doves started to fly at her and then returned to their perch. Alice was gone along with her cat and belongings, it seemed to Kate. The closet door was wide open and the hangers were empty.

Kate closed the door and let Jake know.

Later that night Jake and V entered the room and found only the doves and the robe and the cross and candles. It was V who decided to open the window and let the doves fly which the doves did as soon as open air was available to them.

Alice was gone, and gone with the keys.

It did not quite sink in with Rodney that part of his income was gone let alone the warning from both Jake and V that he would have to change the front door lock on the house. The money was always an issue with Rodney, no matter how small the amount.

As for the robe, the cross, and the candles: Jake would try to sneak them back into the church unseen, to leave them on a back pew where they could be readily seen by the Reverend Dr. McGee.

As for the secret entrance that V and Jack knew about, that would have to wait indefinitely for V to investigate it as he knew that Alice was at large. And for all he knew she could be living in that secret place of places.

Chapter 17

Adelia Is Shown The Club

Saturday, July 30th

Two days later, on Saturday, Jake and V pitched in and changed the front door lock and had keys made for everyone, including Rodney. Due to Rodney's cheapness, none of the "tenants" had a back door key, which saved them in the end. They did not give Rodney his new key. V went into his room while he was showering and exchanged the key on his key ring. Trying, again, to explain would be too complicated with Rodney. It was just easier to get it done. He would not notice as he still did not notice that Alice was gone. He would only notice when she did not pay the next month's rent.

Adelia was still at the house that late Saturday morning when Jake walked her new key to her room. She had been waiting for the replacement key which Jake had made everyone aware of, with the exception of Rodney of course.

"Here you go Adelia.......by-the-way, we're going to go to The Club for lunch in about an hour and we'd love to have you come".

"Well, I don't know.......I mean......I really need to get

some work done."

"What work?" asked Jake with a smile realizing that she was just shy about accepting. "Kate and Oliver will keep you company if you get tired of the rest of us."

"Well, okay then," she said and smiled, feeling warmed by Jake's sincerity.

***

V and Jack were already on the patio in front of The Club when Jake arrived with Kate, Adelia and Oliver. They were not alone as Tim Ferguson was sitting with them, or at least it looked like Tim as he was seated with his back to them as they walked over to the table.

Oliver was the first to the table going over to V hoping that he might find a Ritz, but instead he was going to get an energetic ear and face rubbing from V which was just as good. With Oliver's arrival at the table Tim turned in his chair expecting Jake and Kate but his eyes fell first on Adelia and they remained there, not moving.

"Adelia, you know those two but the one now staring at you is my old friend Tim Ferguson," said Jake with a slight laugh as the three came up to the table.

Pushing his metal chair back with a stumble and scratch of metal against the painted white concrete, Tim came partially to his feet with a look of shy embarrassment written all over his face. "I'm Tim…. ah… nice to meet you…. Adelia," he got out as he extended his hand.

Adelia feeling an immediate connection with this man for some reason beyond her understanding extended her hand and smiled. "Nice to meet you Tim."

Tim, fully on his feet, pulled his chair the rest of the way out away from the table and offered it to Adelia. V Looked over at Jack and grinned, never having seen this behavior in Tim Ferguson although he hadn't seen him for at least three years. Teenagers remember character traits sometimes better than adults.

V found it slightly humorous and interesting at the same

time while Adelia quickly embraced this care from a man, which she hadn't experienced in over a year. Although Harold was as good to her, and carried concern for her, he was a school friend.

"Hi Kate, good to see you again," said Tim after seating Adelia.

"Hi Tim," returned Kate with a smile seeing what was obvious to everyone, "you look more excited now than you probably looked when you found civilization again."

"What?" asked Tim getting caught by Kate's comment as he had turned to Adelia again, "Oh, yeah well that's another story."

"'When you found civilization again', that sounds interesting," remarked Adelia as she took her seat with Tim helping her to adjust it forward to the table.

"That's a long story and I wouldn't want to bore you with it," said Tim to Adelia with more embarrassment and in a tone as though Adelia were the only one present.

"Don't let him lie to you Adelia, it is far from boring," added Jake just as Oliver barked at seeing Carter walk onto the veranda with Margaret. "And Oliver agrees."

"And he sees Carter," said V. And with that Oliver took off for Carter.

Adelia turned in her chair to see where Oliver was going and when she saw Carter she said, "The man in the tennis whites who sees Japs!"

Tim's eyebrows went up and V and Jake laughed.

"I didn't really say anything," said Jake looking at Kate now looking straight at him. "I might have said that he sees Japanese soldiers once in a while but I had to explain what Japs meant."

"Well, he does see them, I can tell you that," said Jack "and they're pretty scary guys," he added with a look on his face as though he saw them too, and V, Jake and Tim started to laugh.

"What?" said Jack looking at them laughing at him.

"Are Japs that funny?" asked Adelia.

And with this they started to laugh even more.

Now it was Adelia's turn. "What?"

And as Carter drew closer in his tennis whites with Oliver bouncing up and down at his side waiting for recognition, they laughed even more.

Adelia appearing puzzled, looked at this man that she just met.

Putting his hand on her shoulder Tim with a laugh in his voice said, "I'll tell you later Adelia, after Carter leaves." Then he smiled warmly at Adelia.

The touch of his hand on her shoulder gave Adelia a feeling of security that she had been missing for a long time. His voice also let her know that he would be completely honest with her about everything he said. The sun felt brighter in such a brief moment for Adelia as a result. As she felt this inner joy the man in worn tennis whites approached. He was another man who had jumped to her defense but she would never know it.

"You all sound like a pack of hyenas," said Carter in his gruff but friendly voice as he reached the table with Margaret right behind him.

"They've heard that before and they're just idiots, that's all," said Kate and they laughed even more.

"Adelia, do you want to go to the bar with Margaret and me for an orange juice while they get over themselves?"

Adelia nodded as Kate stood.

"Adelia this is Margaret," Kate said as Margaret drew up to the table. And turning to Margaret she introduced Adelia, "This is Adelia, the new member of the Luger house who you haven't yet met. I think we'll leave the 'men' and get one of Sam's famous orange juices."

Taking the hint to get away for a moment Margaret looked at the men and said with a smile, "Good idea."

As they headed to the bar the boys started to simmer down and then Carter said it.

"What happened to that godless Jap incarnation? I haven't seen those goddamned birds. Jesus H. Christ, I thought it was gonna kill us all until I told it to go to hell the other night. Room seems empty, guess it listened."

They were all just quietly looking at Carter now waiting for what would come next.

"I heard Dorothy scream and then told it to destroy itself. I think I'll get a scotch, you boys want anything?"

"No, we're good," said Jake.

Oliver followed as Carter headed into the bar.

"Well, I guess that says it," said V and they all laughed again.

"Who the hell is Dorothy?" asked Jake to no one in particular.

"I don't know, first time I heard that name," said V.

"I don't know either," added Jack shrugging his shoulders.

"And don't look at me. I was in the Sahara when the Luger family started to get crazy," qualified Tim.

Changing the subject, "What's with Adelia?," asked Jake turning to Tim with a slightly taunting smile on his face.

"Well, you know," said Tim turning red.

"Jesus, he's turning red," said V.

"What's wrong, I like Adelia," piped in Jack.

"I think we all do," said Jake, "and I think the girl has something for our wonderer here," looking at Tim. "Epstein will be heartbroken."

"Where is he by-the-way?" asked V.

"He said he'd try to get here today but you know him."

"Hey, Carter seems a little calmer today," noted V getting back to what just happened.

"Yeah, he is. I guess the 'it' was Alice. I guess he won't be seeing Japs for a while," said Jake.

"He calls Dr. Wholefield 'the Asiatic'," said Jack.

"What? Dr. who?" asked Jake.

"Dr. Bob," said V. "Since when do you call Dr. Bob Dr. Wholefield anyway?"

"Since he has two beautiful daughters," shot back Jack.

"They're older than you."

"Not by much," defended Jack.

"Wait a minute, so that's who Carter was talking about when he mentioned 'Bob the Asiatic', it wasn't an illusion?" queried Jake.

"Well yeah, I ran into the two of them drinking on the back porch yesterday afternoon. Dr. Wholefield is a strange guy."

"Well don't you think Carter is too?!" said V.

"Carter's Carter ," said Jack.

"Now I remember Dr. Bob. He did, or does have two great looking daughters; forgot all about that," added Tim.

"Why does he call him the Asiatic?" asked Jake.

"I don't know, you'll have to ask him. He just introduced him that way as though he'd known him a while. Strange nickname."

"I'll ask him then," said Jake.

"Jeez unck! I'd be careful, you never know what might set him off," said V.

"Yeah, well Carter is more gruff than anything else."

"Yeah, but it can be strange gruff like out of a movie about nuts," followed V.

"Asiatic probably has something to do with Japs, don't get him to start seeing Japs here, now," commented Tim. "It might not be that entertaining."

"Hell, it could be funny, come to think of it," said V.

"Jeez V," said Tim. "It would probably scare hell out of Adelia."

"Ah, so that's what it is," said V with a smile.

Tim just smiled back. "Yeah, well the girl is nice and all."

"I would say," said Jake.

"Hey, where is Rodney Dangerfield?" asked Tim, changing the subject.

"Ah, good one," said Jake.

"Not bad," commented V with a laugh, while Jack just shook his head.

"Probably see him out on the tennis courts," said Jake now reminded of his smashed pinky joint and starting to rub his hand, trying to bend his pinky now that the cast was gone.

"Look for a guy who looks like he's wearing pink from this distance."

V just laughed, then added, "I wonder what he's going to think happened when he doesn't get Alice's rent? I bet he leaves a note on her door."

Jack just started to laugh at the thought of his father putting a note on the door dressed in tennis whites covered with clay and totally oblivious to what was going on.

V looking at Jack said, "It doesn't take much to get you going."

"Dad can be funny," returned Jack still laughing a little.

"That's an understatement," said Jake shaking his head.

"Don't look now but here comes Carter with a tall glass minus Oliver," said V. "You can ask him about Dr. Bob now."

As Carter drew closer Jake yelled, "Where's Oliver?" just to break the ice.

"Ah, the girls are feeding him that mixed bar snack stuff in a bowl," said Carter as he came up to the table.

"Ah great," said Jake. "Kate knows better, that stuff has Ritz pieces in it."

"You mind if I sit?" asked Carter gruffly, more as a formality as he pulled a chair out between Jake and Tim."

"Not at all," said Tim as Carter was sitting.

As he sat he took a large draw off of his tall drink which was yellow/ brown or amber and no doubt Johnny Walker. He then smiled curtly and with a gruff voice, that just had its thirst quenched, he queried, "So what are you boys up to?"

"Planning to storm the bar when Sam's not looking," said V.

Carter just smiled curtly.

"Carter, do you know Dr. Bob?" asked Jake.

Carter turning to Jake with his head reared back in defense, "Who?"

"You call him 'the Asiatic,'" followed Jake.

"Yeah, 'the Asiatic', Bob, what about him?" said Carter his voice changing and getting a bit more serious as everyone straightened up in their chairs expecting something to happen.

With hesitant nervousness Jake asked, "Why do you call him 'the Asiatic'?"

"Can't you see?" said Carter in a demanding voice.

"Uh-oh," muttered V.

"No Carter, help me, I can't," said Jake taking another tack to try to keep Carter from going off a deep end.

"He looks like a Jap for Chrissakes," intoned Carter who for a moment remembered his homecoming, being welcoming until 1946. This was when the press and the public started talking about combat veterans as individuals to be cautious of, who could be violent especially if they gathered for reunions. The 31-year anger over this had entered his voice.

"Oh, crap," muttered Tim.

Jack was just frozen.

"He's been out there too long and gone Asiatic," followed Carter.

"Out where?" asked Jake easing the question in.

"Amongst them. The Pacific can do that.........I've seen other Marines go Asiatic."

Everyone froze. No one said a thing except Jake.

"I understand Carter. Are you helping him?" Jake asked.

"I watch out for him. Going Asiatic ain't necessarily bad," said Carter calming down with a softer voice.

V's eyebrow went up at his uncle's connection with Carter.

"Carter, let me know if you need any help," offered Jake.

Now putting his drink down, slowly looking at Jake and not saying a thing for a good five seconds, as everyone got nervous again, Carter finally said, "I will, thanks." And he smiled a broad happy smile, in place of his curt smile, for the first time that anyone outside of Jake could remember.

Just as he said this Oliver bounded up bumping into a couple of metal chairs and forcing them to scratch against the concrete of the patio as he came. He was followed by Margaret, Kate and Adelia.

Jake for one brief moment thought of going near the name

Dorothy, which was now another mystery, but he wasn't going to push his luck right now.

"So, are you entertaining the boys?", asked Margaret as she came up to the table.

They all just smiled as Carter calmly said, "You've gotta watch out for these boys." He then smiled again and got up to offer Margaret a seat.

They all stood at this point as Tim and Jake, and Carter added chairs to the table for the women. They all stood until all three women were seated and then sat again.

They were tight at the large round table and Tim was now sitting right next to Adelia.

Kate looking at Tim was the first to speak, "Adelia has an interesting background Tim, somewhat like yours. She's traveled a great deal. She spent some time in Sicily too."

"No kidding," said Tim now looking at Adelia. "I was there on my way to North Africa."

"I spent a little time there," said Adelia shyly to Tim as the others looked on, now cut out of the conversation.

Kate smiled and turned to Jake. "I kept the Ritz pieces away from Oliver if you hear about him getting bar snacks."

"Thank you," said Jake with a smile.

"Has anyone seen Rodney," asked Margaret.

"No, and it doesn't look like a pink man is running around on the court," said Jake.

"He's probably trying to get into the house with his old key," added V with a laugh.

"I hope you threw that away V," said Jake.

"Well we know he picks old cigar butts out of the sink, it's not a jump to go into the garbage for something shiny like money," said V. And Jake, V and Jack just started laughing at the memory of him going into the sink after that butt.

Coming out of nowhere, "Do you all mind if Adelia and I leave? I'm going to show her around The Club," said Tim.

"No," said Margret and Kate together.

As Tim pushed back his chair he reached over and started to help Adelia push hers back. In seconds they were off slowly walking across the field to the tennis courts, talking and not really paying attention to anything else around them.

"Well, I guess Tim is going to disappear again," said Jake, finally, as everyone just sat there for a few moments.

"She's a nice young girl," said Margaret, "a little lonely maybe but sometimes it just takes the right man. Right Carter?", she said as she tugged at his shirt while he took a sip of his scotch.

"Right, right," said Carter putting his scotch down and looking over at Margaret sitting next to him. "And the touch of the right woman can wake you from a long sleep."

Everyone's face, except for Margaret's, registered surprise as no one had really heard anything quite so 'poetic', if that was the right word, come from Carter. But apparently Margaret had, as indicated by her lack of surprise over the statement.

"Say Carter," said Jake, "what if we play some tennis tomorrow?"

"I…I don't know. I'm rusty."

"Well, you're always dressed for it," said V and Kate turned to him and shook her head as to say don't go there.

"I'll cheer you on," said Margaret.

"Cheer what, an old guy with bad eyes."

"Yes," said Margaret.

Carter turned and looked at her, softly kissed her on the lips and then turned to Jake, "Not a bad idea then, tomorrow."

"Tomorrow it is," confirmed Jake.

"I gotta watch this," said V smiling.

"Well, whaddaya know, it's Epstein," said V looking towards the entrance to the patio.

"Jeez, about time," said Jake turning in his chair.

Zach came across the patio with a big smile and once again Oliver was up and off to another one of his benefactors. As Jake watched he thought it funny that Oliver had a category for everyone. Carter and Kate he watched over. V and Zach he went to, to get a treat either to eat or a good scratching and rubbing of the head. Jake, well he always had an eye on him so he wouldn't lose him.

"I see you started without me," said Zach looking at Carter's scotch after reaching the table.

"You want a scotch?" asked Jake.

"Don't mind if I do."

"Well, you know where it is. Tell Sam to put it under my number. Hell, he'd probably like to see you anyway."

"Sam likes to see everyone," said Zach smiling broadly.

"Well, you're right about that," said Jake.

"I'll be right back, anyone else want anything?"

"Nah," said V as Jack shook his head no as well.

"Ah, it's still too early for me," said Jake.

"Thanks Zach, we still have our orange juices," added Kate.

Zach left but was back in minutes with his scotch.

"What happened? I thought Sam would probably keep you there for an hour," said Jake.

"Fire in the garbage."

"What?" said Jake.

"Yeah, the garbage started to smoke after he poured my drink, cigarette I guess. Sam nailed it with half an extinguisher."

Then Jake noticed and started laughing. "What's the white stuff in your hair and beard, looks like snow?"

Zach just grinned. "Fire extinguisher. Whatever it is, powder? Stuff went all over the place when he hit the lever in that little bar area," he said as he took another sip of scotch with some powder sprinkling down from his head as he did so.

"Sam white too?" asked V.

"Not enough to take his humor away," said Zach smiling. "Whaddaya drinkin' Carter?"

"Scotch."

"Salute," said Zach and tipped his glass to Carter then took a long sip from a rock glass full of scotch without the rocks.

"You missed Adelia," said V.

"Really, where is she?"

"Out there," said Jack pointing to the field.

"Yeah, it appears that ol' Tim made the connection before you.........and the girl knows baseball," said Jake.

"Oh well..........baseball too? Win a few lose a few. I drink too much anyway. Pretty girl though."

"But you're lovable," put in Kate as she smiled and laughed.

"They all say that and that's all they say," said Zach punctuating it with a broad smile.

"Hey, did you hear, crazy demonic Alice has flown the coop?" said V.

"I heard," said Zach. "How'd that happen?"

"Don't know," said Jake, "and don't care."

"The birds are gone too," said V. "I never saw two birds fly so fast once we opened the window."

"She probably gave off a high pitched screech that humans can't hear and they flew to that," said Zach before taking another big sip of scotch.

"Really, you're all bad," said Kate.

"She couldn't have been that bad," said Margaret.

"Ask Carter," said V looking over at Carter taking another sip of scotch.

Jake just shook his head at V.

"Ask Carter what?" said Carter gruffly, looking right at V.

"Oh, nothing. Everything's good," said V.

Changing the subject Kate said, "What about lunch? I'll get one of Sam's kids." Then she got up to go inside. As she passed behind Carter she softly patted him on the shoulder.

Alice was not brought up again.

"Hey Zach, did you really run off a train in Germany?"

"Who told you that?" And he just grinned with partially glazed eyes and black hair and beard covered in white dust.

Chapter 18

August 1977

Eleven days later, on August 10th, Son of Sam was captured and the pressure was off of Carter from at least one person. Birdie, sitting in her apartment watching the news that night looked hard at David Berkowitz every time they showed him and tried to see Carter. She came to the conclusion that he did look different and then forgot about Carter. She would never come to the Luger house again with all of those crazy people walking around.

***

Carter was starting to show more sparkle in his face and he was starting to get particularly animated on Friday afternoon the 12th of August as he sat on the side veranda to the Lugers' with Dr. Bob.

Jake was writing on the third floor with Oliver by his side when all of a sudden Oliver heard something that Jake could not hear and he was up and down the stairs. He had heard Carter.

It was a beautiful August day with the early afternoon temperature at around 75 degrees so Jake decided to take a break and follow Oliver to see what he was up to.

Jake was at the halfway point on the back steps when he heard Oliver's weight and toe nails land on the ground floor outside of the kitchen. It had a distinctive sound to it. Jake could also hear the slight echo of the sound of Oliver moving through the large main hall, probably on the way to the side veranda.

When he made it to the veranda, there was Oliver sitting next to Carter who was sitting in one of the wicker chairs talking to someone sitting in the love seat.

Before Jake even stepped out onto the veranda Carter looked up and smiled. "And here comes the fellow who barely beat me at tennis." He then raised his glass to Jake as Jake stepped through the French doors and turned to see who Carter was talking to in the love seat.

It was Dr. Bob, who Jake had never seen up this close and, as a matter-of-fact, had only ever seen fleetingly in his back yard.

"Bob, I'd like you to meet Jake, he lives here too."

"Jake, Bob's gone a little Asiatic but he can hold his scotch," said Carter now looking at Jake.

"Glad to meet you my boy," said Dr. Bob. "My God but you look like a Luger."

"I am," said Jake cordially.

"Where is your father? I haven't seen him recently," queried Bob.

"Well, he's actually my older brother. I was a late afterthought," said Jake and then he smiled.

"Ah, better late than never," said a smiling Carter who would usually punctuate his comments with a sip from his glass, but Jake noticed that this time he didn't.

"Well, here's to afterthoughts," said Dr. Bob smiling as he raised his glass. "I have two of them and they are wonderful girls."

Carter raised his glass but did not drink. Jake now realized that Carter was cutting back on his drinking.

"Do you want a scotch?" asked Carter.

"No, I'm good," said Jake. Turning to Dr. Bob, "Why have you gone Asiatic?"

Dr. Bob raised his glass in the direction of Carter. "You'll have to ask Carter."

"He's starting to look like one of them, as I told you," said Carter as he now took a sip.

In for a dime in for a dollar thought Jake as he said, "Look like one of who?" And now Dr. Bob perked up to hear the answer.

"Like a Jap! Can't you see it with that hat and neck shade?" said Carter nodding towards Dr. Bob who was self-consciously feeling the material hanging down at the back of his field hat, which he had added to protect his neck from the sun. But he wasn't overly surprised having come to know Carter to the extent that he had.

"A Jap like in the war in the Pacific?" asked Jake.

"Well….yeah," said Carter seeming somewhat confused but more rational now than he had been when he first noticed Dr. Bob's appearance.

"The war's been over for 32 years now Carter."

Carter now took another sip. "I know that."

Carter had quickly warmed up to Jake since their tennis match to the point where he was not gruff with Jake. He had also even started to mention subjects of interest to him over the ensuing days since the match. It was almost as if Carter had been in a fog forgetting all the great experiences he had had in life and now he found another man, a young man he could open up to with these memories and enjoy them again.

And it was different than the way he opened up with Kate and even Margaret. It was like he had a male friend again after many years, a male friend who was a friend and somewhat like a son. It was as though he had jumped over a long period that it takes to become good friends and established a friendship with Jake. It was similar, in a small way, to the one he had had with Harpie except the roles had reversed as Harpie had actually been a little older than Carter, like an older brother. Now Jake was like a close friend and son, with the same characteristics of a relationship that smart fathers try to downplay in order to give their sons more independence.

"Who's Dorothy, Carter?" Jake came out with forcefully as he recognized the opportunity to bring up the question as Dr. Bob looked on, now with more curiosity after the first revelation.

Carter hesitated and looked into his glass but did not take a drink for fortification. Jake was able to get the question in without putting Carter back into a defensive but yet guilt ridden fog of illusions.

He looked up and looked right at Jake with the forming of tears in his eyes. "I killed her."

Dr. Bob's ears tweaked at the resounding admission in Carter's voice that he had killed someone.

Not yet knowing who Dorothy was Jake firmly said, "No you didn't."

"But I did, I let Harpie die and I killed her," said Carter as tears slowly ran down his face.

"Who is she Carter?" asked Jake quietly as Dr. Bob sat there frozen with scotch glass in mid-flight to his mouth and concern on his face.

"God, I miss her long brown hair and her eyes which told a story I'll never see again," he said as he started to cry openly.

"Who is Dorothy?" persisted Jake.

"Harpies's baby sister............I killed her."

"What happened Carter?"

"She was hit by a train."

"You didn't kill her."

"I did as if I had pushed her in front of that train myself. They found her with my letter," said Carter looking down at his meaningless drink.

"What letter?" persisted Jake as painful as this was to Carter.

Carter, filled with distress, was responding as something was telling him he needed to get this out after all of these years.

"The letter I wrote to her about her big brother," said Carter now looking up at Jake again.

"That letter didn't push her."

"We were going to get married," said Carter looking down at his drink again. "She was 17 and I was 17. I met her with Harpie on leave, we wrote a lot. We just knew it when our eyes met. There seemed to be no one else in the room. I had never felt that way before. I loved her.............and I killed her. Her best friend Leslie said she was upset over Harpie and wasn't paying attention when they were on the platform in Bronxville."

"Carter, it was an accident do you hear me, IT WAS AN ACCIDENT! She loved you, if anything your letter probably gave her peace after the family got the telegram from the War Department."

Carter looked up and did not say a word.

"How do you feel about Margaret? Didn't she make you feel as you hadn't felt since Dorothy when you met her?"

Carter just looked at Jake.

"I have this belief Carter that we never lose anyone and I don't mean just in our hearts. I feel that everyone we have ever loved and lost are out there looking over us, wanting us only to be happy for ourselves and for them. I'm only a young man with little experience but maybe that's why I see so clearly what I am trying to say to you. If you think of Dorothy smiling at you do you think she would want you to be upset over her? Don't you think that she would want you to be happy and to smile when you think of her and to enjoy your life not only for yourself but for those around you and for her memory?"

Carter looked down and tears dropped into his scotch glass diluting the brown liquid with an imperceptible swirl of white and light brown and then he looked up at Jake.

"I don't know anything about Dorothy, Carter, but the boy is right," said Dr. Bob now putting his glass down on the coffee table next to the bottle of Johnny Walker.

Carter put his hand around the back of Oliver's neck   and

started rubbing the right side of Oliver's face as Oliver looked over at him with concern. Oliver had sat up and looked at Carter when he started to cry. Carter noticed this and smiled a rare smile at Oliver. He could not avoid the reality that man and animal were both concerned about his happiness. Maybe Dorothy was sending a message he thought as he smiled again. He started to feel a great weight removed although he would never quite get over the loss of Harpie and the vision of it happening; he was there, after all, in the sand with Harpie.

Carter put the glass in his left hand down on the table, reached over and squeezed Jake's right knee, smiled and nodded, and said, "You're okay boy.........," and turning to Dr. Bob he added, "Thanks Asiatic."

Dr. Bob just smiled, picked up his glass again and finished off the scotch that was still in it.

Looking back at Jake without moving his hand off his knee he said, "Margaret and I are getting married at the end of the month."

"Alright, damn. Congratulations Carter," exclaimed Jake.

"Congratulations Carter," said Dr. Bob with a heartfelt smile covering his face.

"And I want you to be my best man," said Carter with a solemn seriousness in his still somewhat gruff voice as he looked again at Jake after nodding to Dr. Bob.

"I don't ......I don't know what to say. Yes, I'm more than honored........yes," said Jake with an emotional smile.

"Good then," said Carter then turning to Dr. Bob and adding, "Bob, would you come too, at this point I could not think of getting married without you there."

"You may not recognize me all cleaned up," Dr. Bob said with a smile.

Carter just smiled back and then looked down at Oliver, and rubbing his head more said, "And I want you there too Oliver." And Oliver just looked up at him with tongue out and a smile in his eyes as he was now not worried about Carter, for he could hear the positive change in his voice.

"There we go then. I'll tell Margaret," said Carter while still rubbing Oliver's head.

"Hopefully about me being best man and not that there is going to be a wedding," said Jake smiling.

Carter just smiled getting it. "She knows about the wedding, she gave me the date. I was saved."

"I propose a drink," said Dr. Bob holding his glass just halfway up to his head, and then looking at Jake, "You will need a drink in your hand for us to do this the right way."

Jake jumped up, ran into the den to the small portable bar, grabbed a rock glass and headed out again to the veranda and sitting poured himself a scotch mumbling, "God, it's early."

"Yes but for a good cause," intoned Dr. Bob raising his glass to the height of his forehead and looking back and forth between Carter and Jake to add, "I will try to make this short although my words are meant for a man who I have only known briefly but yet one who has given me a great reservoir of compliments and comments that I could make on his behalf. In keeping with brevity and not to embarrass him too much, I want to say that if there is one man that I know who deserves happiness and, dare I say unqualified love and great companionship, it is Carter." Now looking at Carter and raising his glass just a bit higher he concluded, "Carter, may happiness, friendship and joy fill your life from this day forward in the same way that you have unknowingly filled the people around you with a warmth and awareness that you may never understand and which you will probably deny."

Jake and Dr. Bob completed the toast and drank. Carter sat their not knowing what to do and then he raised his glass part way and simply said, "Thank you........." and then drank as his eyes showed a subtle hint of welling up just short of doing so.

"Carter, let me know if you need any help with anything," said Jake, and adding with a smile, "By-the-way, do I need to set up a bachelor's party?"

"I am beyond that," answered Carter with an embarrassed smile, then he took the last sip from his glass.

***

A wedding was on and it took Margaret to inform everyone informally about the date. There would be no wedding invitations, everyone would get a personal call from Margaret.

Carter seemed even more of a changed man. He was noticed as smiling once in a while. Dorothy never came up again after the conversation on the veranda and Margaret would never hear about her.

On Tuesday, August 16th, Elvis died at age 42 and Rodney finally realized that Alice had left the house. He was also upset that he had no security deposit to keep back from her forgetting that he had not given her change back from her first rent payment. Nor had he applied it to the next month's rent as he had told her he would.

Groucho Marx died three days later on the 19th and Tim and Adelia announced to everyone that they were engaged. Groucho would have seen the humor in it while appreciating that these two people had traveled the Tattooed Lady and actually crossed each other's paths several times and hadn't known it. Adelia had been with a chaperon traveling in a small group in Sicily while Tim, three years older, had unwittingly passed that same group in his travels. He had smiled and nodded at the group not having seen Adelia as she walked out of a bake shop as he passed on. They had been wondering afar in their young lives in their own way as Adelia was sent on the trips while Tim ran away through his travels. In the end they were both looking for something they thought to be nonexistent not realizing that they were walking towards it all the time until they finally met up that day at The Club.

On Saturday, August 20th, Jake was in Fort Lee, New Jersey covering a minor story of interest that was taking place in the main courtroom of the town. It was a dedication to a Fort Lee resident who had never come back from WWII and had gone missing until February of 1977 when his remains were found in the mountains of the Owen Stanley Range of Papua, New Guinea. They had found him, along with three others from his B-25 crew, under or near the remains of a parachute. The Parachute had deployed at impact of the plane with the mountain, it was determined, and blew itself into the jungle canopy which had protected it for years. The jungle canopy was also thin enough to eventually reveal it to a passing helicopter. He was home again.

Jake experienced the deep emotional bond that the man's two sisters and brother still maintained after all of these years as though he had just been lost and it reminded him of Carter.

He could not ever imagine, nor try to imagine, what would go through Carter's thoughts during sleep or awake. Most people have dreams they cannot keep whereas Carter had dreams that he could not rid himself of but only diminish, as he had done with his memories of Dorothy which were now only good.

Jake was gaining a deeper understanding of Carter and thinking this when he walked into a place called the Salty Bagel, not too far from the court house, to get a sandwich. He walked in not paying attention to his surroundings until he heard a familiar giggle but it was different somehow. It was a familiar giggle but it was happy and light and filled with joy, and it attracted his eye. He looked hard, completely dead in his tracks, and saw Alice. She was sitting next to another woman and they were just getting up to leave. As Jake watched he saw them hold hands as they headed towards him and there was no place for Jake to go. He was right in the middle of the bull's-eye and he swallowed hard just as Alice looked up, saw him and smiled.

Alice smiled at him. She was dressed in jeans and a flowery blouse and as she came near her smile stretched to her eyes and she nodded in warm friendship. He found himself nodding back with a smile on his face as she passed by holding hands with another young and attractive woman who was going on about something with great excitement and joy. Jake had no idea what the other woman was talking about   as they passed, he was too preoccupied with his mind trying to wrap itself around someone who looked familiar but was completely different than his memory allowed.

They were gone and out the door in a moment and Jake still hadn't moved from the spot where he had become frozen by what he saw. He smiled to himself again and moved. Then he looked behind himself to make sure that he had actually seen what he had seen and there was a happy Alice with her friend moving off down the street. Jake just mumbled to himself, "Maybe Kate was right all along, maybe she isn't as bad as I thought." But he could not forget how scary she had been.

***

The wedding was getting closer. It was just short of a week away.

Carter was getting married. He was actually getting married and Jake and Kate could not be happier, even Oliver seemed to know and constantly wagged his tail at Carter.

Jake was having these thoughts while driving with Carter in his old blue Chevy station wagon. They were traveling too fast through the small roads from the Englewood Field Club, where they had picked up several round folding leg tables for the reception at the house. The tables were big, round, brown and heavy, the type that seem to be a part of any club with a large dining room. They had transported two at a time on the roof without securely lashing them down; the 'lashing down' was humorous if not dangerous. Jake did not know how he did it but Carter had actually made him believe it was fine and not dangerous as they both held on with one hand out opposite sides of the car. Jake, holding on with his right hand straining on the right side of the car, looked over at Carter to try to get the full sense of the man for the hundredth time even though he thought he had, especially after hearing about Dorothy. Carter had determination written across his face as he held the table with his left hand and drove with the right. He had a mission, to get those tables back to the Luger house as quickly as possible as though the reception were the   same day and not a week in the future.

"Carter, da ya think maybe we're going a little too fast?"

"Nah, we'll be okay," assured Carter as his mind went back to that hole on Tarawa 34 years earlier as again a slight change came over him. "We'll make it Harpie don't worry" as tears started to form. "We'll be okay, ...I promise."

Jake just looked at Carter not saying anything. He knew he was back in hell and he cried inside for Carter but he also knew what to say. This is one thing he learned about the enigma that was Carter because he had become that Carter from 34 years earlier several times since that conversation about Dorothy and Jake had become Harper to Carter on these occasions. A day after that conversation about Dorothy was the first short episode where Carter, in passing, had called Jake 'Harpie'. He had asked 'Harpie' for his agreement on something so minor that it almost went by Jake but for the fact that the subject matter dealt with the M1 Garand rifle and came out of nowhere. Jake had responded as though he were Harper and it worked. Carter came quietly back to the present not knowing that he had left. So Jake knew to expect it and Carter never remembered when he floated backwards in time even if it seemed to him that he had fallen asleep for a second. It was becoming less and less but each episode, although short, seemed to be more intense as the wedding drew closer. This would change after the wedding and the episodes would gradually disappear altogether.

"Carter, thanks. I needed to hear that. I'm okay. I'll always be okay no matter what happens."

"I know Harpie, I know," and then the tears flowed and would not stop as they started to veer into the opposing lane.

"Carter, wake up, wake up. I need you to wake up."

Carter flinched and took firm control of he wheel with his one hand and redoubled his concentration still holding tight to his side of the tables.

"How did we get here?"

"Margaret, the wedding, the tables. We have the tables from The Club. We're good, just watch the road."

"Jesus, I lost track."

"You're okay, maybe just a little too fast is all."

"This ol' bucket drives itself."

Jake just smiled as they took the right curving turn onto Lydecker way too fast as they rocketed towards Chestnut Street. The tables shifted and Jake could feel his arm straining with minimal support from the jerry rigging rope works attempting to hold the tables in place. Carter's Boy Scout memories of tying and securing items in transit had its faults.

"Chestnut's coming up," warned Jake.

The tables lurched as Carter started to brake and as they eased into the right turn the tables slide left before they made a sharp left turn which caught the tables in motion and corrected their movement stopping their motion. Jake just shook his head. You could not have done that if you tried but like everything else with Carter disaster averted its attention someplace else.

They slowed almost to a stop and turned left into the driveway at 224 King Street, or the Lugers'.

Hell was left back on the road as Carter directed his attention to the tables and the wedding to come. He finally seemed happy in his own protected way even though he seemed at times to be a person who should not be allowed to experience happiness. Harper would always be with him, always. But maybe he could smile at Carter happy for him in the same way that Carter now felt Dorothy did. The demonic Japanese soldier with the grenade seemed to disappear altogether. Only Carter knew of this particular demon and could see him, a demon that he never thought of but met in his sleep or during periods where he allowed himself to relax, or on occasion when he saw Alice. He did, as well, openly acknowledge the fearful presence of Japanese soldiers on other occasions, which everyone knew about. Margaret had changed the way he was affected by helping to lessen the effect of the demons with her presence. And Alice had unwittingly walked that one particular demon out the front door of the Lugers' the day she left after her confused and embarrassing failure with

Adelia and her run in with and condemnation from Carter. The demon was held back from returning because it had no right to Margaret's life. It had no grievance with her, she did not know Harpie, she was not responsible for him. She would be protected from the sight of brains and blood on green and sand. She would be protected from all of the demons. He could protect her where he could not protect Harpie. She was his responsibility and he would do everything he could to keep her in a safe place as he never had the chance to do with Dorothy.

After they set the tables up, they went back for two more and this time Jake did the 'lashing' with extra rope from Sam.

***

The tables, brown in the sun, radiating out from the sprawling old magnolia gave Carter a feeling of completion and relief as Harpie did not come back again on the second trip. Carter fully understood and completely embraced what he was actually doing in the moment with no shades of the past to alter its color at least for the rest of this day. No sweat soaked sage green cotton herringbone twill, no red in white sand or gray/yellow on the face of a fanatic with a grenade, just the beauty of a late summer's day in Englewood, New Jersey.

Carter did not need a drink after finishing his task. He just sat down on the steps off the side veranda, looked at his handy work and smiled. Jake seeing Carter getting lost in his happiness as he stepped onto the veranda, stopped and slowly stepped backwards not wanting to disturb him. Then he turned and headed in through the opening, protected by the French doors, which had seen so many people pass through its portal since 1880. The house had been completed in that year for a businessman from St. Louis who summered in New Jersey across from the great city of New York and now the great house was hosting the event of the year.

It was good to see Carter at peace at the moment. There was something quite important about the man. He seemed   to be lost in a middle world fighting with the demons and experiencing periods of great lucidness when in the presence of Margaret. Jake noticed that even now when Margaret was not near he was living in more and longer periods of lucid happiness with the thought of Margaret near. He was important to many besides Jake and seeing this brightness shine through the hazy darkness gave Jake satisfaction and a relieving happiness. It was as though Jake had been drowning and then saved realizing again the importance of life and it had in reality been Carter who was drowning not Jake.............Carter was just a significant man......in his own way.

***

The wedding was at hand and the day was a cool late summer day outside as everyone gathered inside St Paul's where the ceremony was to be held. Margaret, twenty years younger than Carter, was radiant and she glowed with happiness having Carter by her side. It is something uniquely important when one individual is brought back to life by another. There is a connection that transcends time. This is what happened the first time that Margaret and Carter had met on the patio at The Club with Carter's friends around him. Everyone had seen it as those two just looked at each other as though they had been searching an eternity and while not looking had found what it was that had made them searchers. Everyone around them that day at The Club had felt a change in themselves. This man meant a great deal not only to Jake but to everyone else present at the wedding.

And with this wonderful woman at his side the two of them represented a symbol of exaltation, 'something to protect and run to in one's mind when in doubt about things around you,' Jake had thought. He had never thought this way until he had met Carter and then Margaret at his side. There was an honesty and a perfect imperfection about the two together.

Jake was the best man that day. He got to hold the ring so that Carter would know where it was. It was one of the greatest days of Jake's life. Most people there felt that way. These two had given everyone a piece of something that they were otherwise missing and at the same time unaware that they were missing something until meeting Carter and Margaret together.

Tim was there with Adelia. V and Jack were there with Sally. V kept looking around the nave, one he was familiar with but one where he would always be haunted by Alice, expecting her to come out of a dark corner at any moment. Jake only told Kate about seeing Alice in Ft. Lee so she remained a specter at large for others. Jake found it humorous to leave it that way.

Zach was in the front pew with Kate. Oliver was at the altar with Carter and Jake.

Everyone they knew at The Club was there along with Bea from the store.

Dick Baxter was there next to Dr. Bob and his wife. Dr. Bob was dressed up and looked different. Dick Baxter was making Dr. Bob laugh about something as they all waited for Margaret.

Even George and Gladys Johnson were there, although they were a bit nervous about the church since the night they had heard the voice of the 'ghost'.

Birdie had been invited by Rodney but as she never wanted to again set foot in Englewood, N.J., let alone attend the wedding of a possible serial killer, Rodney sat alone. But Rodney being Rodney, he had enough company and he could be seen by everyone as he was dressed in a loud pink shirt with a patchwork multi-colored tie topped by an emerald green blazer. Who knew who was dressing him this day but it seemed to fit, in a bizarre way, with his nose which now looked like it belonged to a retired boxer.

As for Carter, he was not in tennis whites. He was in a brand new dark navy suit from Brooks Brothers that Jake had helped him pick out. He wore a light blue Oxford shirt with the suit and a subdued green and black striped bow tie, a real one he had to figure out how to tie as it had been so many years since last he wore one. He wore a bow tie as Margaret liked bow ties and she loved green, and Carter loved her.

Alice's red circles were no longer in the church with the exception of one of them, until Oliver rubbed up against it. The first of Alice's red circles was found by the old man who would use the occasion of a funeral or wedding to make his thorough cleaning rounds of the church. In talking to Jake about preparing the church he mentioned in passing, "I found some small red circles in chalk in some strange places around the church, and even under the pulpit lectern, almost like a little infestation. The damnedest thing I tell you, like the mark of the devil, but they came off easily enough." While he men- tioned this a little red circle lurked in plain sight at the lower corner of the front pew. But it was not noticed by either Jake or the old man, even as they were now both acutely aware of these circles, as it blended well with the dark wood it had been drawn on. Before reaching Carter at the altar, however, Oliver had a need to itch the scars from Alice's white cat and the front pew was handy. As he itched the old wound the last of Alice's red marks vanished for good.

When the organ started the Wedding March everyone stood up and turned to see Margaret. She was dressed in a white wedding gown at the head of the aisle on the arm of Sam, who she thought could be the only man to give her away to another Marine. As they came down the aisle Margaret was nervous and Sam smiled with joy at a room filled with people whom he knew so well for the joining of two whom he loved.

The wedding ceremony was flawless and the ring was produced at the appropriate time, although Carter started checking his own pockets before he saw Jake's hand in front of him holding the ring.

The bells peeled as Margaret and Carter started to walk out followed by those in attendance. As they filed out V, Jack and the Johnsons looked up towards the bells with nervous caution written on their faces preparing for an 'I-I-I-I umph' that thankfully never came.

Everyone walked up the hill from the church following behind the couple on their way to the Lugers' and the reception on this late summer day. Carter had not had a drink in the three days leading up to the wedding but he would allow himself one or two at his own reception.

There had been a slight rain, not to amount to much, while they had been inside the church and it was a crisp 64 degrees for the end of August.

The sun was full for the reception with drops of water on the green magnolia leaves that reflected the sun like many jewels as everyone gathered in celebration.

Oliver was walking around looking for easy marks. If he looked up just right at someone with food in their hand or taking an Hors d'oeuvre off of a platter he would get some. He was on the way to a bad stomach.

Luckily V and Sally were not bartending as Sam had a friend come in to do that.

Both Margaret and Carter liked the banjo so they had hired a banjoist to walk amongst the people and play. He wore a straw hat and a red and white striped blazer playing a great many Dixieland pieces as he went.

There were well over a hundred people on the side and back lawn of the Luger house and the air was filled with laughter and the loud voices of story telling and recognition of stories remembered.

Tim and Adelia spent time leaning up against a large lower branch of the grand magnolia talking non-end. They would never run out of things to talk about and could go on for hours forgetting about everything else around them.

Jack was with V and Sally, and Zach was with Jake and Kate all on the side porch. The six of them had taken up temporary residence on the side veranda of the wrap around porch occupying its love seat and wicker chairs and an added chair from the den. They were busy telling stories and enjoying a great day for everyone, including Oliver.

Dr. Bob and his beautiful wife could be seen continually mingling as everyone knew who he was but had, for the most part, never seen the man. When word spread that he was there a constant flow of people introduced themselves either in a group or individually.

Dick Baxter was surrounded and telling stories again and one in particular about two doves flying across the room at another party earlier in the summer at the house. He also told a story about a screaming Englishman running up the same back lawn that they were standing on. The laughter was infectious even if one didn't know what they were laughing about.

Birdie was not present but Rodney was. He was busy stuffing Hors d'oeuvres in his mouth as though they were Chef Boyardee raviolis. He was nodding his head at people as they talked to him but he really wasn't listening. Luckily none of the conversation directed at him needed an informed response other than a head nod.

The reception headed into the early evening when Carter and Margaret gave their thank you to the gathered group and made their departure for Cape Cod. There was a roar as they got into Margaret's Saab with tin cans, mostly Chef Boyardee, tied to the rear bumper courtesy of V, and Jack, and Jake.

They were off down the street and then right to Lydecker accompanied by a roaring cheer from all gathered led by Dick Baxter and a cacophony of tin cans bumping along the road.

The Chef Boyardee cans could be heard up to half a mile down the road as the late summer air carried their sweet sound of happiness. And as the last of the distant cans were heard, during a brief moment of silence, everyone started to laugh.

The house was strangely empty that night as Carter was no longer a member of the household and upon his return from the Cape he would go straight to Margaret's where everything that he owned had been moved. Jake, on the third floor, was thinking of this and how he would miss having Carter close at hand, when all-of-a-sudden Oliver farted audibly. Even Kate heard it as she moaned in dreaded anticipation, "Ah, God!" The reception had been too rich for his stomach but he was oblivious, lying quietly stretched out on the floor, as Jake got up from where he was sitting and opened the window wider while Kate gasped in anticipated relief and thanked him.

Chapter 19

The Final Chapter

The end of August would see the boys getting ready to return to school from New Jersey as they had never returned to the Cape that summer of 1977. And on August 29th Lou Brock of the St. Louis Cardinals broke the 49-year mark of Ty Cobb's 892 career stolen bases on his way to going past Billy Hamilton to 938 career stolen bases. This was big to Jake, a Yankee fan, who watched the Cardinals just to watch Lou Brock. All in all it was a good month and a man he loved almost as a father was coming out of a 34 year intermittent fog to become complete and whole again, and mostly sober.

***

Six months later Carter started suffering from lower back pain. He thought that maybe he was feeling things that had always bothered him but because he was always inebriated he hadn't felt them. Now sober he felt them. Margaret knew it was more.

They went to Sloan-Kettering in the city. It was cancer and it was prostate cancer which had not been noticed early, had metastasized and was spreading. Treatment would take time away from Carter and Margaret and as it would turn out they had precious little left.

***

Carter died seven months after the happiest day in his life and with him a little piece of all of us died. He lived without the demons for the better part of a year. And in the end he and Harpie and Dorothy walked off into eternity together but he carried Margaret in his heart when he went. And he went knowing how to smile again and knowing that he did his best to protect the woman that he loved most.

Margaret had had Carter and in her heart she knew that she would have him again in time. She knew that in the end they would be together again. And she would swear that Carter came to her one night and let her know this and that every day since that night she had his warmth and love deep inside her soul. Carter had given her a smile too. He had given her love that she never knew that she could feel and she was simply thankful for that.

Margaret knew, 'It wasn't over but just the beginning'.

ABOUT THE AUTHOR

Mr. Lowe started life as a journalist and wound up on Wall Street. He was born in Englewood, N.J. which explains his choice of that town for the setting of this book. He has lived in England and in the American West but in the end has always returned to Bergen County, New Jersey where he now resides.

www.ingramcontent.com/pod-product-compliance
Lightning Source LLC
Chambersburg PA
CBHW020726210626
46807CB00016B/175